I0536358

The Silver Rings

J.J.Anderson

The Story Bazaar

The Story Bazaar
BM6231
London WC1N 3XX
www.thestorybazaar.com

The Silver Rings by J.J.Anderson. -- 1st ed.
ISBN 978-0-9932106-8-6

The Silver Rings is Book II in the Al Andalus series of stories.

Praise for *Reconquista*, Book I in the Al Andalus series of stories

Reconquista was long listed for 2016 *Mslexia* Children's Novel Award.

Jerez 1264

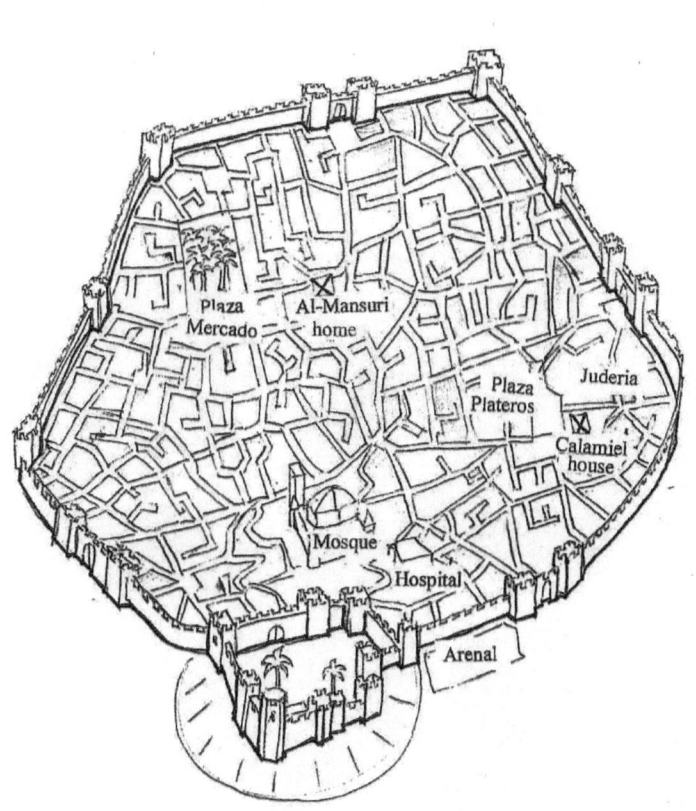

Plaza Mercado · Al-Mansuri home · Plaza Plateros · Juderia · Calamiel house · Mosque · Hospital · Arenal

v

CONTENTS

Prologue

Part One
In the City

Part Two
In the Mountains

Part Three
Home

Epilogue

Prologue

In 1264, after months of siege, the city of Jerez in Al Andalus, now southern Spain, fell to the army of King Alfonso X of Castile and Leon. The lives of five young townspeople, Nathan, Rebecca, Atta, Miguel and Ben were turned upside down. Four of them left their homes and one set out to find them.

It is now March 1265 and all of them have returned to Jerez, but they find that much, not least themselves, has changed.

Part One

In the City

1.

The Scapegoat

'Harlot!'

Rebecca spun round, skirts swirling about her ankles, as the shout rang out across the cobbled square. Laughter sounded from the concealing shadows. The insult was meant for her, of that she had no doubt.

The stir and bustle of the early morning market faltered for only a moment, before continuing as if nothing had happened.

Ignore them. Don't react.

Unclenching her fists she turned to face the market stall once more. None of the other women standing in the queue looked around, though they must have heard.

Calm. Be calm. Brazen it out.

Today was the first time since her return that she had ventured out alone. Uncle Simon had taken to accompanying her, glowering at anyone foolish enough to criticise her openly, but he couldn't defend her from the silences, nor the snide remarks made just loud enough for her to hear them. The townswomen referred to her as 'the runaway' or worse.

This morning she had slipped out without Simon, anxious, for once, to be by herself.

She stamped her feet in the cold.

This was taking a long time.

Glancing up at the sky, Rebecca saw the glow of gold in the east. The flickering torchlight grew weaker as sunrise approached and the finches were already chattering in the palm trees. Orange-tiled roofs caught the first rays of sunlight and grey shadow retreated down the white-washed walls. High in their wide nest atop the watchtower the storks awakened, clack-clacking.

At the foot of the tower stood the spice stall, a patchwork of bright colours and perfumes. Senora Lopez scooped up her scented wares, pouring golden turmeric, red pimientos or black, pungent peppercorns into cones of palm leaf, twisting them closed with a flick of the hand. Her cheeks were rosy in the cold, her black hair drawn back into a tight top-knot. Like the other traders she was a regular visitor to the market. The city no longer went hungry.

Rebecca blew on her hands as she waited. Her head was wrapped in a thick, woollen scarf and she wore a heavy shawl around her shoulders against the February chill. A wicker basket hung from her arm. She should be served soon.

Most of the women waiting at the stall she had known for years. Though she had never been an outgoing girl, or popular - she had kept to herself and looked after Simon and her cousin Nathan - people were civil, sometimes friendly. She used to belong.

Not any more.

They talked amongst themselves, but no one spoke to her. Among them stood Sheba Barruch, coat buttoned up to the chin of her pale face, long plaits tucked beneath a hood. Why was she smirking?

Around Sheba people were coming up to the stall and being served. Everyone was being served, but not her.

Senora Lopez was ignoring her, it was obvious to them all. No one met her eye.

'Excuse me...' she said, raising her hand to attract the stall-holder's attention.

The woman looked at her, hard-faced. Then she turned her back.

Rebecca gasped.

It was so unexpected and from an outsider too. It took her by surprise.

She felt blood rush to her face, burning with shock and indignation. Now everyone was looking at her, their eyes curious and cold. Everyone had seen the snub.

Rebecca drew breath to protest. She wanted to upend the trays of spice onto the cobbles, send the little boxes spinning across the square, contents flying. Then she caught another glimpse of Sheba's face, sharp, sly and gimlet-eyed, eager for more drama, waiting for her to start complaining.

It hit her like ice-water.

She wouldn't rant. She'd not give them the satisfaction.

But she had to get out of the market square.

As she hurried away her winter boots slipped on the dew-covered cobbles and she almost fell – that would be something else for them to laugh at.

The narrow streets of the Juderia passed in a blur as she fled homewards, eyes stinging. She dashed the tears away with the back of her hand.

Don't cry. Don't let them know they'd hurt her. That's what they wanted.

Up ahead was the blue painted gate which meant home and sanctuary.

She fumbled with the key, wrenched open the gate, then slammed it shut behind her. Breathing heavily, she leaned back, her head against the wood.

In the courtyard all was peaceful. Budding jasmine climbed around the porch and green shoots poked from the soil in the small kitchen garden by the stables. She began to relax.

There was a thump on the gate.

She leapt forwards, heart pounding.

'Strumpet! Filthy strumpet!'

The yelling came from immediately beyond the stone wall. It sounded like children. They must have followed her from the market.

'Sailor's drab!'

A volley of blows struck the gate. They were throwing something. The gate shook with each thud.

'Harlot! Harlot!' They chanted.

She fled the sound.

Inside, through the hall and living room, she abandoned her basket and stumbled up the open wooden stairs to the first floor. In the bedroom, she grabbed the rungs of the wooden ladder and climbed up to the attic.

8

Dust motes floated in the shafts of sunlight which pierced the window shutters. The dry air was stale, but it was quiet here and safe.

Rebecca caught her breath, trying not to weep.

Was this her life now - unable to walk the streets without fear or humiliation? Why were they doing this? Why were they taking everything out on her?

Her own people didn't want her any more.

How could they? How dare they!

She paced back and forth, fists clenching again. A kick at the open trapdoor flipped it closed with a crash.

Twelve months ago she had been an ordinary girl, living an ordinary life in her uncle's house in Jerez, bickering with cousin Nathan. Then the armies of the King had come. The besieged city had resisted, starved, then fallen and she had made the decision which had changed her life.

She had run away.

She stamped towards the sky-light window. Propping open the shutter, she sat on the sill, her back against the window jamb and her knees drawn up to her chin.

The pan-tiled rooftops angled this way and that until they reached the castle battlements, where the flags of the King fluttered in the blue sky. She saw none of it, looking only inward as tears ran down her cheeks. What was to become of her?

If only....

She dragged off her headscarf and used it to wipe away her tears. Her soft brown hair no longer fell about her face, she had cut it close

9

to her scalp to disguise herself as a boy. It was growing again now, but still wasn't long enough to tie back with a band.

If only she hadn't....

She sniffed. No, she wouldn't change things. Think of what she had seen, what she had done.

Riding the swell of the great ocean, she had passed through the Pillars of Hercules into the Middle Sea. She had seen the shores of Ifriqa, she had wandered in the spice market of Algeciras, its jewelled colours and heady perfume so much bigger and better than Senora Lopez' stall. She had done more than those petty, small-minded women at the market could even dream of.

In the galley of the Teresa she had worked as cook's boy, a trusted comrade-in-arms. She had been part of the sea battle.

She had met the King.

It was worth it. Of course it was worth it.

She'd tried to tell them about it, the women. What a world there was out there, if only they chose to visit it. But they didn't want to hear. Most of them had never travelled beyond the city walls.

What did they know?

Babies and back-biting was all their closed lives allowed. Many of them couldn't even read.

Those hard days at sea, so full of peril, seemed carefree and happy now - climbing up to the look-out's perch to sit in the crow's nest, legs dangling above billowing sails, as the Teresa heeled over and forged through the white-capped waves. She and Miguel, with his chestnut curls blowing in the cold, clean wind and his crooked smile. Together they had faced down danger and even death.

10

She hadn't seen him since their return to the city and they had been back almost a week.

Where was he? Why didn't he come?

She knew he was still in town. His friend, Senor Thomas, had told her. Thomas was the English doctor who lodged in the room over the smithy next to their house. So Miguel had every excuse to call, he just didn't choose to.

Hah!

If he didn't care, then neither did she.

But...

She gnawed at her lip.

What would become of her?

Other girls her age were married by now. Yet for her to settle down to such a life, after all she had seen, it was unthinkable. And there was only one husband for her.

She'd turned down one offer already. Poor Ben Isaacs had looked so dejected when she had refused him, but there was nothing else she could do. She could never be the sort of wife he wanted.

Rebecca shivered. She slid from the sill and closed the shutter behind her. In the half-light she bent to re-open the trapdoor and clambered down the ladder.

Morning sunlight shone into Nathan's little bedroom.

His dark woollen cloak hung on the peg on the back of the door. Light reflected on a metal button lying on his table and she picked it up, turning it over in her fingers. He had demanded that she sew it on for him, she remembered the argument which followed.

It was as he had left it. No one had seen him since he and Simon had quarrelled.

11

She had asked about that day, but all Simon would tell her was that they argued about the smithy. Afterwards Nathan had left and not returned.

Without him the house seemed empty, bereft of energy and vitality. He would have walked beside her in the town. He would have found a way to stop the insults and abuse.

Now he could be anywhere. He could be lying injured somewhere, or dead, killed in the sea battle. Surely they would have heard if he had died?

The men in her life were a trial to her. Cousin Nathan, Uncle Simon and....

No. He hadn't come and he wasn't going to.

She wandered out on to the landing and down into the living room.

Empty chairs sat by the wide stone hearth, its embers still smouldering from the night before. There was no sign of her uncle, he must have gone out, probably looking for her.

Had he heard about the latest insults? Had the gossips told him? She hoped not. It would only distress him and he had cares enough.

During the day he prowled around their little compound, or walked the streets of the city seeking news of his son. The forge next to their house was cold and smoke no longer rose from its chimney. Ever since Rebecca could remember, Simon had made beautiful things from the silver stream of metal, but no longer. At night he gazed into the flames in their hearth, far beyond her reach.

Then she was grateful to their lodger, Senor Thomas. He spoke with Simon, drawing him out of the darkness and despair into which he would sometimes descend.

How could she wallow in self-pity when her Uncle's troubles were so much worse?

Her basket lay on the stone floor. Sweeping it up into her arms, she took it into the adjoining kitchen.

As she put away those few items she had managed to buy, Rebecca pursed her lips. She must convince her uncle that all would be well. She would ignore the shouting children, the spiteful comments and glances. It would be almost unbearable, but she would have to bear it.

She heard the outside gate slam. That would be her uncle.

Rebecca wiped her eyes with the back of her hand, straightened her clothes and stood up straight. From now on she would hide her sorrows.

'Rebecca,' she heard him call. 'What's all that dirt on the gate? Where are you? Are you all right?'

'I'm in the kitchen.'

She forced a smile as he entered.

His grey eyes met hers, questioning. Worry was etched upon his face, his mouth a thin line and his jaw taunt. He looked so helpless, this big, strong, kind man, who had been a father to her for most of her life and cared about her so much.

She had already caused him pain and anxiety when she ran away. Now she must make recompense and do whatever she could. For him.

'I'm passable well,' she said. 'Let me make you breakfast...?

13

2.

The Hero

Ben yawned.

He rubbed his bleary eyes and watched milky skeins of steam rise from the bowl of porridge in front of him, twisting and vanishing into the air. Elbows on the wooden table, he stirred the porridge with his spoon.

The nagging ache in his left arm returned and he shifted position. Today the bandages would be removed. Just as well, they had begun to chafe.

Around him the stone-flagged kitchen was full of activity. His sisters were binding herbs for hanging as his mother chivvied and fussed. Maria, the plump kitchen maid, washed dishes in a bowl by the window. Her back was to the others and she sent sidelong glances and smiles his way.

Ben ignored her. It wasn't her place to flirt with him. His mother would soon put a stop to that sort of behaviour from a servant. The girl would never have dared do that before.

Only yesterday he had overheard her talking with her friends in Plateros Square. They were clustered by the fountain and hadn't seen him approach.

'So the Isaacs are back then,' one girl said.

'Much good running away did them,' said another. 'And you've got your old job back?'

'At better pay,' Maria replied. 'They're not so high and mighty now. Everyone knows that they ran before the siege, leaving the rest of us behind. Young master might be a hero, but I think they're just grateful to be back home.'

'Reckon those pirates taught them a lesson,' a third said and they all giggled.

What could these silly girls know about pirates - nightmare monsters with which to frighten children? Ben had met the real thing and didn't ever want to do so again.

The girls had fallen silent when he passed them, watching him from the corners of their eyes. He had wondered if he should speak, but then the blue gate to the courtyard of the Calamiel house had opened and Rebecca stepped out.

Unprepared for such an encounter, Ben hurried away.

He couldn't face her right then, though he knew the Juderia was too small for him to be able to avoid her for long.

It was her kindness, her gentleness when she refused him that had hurt him the most. She hadn't even considered accepting his proposal. Even before the words were out of his mouth she must have been thinking how to let him down gently.

Ben closed his eyes and cringed inwardly, his stomach clenching. It was too humiliating.

His only consolation was that no one else knew of his rejection.

Last Spring, before the siege, before the armies had come, he had been so sure she would accept him. Had he been wrong then too? Or had something happened to change her mind since?

Ben had heard the gossip. Everyone had. Folk said she had shamed her uncle, the man who had brought her up as his own. Running away and sailing the ocean, the only woman on a ship full of men, sailors and brigands. He didn't believe half of what was said of her, but maybe he hadn't ever really known her as well as he thought. Now she was a scapegoat.

'Ben. There you are.'

His father's voice broke into his thoughts.

Solomon stood in the doorway wearing outdoor clothes. His beard and eyebrows looked greyer in the morning light.

'I'm going to de Faro's, the goldsmith, on business, will you come with me?'

'Gladly, but I must go to the hospital this morning.'

'Yes, I know.' Solomon hesitated. 'But walk with me anyway. It's not far out of your way. I'll be carrying some gold, so would welcome someone to walk by my side.'

His father never used to worry about robbery. With all the patrols and the curfew the city streets were as safe as they had ever been. The soldiers saw to that. Yet still, it seemed, his father didn't feel safe.

To all outward appearances his family had resumed the life they had left behind, in their old house in the Juderia. They had escaped the siege and then the pirates. Yet Ben felt their good fortune to be precarious, as if it might be snatched away at any moment. In

17

reality, things were different now. He heard whispers in the night and sometimes there were dark circles under his mother's eyes in the mornings. She felt it too.

Ben swallowed the last of his porridge, pushed the bowl away and went to get his cloak.

Outside, he and his father sought the sunny side of the street, to feel the warmth of the February sun as they walked through the narrow lanes of the Juderia.

Many houses still lay empty, their windows and doors gaping or boarded over. There were sudden empty spaces where dwellings had once stood. Sunshine penetrated into these patches of waste ground, and weeds and seedlings grew among fallen masonry. One or two leggy saplings were already reaching up into the light.

'There are rumours that people from the north are coming,' Ben said. 'Foreigners - to re-populate the town.'

'Coming where they're not wanted,' Solomon replied.

The new people would move into the town, just like the shrubs and bushes had colonised the empty waste ground. But they wouldn't find life easy.

As they walked Solomon greeted townsfolk and sometimes stopped for a brief word. He was well regarded, that was certain, no matter Maria's gossiping. The Isaacs name was still a respected one.

There were greetings too for Ben and people shook his hand, although a full week had passed since his name had been listed in the King's proclamation, alongside those of the captains and other notables who had fought in the sea battle. King's soldiers hailed him too - he had acquired a phalanx of new friends, young soldiers of his own age who had taken part in the dawn raid on the pirates.

It was ironic. He'd always been the last to be chosen when the city's young men trained on the parade ground and had always disdained athleticism and physical prowess. Yet now he was a hero. He smiled and nodded and said little.

Ben sensed his father's mood lightening. The congratulations for his son had cheered him.

'I'll carry on to the hospital now,' Ben said as they approached the de Faro house.

His father's hand darted out from beneath his cloak as if to clutch at him and Ben fought the impulse to flinch.

'Wait just a moment,' his father said.

This nervy, frightened man didn't resemble his father at all. Where was the shrewd and confident merchant he had always known?

Solomon rapped on the door. When it opened Ben hid a sigh of relief. Not looking back, he lengthened his stride as he walked away.

But who was this coming along the street? Handsome Miguel Delgado, dressed in fine boots and a long cloak, wearing a sword at his hip as if he knew how to use it. He had been on the *Teresa* at the same time as Rebecca.

Ben frowned. Could anything have happened between them? Unlikely. The Delgados were an old and wealthy Christian family, but still... Ben watched him covertly.

The young nobleman passed him by without a glance.

Ben's gaze followed Delgado until he rounded the corner. The man had a reputation for loose living, not unusual for the first-born son of an aristocrat, but still.... Maybe there had been something?

19

For now he dismissed the thought as he walked on. The front of the hospital lay just across the paved square.

Ben passed beneath the awning which shaded the front of the building, through the doors into the long, lamp-lit room.

The hospital reached back into the stone of the hill upon which the town had first been built. Near the entrance charcoal braziers burned for warmth and, deeper in, oil lamps illuminated the rows of beds. For a brief moment he was taken back to the day of the sea battle, his head pounding, bandaged and bloody, his arm in a crude sling. The hospital had been crowded with the wounded and dying, the doctors and their helpers desperate to help them as they cried out in pain.

Now all was quiet and he recognised only a few patients.

Ben walked over to where Senor Thomas was speaking with a patient.

The doctor looked up and smiled and Ben smiled in response. He liked the tall, loose-limbed Englishman, only a few years older than himself. And Thomas was a useful contact, he belonged to the King's court and, of course, he lived as lodger with Simon and Rebecca Calamiel.

'Hello Ben. Let's have a look at that arm.' Senor Thomas drew Ben over to the window for better light. 'Take off your shirt, please.'

Ben did so and sat on a high stool. Thomas removed the bandages and his expert, long-fingered hands felt around Ben's shoulder joint and along his arm. He manipulated his elbow and wrist, back and forth, side to side.

'Your muscles are mending well,' Thomas said. ''Though I don't recommend any hand to hand combat for a while. Have you had any repeat of the deafness you experienced after the battle?'

Ben shook his head.

'Good. It's possible that there's no lasting damage,' the doctor said. 'You may dress again. Though I wasn't jesting when I said you shouldn't be doing any fighting. Were you planning on doing so?'

'No.'

Why would he be going to fight?

'Why?'

'I wondered, because....,' the doctor lowered his voice so that none but he could hear. 'There's to be an expedition to rescue Don Reza. I thought, perhaps, some of your soldier friends may have mentioned it to you.....'

'No.'

'Maybe they are trying to avoid word getting out,' Thomas shrugged. 'There's a meeting the day after tomorrow. I'm going. Will you come?'

Would Simon be there? He was Don Reza's friend. And maybe Rebecca too? Ben's hopes rose, he couldn't help it. But it would not be the place for women.

'I... Where is this meeting to be held?' Ben pulled on his shirt, turning his reddening face away.

'The new barracks near Plaza Mercado,' Thomas replied.

Ben nodded, drawing his shirt string tighter. Maybe he could go along, to the meeting at least.

'Yes. I'll be there,' he said, his voice firm.

'I'll let them know,' Thomas replied.

3.

The Heir

The golden light reflected in the little glasses of amber sherry-wine.

Miguel gazed at them as he sat in a high-backed chair behind a desk in the room which he still thought of as Father's Study. The coffered ceiling and wood panelled walls were warmed by the sun from the tall windows behind him. The room glowed in the light, its surfaces dappled green and blue, the colours of the Delgado coat of arms set into the casement glass.

On the far side of the desk sat two men.

Ludovico, a thick set, older man, was steward of the Delgado estates. He gave Miguel a thin lipped smile from within a short grey beard.

'That's all for now,' he said. His fur-lined sleeve brushed the parchments and papers awry as reached across the desk to collect them up.

Finally.

Miguel tossed down the quill he was holding,

The man had been his father's faithful retainer for years and, doubtless, saw it his duty to guide his old master's son. But he didn't have to be so damned condescending about it.

At Ludovico's elbow sat Bonifaz, young lawyer to the family. His father, like Miguel's, had died during the siege. His close cut gingery curls above a pale face contrasted starkly with the dark coloured robes of his profession. Not much older than Miguel, he was someone less hide-bound by tradition.

Miguel glanced across to him with a conspiratorial smile, but today Bonifaz was fidgeting and looked uncomfortable. His grey eyes shifted to Ludovico, then back to Miguel.

Something was brewing, that was for certain. There was no love lost between these two and they rarely saw him together. Ludovico regarded Bonifaz as new fangled and too ambitious – he had said as much - and Bonifaz considered the older man a reactionary, living in the past. But today they were up to something.

Miguel looked from Bonifaz to Ludovico.

'Well?'

'We've talked about the Delgado property, feus, rents and tenants,' Ludovico began. 'Your obligations and the financial decisions you will need to make. You are in a unique position, as an existing Jerezano nobleman, whose title the King has recognised, despite....' He paused, licking his lips as if they were dry.

Bonifaz pushed one of the little glasses of wine towards the steward. Ludovico ignored it and, hesitantly, met Miguel's gaze.

'Despite your family's part in resisting the King. But there is one other matter,' he said. 'Were your father alive, God rest him, I am sure he would speak with you about it. As it is, it falls to me...' The steward spread his hands. There was a silence.

'You will be seventeen next birthday,' Bonifaz spoke, prompting the older man, who cleared his throat.

'You'll be seventeen next birthday and should be thinking about securing the future of your house.' He looked at Miguel, a hopeful expression on his face.

So that was it.

An heir.

It was bound to arise. Many sons of noble houses were betrothed as children. Marriage was a dynastic concern. Had his mother lived she would have seen to matters and, even so, if it hadn't been for the war he would probably have been married already. His parents had paraded enough 'suitable' girls before him, but he hadn't agreed to wed any of them.

Miguel glared at them. They shifted in their seats, both sets of eyes cast down at the huge expanse of desk between them and him.

'Your father had a list,' Ludovico reached inside his document case and drew out a roll of parchment. 'It was in his papers.'

'That's personal. A family matter.'

'Don Carlos didn't think so,' Ludovico answered too quickly, on the defensive now. 'He asked me to explore the current state of the girls' fortunes. I'll have to do it again, now, of course. Things may have changed.'

'Give me the list.' Miguel reached out for the scroll, which Ludovico placed, with some reluctance, in his palm. Ludovico and Bonifaz exchanged looks.

He rested back in his chair and unrolled the parchment. Yes, there were names he recognised, the obvious choices for a wife of the Delgado heir. Some of them he'd seen, they had visited from Toledo or Burgos, with their parents and trains of servants. Others he had vague memories of, from childhood family visits, when he and his younger brother Juan had accompanied his parents to their lands further north.

Juan was dead now. Father, mother, Juan, all dead.

He let the scroll spring back into shape and looked across the desk.

Ludovico's expression was anxious, but determined, his hand still half out-stretched. Bonifaz was watching Miguel's face, eyes wary but calculating.

Each of them would have their preferred candidates. He wouldn't be surprised if goodwill presents had already been offered, though he doubted Ludovico would have accepted, the man was pompous but honest.

It was tempting to tear the list in two.

Before he could do so there came a knock at the door.

'Come in.'

Mercedes, the little house maid, bobbed a curtsey as she entered.

'Begging your pardon, Sirs,' she said. 'Senor has a visitor, Don Iago de Torlona. He is in the receiving salon.'

'Thank you, Mercedes, I'll attend him shortly,' Miguel leaned forward. 'Very well, gentlemen, I will consider on my future wife.'

Ludovico sat back, relieved. Bonifaz smiled. Both got to their feet and, bowing and nodding goodbye, followed Mercedes from the room.

Well, he supposed, it couldn't have been easy, bringing that up. And they were right, the Delgado family would need an heir.

Miguel had no intention of settling down and running his estates, he wanted to do things, to see things, he wouldn't always be at home. He was content to leave the running of the estate to Ludovico – the man had served his father well. But an heir was required and he needed to marry.

Miguel stood and turned to the window. Looking out, he did not see the courtyard beyond the glass. He saw the waves rolling across the ocean.

There could only be one wife for him. One who would go with him wherever he went, not sit in a house, however grand. He remembered the crow's nest on the Teresa the salty sea-wind blowing in his hair, and hers. Her face pale and delicate, above the blade of Don Raul's knife at her throat, her grey eyes wide with fear.

He had not seen her in the week since their return to Jerez.

It had been necessary. There had been business to do, arrangements to make without letting his household know his purpose.

There were difficulties and very real obstacles, like her religion. Her family might not like the idea of a Christian son-in-law, though his wealth and status might be some compensation. But Rebecca Calamiel, niece of a silversmith, however respectable and skilled, would not be considered a suitable match for the head of the Delgado family. Were they alive, his parents would never have allowed it.

Miguel felt a twinge of guilt. He shouldn't be glad that his parents could no longer object.

So he had to ensure that there would be no letters addressed to far-flung Delgado kin from Ludovico or Bonifaz, complaining that he was sullying the family name.

It was hard to keep away from her, but he made himself do it. Yet now, he found, he was nervous of seeing her. How would she receive him?

Miguel heaved a sigh. First things first, he should go and meet his visitor.

He walked briskly along the wide corridor to the salon, trying to recall all he knew about Don Iago de Torlona.

One of Ludovico's more useful ideas had been to seek out information about the noble followers of the King, who they were and where they fitted into the hierarchy of the court. Don Iago was the King's Falconer, a Christian knight and now the owner of a palace near the Alcazar, formerly the property of a wealthy Muslim family, but gifted to him by his liege lord the King.

It was courtesy to receive him and good policy too, Don Iago might be useful. Miguel's own title and lands had been confirmed, but his position wasn't unassailable. After all, the Delgados had fought with the city's defenders.

The double doors to the receiving salon were ajar and Miguel could see his caller, facing away from him, looking around the room. He was shorter than Miguel, with a wiry, sinewy build and wore his black hair long, tied back at the nape of his neck with a strap. His sleeveless leather covered a blue silk shirt and black hose.

Good day, Don Iago,' Miguel said, entering the room and bowing formally.

The man turned.

Miguel blinked in surprise, forcing his expression to remain welcoming.

One of the man's eyes was sightless and whitened, amid a mass of reddened flesh. In one swift movement Don Iago pulled his eye patch down to cover it.

Damn. He should have remembered.

Ludovico had told him the story of Iago's injury. In search of an eagle chick to train he had climbed up to an eerie, but the mother, a strong and powerful bird, had returned to the nest and attacked. Don Iago had been lucky to escape with his life, but without one eye.

His other eye was a soft dark brown. In his early twenties, Miguel guessed, and good looking, were it not for..... Still, the eye-patch lent him a saturnine air, which some women might find attractive. And he was rich.

'Don Miguel,' he shook Miguel's proffered hand. 'Thank you for receiving me without an introduction.'

'My pleasure,' Miguel replied. 'You are welcome.'

The two young men stood, looking each other over.

The Torlonas were not old nobility. Don Iago owed his status and position to his father, also Royal Falconer. This was no sinecure, for it was widely known that the King loved to hunt and kept many fine birds. He rode out hawking whenever he was able. So the falconer was a practical man.

But why was Don Iago calling on him?

'Do you hunt, Sir?' The visitor asked.

'It has been known,' Miguel replied, smiling. 'Though not of late. All my family's hunting birds were killed during the recent siege.'

And they had tasted well enough.

'Ah, yes, I can see how that would be,' Don Iago said. 'I'm sorry.'

'The fortunes of war.' Miguel shrugged.

'But then...' Don Iago paused. 'Perhaps I may offer you one of my birds. Not the King's, naturally, which are the very best, but I have more than enough. It would be some recompense for the loss of your own.'

'Thank you. That is a very generous offer.'

'Not at all. A gentleman should never be without hunting birds, otherwise people like me would be idle.' Don Iago grinned. 'Perhaps you would call upon me and choose your falcon. And, I hope, meet my sister. Beatriz is widowed and now keeps my house for me.'

So that was it, back to the question of marriage. The bird was but a lure, to entice him to see the sister. Was every one trying to marry him off?

'I would like that,' Miguel bowed. He had little choice. To reject such an offer from one with the King's ear would not be wise.

'Perhaps tomorrow morning?' Don Iago returned the bow.

'I look forward to it,' Miguel reached for a little silver bell, which sat on a low table. At its ring Mercedes appeared. 'I will call on you tomorrow.'

'Until tomorrow.' Don Iago smiled and followed Mercedes out.

4.

The Good Son

Atta lifted the ewer high and poured.

Cold water ran over his head and shoulders, slicking his long black hair to his scalp and neck. By heaven it was cold.

He shuddered as it ran down his naked body. Reaching for a towel, he could see his own blurred outline in the polished wall tiles. He was still very thin, but his muscles were taut and strong when he flexed them as he dried himself down. His body had hardened. Quickly, he pulled on a heavy cotton robe.

He was fresh and clean and ready for mosque. Except that there was no mosque to go to.

Atta left the cold room of the baths and wandered into the salon, rubbing his hair dry. Here the air was warmed by hot coals in braziers on ornate stands. Gold-fringed cushions littered low divans and he threw himself down onto one of them.

He rolled on to his back and looked up at the carved and painted ceiling.

The Ambassador's residence was luxurious, a far cry from the apartment where he had lived with his father near Plaza Mercado.

He shared this new home with his Uncle Mustafa, Ambassador from Emir Mohammed of Granada to His Majesty King Alfonso of Castile and Leon.

Turning his head towards the window he saw the top of the minaret reaching up into a blue sky. It had recently grown taller, with the addition of a bell tower. The sound of bells was one of the first changes he'd noticed upon his return to Jerez. They rang the hour and they rang to summon the faithful to prayer. The muezzins called no longer.

He levered himself upright and pushed his feet into his shoes. He must be ready for the King's Cavalry Lieutenant who was coming to discuss plans to rescue his father.

Atta's footsteps echoed as he walked through the empty rooms of the residence.

He found Lieutenant Riccardo already in the salon, sitting to study a large map unrolled on a low table before him. He rose when Atta entered and smiled. There were well-worn creases in his sun-tanned cheeks and about his dark eyes, beneath a tight thatch of curly black hair.

'Please, sit,' Atta said, indicating the divan. 'That's a fine map.'

It showed the coastline of the Bay, with the course of the Rio Guadalete winding to Jerez and beyond. The blue line of the river crossed the plain to the hills and valleys and thence to the high sierras to the east. There were fewer details shown in the mountains, but Atta knew that high country, the deep defiles and snow covered valleys.

'Here,' the cavalry officer stabbed his finger down, his voice echoing in the large room. 'This is where we are headed.'

Atta sat by Riccardo's side and leaned over to look, folding his long legs cross-wise beneath the table.

'Yes, I think that's where I found the entrance to the valley,' Atta said. 'But I can't be sure. I was trekking all through the night in the dark.'

'Don't worry,' Riccardo assured him. 'Our scouts will reconnoitre the ground.'

'But the bandits will know we're coming.'

'They will have look-outs, Atta, of course they'll know we're coming.'

'But what about my father? If he's there, won't they kill him when they see us?'

'No, I don't think so,' Riccardo shook his head. 'Bandit groups like this wait out the winter in camps, abducting people to work for them. Come spring they'll disperse – one of the reasons why we must set out soon. But they were very lucky to come upon someone with your father's skills. This is good. It means they're unlikely to harm him, he's simply too valuable to them. And, after all, they don't know we're looking for him. As far as they know, we're just conducting a military exercise.'

It sounded convincing, the cavalryman knew his business.

'We'll attack their camp,' the Lieutenant continued. 'But the bandits will probably run, heading for the high mountains. Anyway they'll probably be too busy defending themselves to think about your father.' He sat back in his chair. 'I just wish we had time to get someone on the inside, it would have made things so much easier.'

Atta frowned.

33

He had suggested exactly this, to get a spy into the camp, on their journey back to Jerez but Uncle Mustafa had not heeded his advice.

'How many men do you have?' A deep voice asked.

Atta looked round sharply. He hadn't heard his uncle enter, but there he was, towering over them. Fresh from his daily exercise, his right hand was hooked into a wide leather belt, below his curling beard, which glistened with sweat. In his left hand he held a towel.

The Lieutenant began to rise.

'No, sit. Sit.' Mustafa strode around to the other side of the table and lowered his massive frame on to another divan. He mopped his shiny brow and neck with the towel.

'I have thirty men,' Riccardo replied.

'We have another ten. My nephew and I will bring our guards - for protection,' the Ambassador said.

'Sir, your safety is paramount,' the Lieutenant began to protest but paused, uncertain, as Mustafa's mouth twitched into a smile.

Atta smiled too. The thought of the giant swordsman needing protection seemed absurd. His uncle practiced with the scimitar for an hour every morning and wrestled with his guards - none of them wanted to fight him.

'But, sir,' Riccardo persisted. 'This is a military operation ordered by his Majesty the King.'

'And you are in command of it. Yes, Lieutenant, I understand,' Mustafa said. 'My guards will be under your orders for as long as the mission lasts. I will instruct Major Rashid, their commander, to take his orders from you. Now, if we have correctly observed the military hierarchy,' he got to his feet, 'I must bathe.'

Lieutenant Riccardo had a wary look in his eyes, but he said nothing more.

Atta understood. This mission was dangerous enough, without the Lieutenant taking along soldiers who owed their allegiance to the Emir, his King's recent enemy.

The new found peace was fragile and it was said that the King was, even now, in Sevilla raising more troops for an attack on Granada. The truce might fail any day, but it had to last long enough to allow his father's rescue.

'I too must take my leave,' the Lieutenant said, also rising. 'Forgive me, but I must return to the Alcazar.'

He bowed to them both and strode away.

The Ambassador watched him, one eyebrow raised.

'He's uncomfortable about our guards,' Atta said.

'That's as may be, but they're coming,' his uncle replied, his mouth a thin line. 'And he's clever enough to know that the King's Vizier would support me, if it came to it. Now, the baths!'

'Uncle, I'm going to the hospital and I'll visit Simon and Rebecca on the way, for news of Nathan,' Atta hesitated. 'I want to go alone, without the guards.'

He paused. It was ridiculous, having to ask if he could walk the streets of his own town alone. It was bad enough having guards within the house, there was no privacy anywhere, but his uncle insisted that they accompanied him when he went out.

Jerez was his home, the place where he'd grown up, he didn't need guards. And he certainly wasn't going to take them to the Calamiels, they had had their fill of soldiers.

Mustafa looked down at his nephew and nodded his assent.

35

Quickly, before he changed his mind, Atta hurried to collect his cloak and medicine satchel. Out into the cool air he headed for the Juderia.

The town felt busy. People were out and about. There were many fair north-men from Leon or Castile and some looked at him, curious. He was unusual now, the Ambassador's entourage were the only Moorish faces in Jerez, all others had fled or been driven into exile. There had been convoys of refugees after the siege, on foot or with pack animals, thronging the roads beyond the walls and disappearing into the countryside. He and his father had joined one of them months before.

As he approached the blue painted gate, he heard raised voices in the courtyard beyond.

'I didn't say you shouldn't go out.' That was Simon. 'Only that you take more care, be less... challenging.'

'I won't skulk in the shadows. I just want to walk the streets of my home town.' Rebecca's voice answered.

'Then let me come with you.'

'No. I must do this myself. Not give in to them.'

Atta slowed his steps, knocked on the wood and opened the gate.

'Just be sensible,' Simon said, leaning forward, hands outstretched and palms upwards, with an exasperated look on his face. 'Oh, Atta, it's you.' His hands dropped to his sides.

Across the courtyard, Rebecca stood, hands on hips, lips pressed closed, chin up-tilted. Clutching a scarf in one hand, she wore coat and boots as if she was going out. Once more it struck him how different she looked, with her suntanned skin and short hair.

36

From the words he had overheard it seemed that she had changed within too, that she was much more sure of herself.

Her wide grey eyes were now full of indignation and he sensed that anger wasn't far beneath the surface. She radiated tension and a deep unhappiness.

Oh dear. Clearly he had arrived at the wrong moment.

'I..er.. hope I'm not disturbing you,' he said, looking at first one then the other.

'No, no,' Simon recovered his composure. 'Please, come in,' he indicated the house.

'Yes,' Rebecca smiled, too brightly. 'Tell us all your news.'

'Gladly, but I'm looking for news from you. Have you heard anything of Nathan?'

'No.' Simon's mouth snapped closed upon the word. His eyes grew blank and unseeing.

Rebecca's stance softened. She came over and gently laid her hand upon her uncle's arm.

'We would have heard if.... anything had happened to him,' she said 'You mustn't give up hope.'

'Hope. What should I hope for? He chose to go.'

He shook off her hand and marched into the house.

Rebecca pulled off her coat and grimaced at Atta as they followed him inside,

A fire burned in the living room hearth and Atta hung his cloak on the usual peg in the lobby. He joined Simon and Rebecca at the table.

Simon's face was heavy and immobile, while Rebecca gnawed at her lower lip. Neither spoke.

37

What could he say?

'There's to be a meeting,' he said to Simon. 'To plan my father's rescue. Will you come, sir? We need a man who knows the countryside.' Atta hesitated. Simon had learned much about the countryside when he was searching for his runaway niece.

'I don't know the mountains, Atta,' Simon answered. 'Though I would like to help.'

'The bandits are camped in the foothills, we think,' Atta said. 'Not the mountains.'

Simon didn't reply.

'When is the meeting?' Rebecca asked.

'The day after tomorrow,' he said. 'We set out soon after.'

'So soon...' Rebecca whispered then looked at her uncle.

'It can't be soon enough for me,' Atta murmured. 'Every day my father is held is a day when he could come to harm.'

Simon reached over and patted him on the shoulder.

'And it's best to go before news of our plans can leak out.' Atta looked at Simon. 'Will you come with us?'

'I'll attend the meeting,' Simon said. He gave his niece a sharp look. 'I'll think about coming along, though there are other things to consider.'

Rebecca pushed her chair back and stamped out into the kitchen.

Atta looked, questioningly, at Simon, who shook his head.

There were undercurrents here, things he knew nothing about. Unable to think of anything else to say, Atta stood.

'Well, I'd best be on my way to the hospital,' he said.

Rebecca was in the kitchen doorway, her face closed and guarded. How could he help her?

What if.....?

'Why don't you come with me?' He asked her.

Her mouth opened but no sound emerged.

'It's not her proper place...' Simon began.

'Yes.' Rebecca answered. Her eyes shone.

'High-born ladies attend there now,' Atta reassured Simon. 'The Lady Beatriz, sister of Alfonso's Knight, Don Iago, comes every other day.'

'I'll bet she doesn't get her hands dirty,' Simon said. He seemed reluctant to let his niece go.

'She's nobility, she wouldn't clean the floor,' Atta replied. 'But she helps with the patients.'

Simon frowned. 'My niece may not have noble blood, but she is no one's skivvy.'

'I'll remind you of that when the floor wants cleaning,' Rebecca said, smiling now.

Atta turned to Simon, who seemed to be deliberating.

But Rebecca was at the doorway, pulling on her coat again. She had decided for herself.

'I'll be coming back this way later, this evening,' he said.

'There Uncle,' Rebecca arched her eyebrows. 'I'll have a chaperone to protect me and I won't give our neighbours more cause to complain.'

'Very well,' Simon said. 'See that you're back before dark.'

The sun was high and shadows were few as Atta stepped out on to the narrow lane. He shot a glance at the young woman walking at his side.

What did she mean - ammunition? Were things so bad for her?

'Have your neighbours been... unfriendly since your return?'

'You could say that.' Rebecca kicked a stone up the street. 'My uncle worries too much. It'd be good if he came with your expedition. Give him something else to focus on.'

So, she wasn't going to confide in him and had neatly changed the subject.

'I hope he does.' It would be good to have him along.

Soon they reached the paved square in front of the hospital. On the facade of the low building directly opposite them the striped awning had been put back into its place.

Atta felt a shock, a jolt almost like a blow. It looked just as it had before the siege. The last time he had seen it like this was the day the city fell. The day Juan died.

'Atta.'

There was someone touching his arm. It was Rebecca, a look of concern on her face.

'Sorry,' he said. 'They've put the awning back. It surprised me.'

It was dark inside the hospital, made darker still by the awning. Atta and Rebecca stood on the threshold, allowing their eyes to adjust. He nodded a greeting to the two helpers working that day as they noticed his arrival. Over to one side he saw Senor Thomas' fair head. The surgeon waved and came towards them.

'Rebecca, I didn't expect to see you here.'

'I've come to help,' Rebecca said. 'If you'll let me.'

'Of course, thank you,' Thomas replied. 'It's getting to be quite a tradition in your family.'

'I've never done any nursing before.' She sounded hesitant now.

40

'Don't worry, we'll teach you. Even Nathan managed.' Thomas smiled. 'Come. Let me introduce you to Pepe, he's one of our orderlies. He'll show you what to do.' He gestured for her to follow him.

Atta watched as Thomas lead Rebecca away. She would fit in here, he was certain and it would take her mind off her other worries.

Then he walked beyond the pierced wooden screen to where the surgeon's table lay and prepared for work. He removed his heavy cloak and turned back the sleeves of his shirt, but he left the leather apron on its hook. There would be no surgery today.

A leather box sat on the table before him. Opening it, he checked the instruments - lancets and scalpels, forceps, retractors - all had belonged to his father. It was impossible to be here without being reminded of him.

Atta's chest tightened as he imagined the tall, gaunt figure weaving between the rows of beds, advising, questioning and soothing, dark eyes lit by compassion. Where was he now and in what peril?

He shook his head, dispelling such thoughts, as he pulled on the cotton coat he wore when he examined patients. There was no point in speculating, he'd find out soon. Time to get on with things.

As he stepped from behind the screen he spotted Rebecca on the other side of the hospital, coatless, with sleeves rolled up to her elbows. A girl with short hair. She unwound bandages from the chest of her patient, a former galley slave named Pablo.

At his bedside his friends watched, a huge black-skinned man and a small fellow with a broken nose – he'd seen them here before.

Both were freedmen, former galley slaves, who had taken part in the sea battle, somehow breaking their chains. Many slaves had been brought to the hospital, all of them carrying the scars of captivity, the marks of irons and the lash. Their new wounds were laid upon old ones. Atta had not seen the like before.

Now they laughed, the black skinned man's rolling guffaw beneath the other, lighter voices. Rebecca seemed at ease in their company, chivvying and jesting, lightening their spirits. She would do very well here. There was more than one way for a hospital to heal the sick.

Pleased, Atta turned to his first patient.

5.

Eid-al-Adha

Atta raised his face to the afternoon sun. It was Eid-al-Adha and the day after he had taken Rebecca to the hospital. He had said his prayers and now stood at the edge of Plaza Mercado, the large square near where his old home had once stood.

Tall palm trees formed an avenue in the centre of the square and lined its perimeter. The space between was filled by market stalls. There were no shades or awnings aloft today, for the stallholders were glad of what warmth the sun afforded. They shouted their wares over the noise of the crowd of shoppers.

'Good bread, baked today!'

'Fresh fish, caught this morning!'

He could smell the fish stalls' salty tang. There had always been fishermen and their stalls at the market, selling that morning's catch.

Goats and sheep bleated in their pens, as all around was colour and bustle. Patterns of glossy vegetables or cuts of meat, dark red rimmed with yellow fat, arranged upon the counters. At a baker's stall there was the aroma of freshly baked bread and cinnamon from

43

new made pastries. Atta immersed himself in the sights, smells and sounds. It all felt familiar. It all felt like home.

Yet there were additions.

In the centre of the square was a new drinking fountain. Men sat on its stone plinth enjoying the sun, laughing and throwing dice, calling out in strange accents. Their clothes were an odd mixture of heavy northern hides and southern finery. Newcomers.

Close by at a stall, a large man stood. He wore leather boots and a jerkin beneath his winter cloak with a jewel-handled scimitar pushed into his belt. Atta glanced, covertly, at the weapon. It was a ceremonial sword, not for everyday. No one wore such a sword to the market.

Most of these folk were new, not the people he had known, or even people like them. They were people who sought better fortune in the conquered lands, mercenaries, traders, craftsmen and their families who followed the King's army.

His gaze was drawn to another man, a figure who looked vaguely familiar. He wore a cloak with a hat drawn low over his face, even in the sunshine. Was this someone he knew? Someone from before?

Atta jumped, startled, as a bell tolled four close by.

The ringing came from scaffolding on the north-west side of the square, where the partial outline of a building rose up from the ruins of another. Another church, its unfinished walls festooned with ropes and spars.

What had he expected? Everything changed.

His market square existed only in the memory now. He began to regret coming here, but it had seemed the closest he could get to his old life. Especially today, at Eid.

No, he had lost the sense of the old market place. It had gone.

He quickened his steps, heading to a road off the south side of the square. The few people ambling along it paid him no heed, yet he felt he was being observed.

The hairs on the back of his neck began to rise.

Was someone watching him?

He had felt it in the square too, this discomfort, but had mistaken it for his own alienation. Now Atta was sure - someone was following him.

He stopped and bent to adjust his shoe, taking the chance to look around.

At the edge of his vision he caught sight of the same figure, the man he had thought familiar, hovering at the corner of the square. Atta looked up quickly at him, to try and see his face, but the figure turned away, disappearing down a side alley.

Surely, he knew this person.

Quick. Follow him.

The alleyway was in deep shadow and there was no sign of the watcher. Buildings on each side were already shuttered and closed against the coming night.

He would have to follow if he was to find out what was going on.

Gripping the hilt of his dagger Atta hurried along, glancing to either side. If someone was waiting to jump him, he'd be ready. He slowed his steps as he reached the alley's end. Either the watcher had entered one of the houses or he had sprinted along the length of the alley.

It was lighter here, where the buildings stopped, though daylight was beginning to fade. In front of him was an area of waste ground, covered by tents and gimcrack dwellings. Smoke curled upwards from cook-fires and Atta could smell meat roasting.

He inhaled deeply - that smelled like roasting mutton.

Could someone be celebrating Eid? Were there people of his own faith here? It would be so good to share the feast day, as he and his father had used to do with their friend and neighbours. Did some Moors remain? He had to find out.

The sound of laughter drew him in, along wooden planks which formed a rough pathway between the shacks. Turning a corner, he came upon an open space where a group of rough-clad men sat around a bonfire. A spit bearing a sheep turned above the fire.

He stopped.

These men weren't celebrating Eid, they looked unwashed and there was a pervading smell of alcohol. In the dusk the bright glow of the fire lit their faces from below. More than one of them looked up at his sudden arrival among them.

Maybe this wasn't such a good place to be. He dropped his eyes and began to edge carefully around the group. He had almost reached the south side of the clearing when his eye was caught by a sudden movement.

It was him again. The watcher. He was flitting along the other side in the shadows.

'Hey!' Atta cried out and started forward.

On the bonfire a branch crackled and broke. His quarry stopped and turned to look back. The fire flared and lit the scene.

What? It couldn't be.....

But it was. Atta was certain.

It was Nathan.

Then he was gone, slipping between two of the cabins.

He had to follow.

But men who, moments before, had been sitting at the fire were now clustered around him. One carried a flaming brand, another held a club.

'What are you doing nosing about?' The first said in unfriendly tones. 'This is our camp, see.'

Another thrust his face close to Atta's. His breath smelled rank. 'And who are you?'

Keep calm, Atta told himself, but his heart began to beat faster.

'I - I've just been to the market....'

'So?' Another called from beside the fire. The man with the club stepped forward, hefting it in his hand and slapping it on to his other palm.

Atta began to retreat, stumbling backwards. He reached for the hilt of his dagger, but let it go. Better not give them an excuse to attack him.

Away from the bonfire he couldn't see his way. The men drew closer.

'Stop!'

A large figure seemed to come out of nowhere, to step in front of Atta. The closest man fell back, with an exclamation, as the other lowered his club.

'I know this man. It's the doctor.' Firelight reflected on his rescuer's dark skin. 'From the hospital, don't you recognise him? He's been treating Pablo and the others.'

Atta relaxed.

It was the big man who had been at the hospital, at the bedside of Rebecca's patient, only the day before. Were the men here the former galley slaves? Was this how they lived now?

'Come,' the man indicated that Atta follow him, as the others returned to the bonfire. 'It's not safe here. You need to leave.'

Atta hurried to catch up as the man strode off. In the growing darkness he could barely make out the way, but his guide didn't hesitate.

'They aren't bad men,' the man said as they walked. 'But suspicion breeds suspicion and the townsfolk here don't like us. Some of my comrades will strike first and ask questions later, they don't take kindly to interlopers.'

'I meant no harm,' Atta replied. ''Though I thank you for your help. I thought I saw my friend.'

'Is your friend a freedman? We are all former slaves here, from the galley *Hebe*.'

'No... I... yes...'

Why should this man know Nathan? His presence in the camp could be a coincidence. Yet Atta had a nagging sense of something eluding him. A piece of the puzzle was missing.

Lantern light shone up ahead as they had emerged from the shanty camp onto a steep cobbled road which led back down into the valley.

'I'll leave you here,' the man said and turned to retrace his steps.

'No, wait!'

The man stopped and looked back.

What could he say?

'Nothing...I'm sorry. Thank you.'

The man shrugged and went on his way.

Atta started down the sloping road, his brow furrowed. Had he really seen his friend?

If it was Nathan, why was he hiding and why had he run? Did their friendship mean nothing now? Was he in some kind of trouble?

Tomorrow he would return and search, perhaps with a guard or two. But no, he couldn't bring Emiri guards here. It would be asking for trouble. And tomorrow was the expedition meeting.

Atta came to an abrupt halt.

He couldn't search for his friend and plan to rescue his father. He couldn't do both.

With heart and mind torn in two, Atta began walking again, down into the valley.

6.

Casa Delgado

Miguel contemplated his reflection in the long mirror.

Not too bad, not bad at all.

He wore a damson coloured doublet, over a crisp white linen shirt and dark hose, girt about with an embroidered and jewelled sword belt. He'd finally decided to abandon the black of mourning. It was nearly five months since Juan and his father had died and it seemed much longer.

His curling, chestnut hair fell over his collar, to just below his chin and jaw-line. He rubbed his palm over the smooth, closely-shaved skin. He had arranged for a barber especially.

Yes, it would do.

Reaching into the leather pouch hanging from his belt he withdrew a small box. Inside was a ring, with a brilliant diamond in its bezel. The gem was set into the golden Delgado crest, of a heron with a fish in its beak, forming a circle. It had belonged to his mother and his mother's mother and, probably her mother before her.

Miguel turned the ring over in his fingers and the sun reflected in the diamond to scatter sprays of colour on to the white walls of his room.

An image of Rebecca filled his thoughts, her eyes which twinkled when their owner teased and grew cloudy when she was troubled. He would see her later tonight. His pulse quickened at the thought.

He would offer her the ring tonight.

He had reason to visit the Calamiel house. It was Captain Morientes' last night ashore, he and the *Teresa* were sailing from Cadiz on the morrow, and Miguel was celebrating with Thomas and the Captain this evening. They would visit the Calamiels to collect the Englishman.

Maybe, if all went well, they might have something else to celebrate?

And yet.

What if she turned him down?

Miguel smiled, it wasn't likely.

There was a soft knock at his door. His hand closed over the ring.

'Come in.'

'Guests, Sir.' It was a servant. 'Captain Morientes and Don Iago de Torlona, in the grand salon.'

'Thank you, I'll be with them presently,' Miguel dismissed the man.

Miguel had visited Don Iago that morning, as agreed. They had talked easily and Miguel found that he enjoyed the man's company. It was difficult to think of him as an enemy, as part of the army

52

which had killed his own father and brother. Miguel had also met his sister, widow of a fallen soldier of the King. An attractive young woman, but not for him. Something he hoped he had made plain without giving offence.

He had invited Iago to this evening's jaunt, in part out of courtesy and because he liked him but also for policy. Right now Thomas was at Court, but at some time in the future he would be going home to England. One never knew when one might need a man with access to the King. An ally was an ally, when all was said and done.

Now Don Iago awaited him in the salon downstairs. He shouldn't keep him and the Captain waiting.

Miguel placed the ring back into its box and snapped the lid shut. Then he hesitated.

He had deflected any interest from Doña Beatriz only that morning. Now he was planning to propose to a Jewish silversmith's niece in front of her brother, Don Iago. With reason, the nobleman might think it a grave insult.

Damn, damn, damn.

Why had he invited Don Iago?

Because he was head of the family now and had to think of the future. Yet he hadn't really considered what this might mean for him tonight. Damn. This problem was of his own making.

Could he speak with Rebecca privately?

Miguel put the ring box into the drawer of his bedroom cabinet. Perhaps he shouldn't offer it to her tonight after all. Still undecided, he descended the wide stone staircase to the ground floor and strode across the black and white chequer-board tiles to the salon.

Inside the lamps were lit, though the last of the daylight filtered in through the windows. There was a fire burning in the wide hearth.

Don Iago sat on a wide divan, while the Captain stood to one side of the fire, his elbow resting on the high mantelpiece. As he entered both were smiling and Miguel got the distinct impression that he had been the subject of their discussion.

'Don Miguel,' Don Iago rose and bowed.

The Captain gave him a mock salute. 'Dressed for the town, I see,' he said, eyeing the doublet.

'In your honour,' he retorted as he bowed to Don Iago.

Don Iago smiled and acknowledged him with an elegant gesture of his hand.

'Are you ready?' The Captain straightened up. 'We go first to collect Thomas, Senor Thomas of Whelmstone. Do you know him, Iago? He's physician to the King.'

'By sight only.' Iago stood. 'I look forward to meeting him.'

'He lodges with the Calamiels. He was billeted on the family after the siege, but they are friends now, he and Simon Calamiel and his niece, Rebecca.'

Ears pricked, but unwilling to join the conversation, Miguel led the way back into the hall.

The ring. Should he take it just in case he got the opportunity to propose?

He glanced towards the staircase.

No, the Captain was already at the main doors with Don Iago close behind. It was too late. Tonight he would say that he would return tomorrow to speak with her alone. He would propose then, before the expedition set out. That's what he'd do.

They walked through the darkening streets, pools of light preceding them as the lamp lighters went on their rounds. As the Captain told Don Iago about Rebecca and her disguise on the *Teresa* Miguel pressed his lips together, determined not to be drawn into their discusstion. It was with something like relief that he saw the blue painted gate up ahead in the lantern light.

'Here we are,' he said and raised his hand to rap on it. But the gate swung open.

'Oh.' A bearded older man stepped back, a look of surprise on his face.

'That's alright, father,' said a young man, just behind the elder, his high forehead catching the lamp light. Of a lighter colouring, his pale eyes were wary. 'It's just visitors come to call on Simon.'

It was Benjamin Isaacs. What was he doing here?

'Of course, of course,' the older man stood back from the gate and gestured for them to enter, looking them over.

'Come, father,' Benjamin Isaacs placed a hand on the older man's shoulder. 'We must go.'

Miguel watched him lead his father away, walking protectively by his side. Isaacs was rich, Bonifaz had said, a rich Jewish merchant. Benjamin was his only son, who was a good friend of the Calamiel family and unmarried.

Rebecca's uncle came out into the courtyard, his initial look of surprise swiftly replaced by a smile.

'Captain, you are always most welcome,' he said, reaching out to take the Captain's hand. 'And Miguel Delgado, your younger brother used to be here so often, but we hardly see you at all. Welcome to my house. Thomas awaits you.'

Miguel was busy scanning the courtyard and the front of the house, but he acknowledged the smith with a shallow bow. Where was Rebecca? Had Benjamin Isaacs called to see her?

'May I present Don Iago de Torlona,' the Captain said, as Don Iago made a low bow.

'A pleasure to meet you, Sir,' Simon returned the bow. 'Please, come in. Welcome to my house.'

As he turned to enter the house a slim figure slipped into the courtyard.

Miguel's insides did a somersault.

Her short hair only emphasised her long slim neck and delicate heart-shaped face above a wide-necked blouse. The laced bodice and full skirt showed off her lithe figure. How could he ever have mistaken such a creature for a boy?

The look in her eyes was cool and appraising.

'Ah, Rebecca.' Simon said. 'May I present my niece, Don Iago, Rebecca Calamiel.'

'Senor.' Rebecca curtseyed low and bowed her head, demurely, but when she looked up her eyes were bright with the curiosity which he remembered from her early days upon the Teresa. 'What brings you all to call on us?'

'I return to sea tomorrow,' the Captain said. 'So I wished to say goodbye. And we come to collect Thomas, of course.'

'How long will you be away?' Rebecca asked, as she and the Captain strolled into the house, Simon and Don Iago following. Miguel brought up the rear.

The living room was warm and well lit. Thomas was hurrying down the stairs towards them.

'Here he is!' The Captain said. 'Thomas, you know Don Iago de Torlona I think?'

The courtesies continued.

This was hopeless, he needed to speak with her alone.

As if on cue Rebecca walked away into the kitchen. This might be his chance.

Miguel followed after her.

She closed the kitchen window, shutting out the sounds from Plaza Plateros, but she didn't meet his eye. With quick, neat movements she placed a flagon and goblets on to a tray on the kitchen table.

Standing on the other side of the table, Miguel hesitated. Now it came to it he wondered what to say.

'How are you?'

'I am well,' she replied. 'You must be very busy. I haven't seen you since we returned.'

'Yes...'

A slight line formed between her eyebrows, the suspicion of a frown. Was she displeased? He could explain.

'There've been many things to do, to make sure everything would be ready....'

That didn't sound convincing, even to him.

What should he say, when he wanted to say so much? He moved around the table, stopping short of embracing her, but standing very close. He would tell her that he wanted to take her in his arms, that he wanted to be with her always.

'Oh, I've no doubt,' Rebecca picked up the tray and held it in front of her, a barrier between them. 'So much of such great importance.'

So she was displeased. Angry, maybe?

'I haven't forgotten...our time on the *Teresa*,' he hurried on. 'I just wanted everything to be ready...'

'So you said. Ready for what?'

'Rebecca?' Simon called from the living room. 'You neglect our guests.'

'Coming, Uncle.' Rebecca rolled her eyes and swung past him into the living room.

Damn.

He followed close behind.

'Wine, gentlemen?'

She filled his senses as she handed around the goblets of wine. He was aware of nothing in the room but the young woman beside him, of her deftness and grace, the perfume of her, the light of the lamps on her hair.

He had to speak to her. She seemed to be waiting for him to say something.

'Was that Ben Isaacs I saw just leaving?'

'It was,' Rebecca replied. 'He and his father sometimes come to call. Solomon doesn't go out much alone these days.'

'No....'

There was a silence, but the others filled it.

Her face was turned slightly away from him and she seemed guarded, restrained, but very aware of him. His body was attuned to

58

her every movement, his skin fizzled, anticipating the electricity of her touch.

What could he say, within the others' earshot?

'You look very fine,' she said to him, smoothing down her woollen skirts.

'Yes, no, not especially.'

He was talking jibberish. He didn't seem to be able to get the words out? It hadn't been like this before, on the *Teresa*.

'There is to be an expedition,' he said. 'Tomorrow. To the mountains, to tackle the bandits.'

'I know, Atta told us. My uncle is going with it, as a guide.'

'I have been asked to,' Simon said, with a sharp look. 'Though I haven't yet decided whether or not I shall go.'

'I'm going...' He had to tell her he would be away, but she spoke at the same time.

'Are you...?' Her wide eyes were fixed on his face.

'Please,' Miguel gestured that she should speak.

'No, no, you, please.'

The room had fallen quiet.

Someone had addressed him directly, but he didn't know what had been said. He looked from face to face for someone to give him a clue.

'Are you ready?' The Captain prompted him.

'What? Yes.'

Miguel upset his goblet as he put it down onto the table.

Rebecca caught and righted it. She had made no sound but he sensed her disapproval. Why was he so clumsy?

Why was everyone looking at him?

'Right, well, we'll be going then,' he said.

'Good fortune go with you,' Rebecca said, but she wasn't looking at him. She stepped forwards and took the Captain's hands in her own as she looked up into his face. 'And return safely.'

'I plan to,' the Captain replied, gently. 'Take care, it's not going to be easy.'

'I know.' Swiftly Rebecca reached up on tiptoe and kissed his cheek.

'I am honoured,' he said, cornflower blue eyes glinting with amusement. 'Be careful, you'll be making the others jealous.'

'And I am honoured to have met you,' Don Iago bowed to Rebecca and Simon. 'I hope we will meet again.'

'Sir,' Simon looked pleased by the courtesy. 'Let me show you out.'

So saying, he led the way out into the courtyard. The other men followed, but Miguel hung back. He turned to Rebecca, who was collecting up the goblets.

'Rebecca...'

She looked up at him expectantly, but her eyes glistened with tears. He found himself speechless, unable to turn away.

'Miguel, are you coming?' Senor Thomas' call broke the spell.

'I must...' he looked out into the courtyard where the others were standing, waiting, then back to Rebecca. His friends wanted to be on their way. The temperature was dropping now the sun had set and they were looking forward to their evening. But how could he leave?

'I'll come back,' he said, in a rush.

'Go,' she said, coming around the table to usher him out and reaching out a hand. 'Return tomorrow, tomorrow morning, before you leave. Now go!'

Slowly, Miguel walked into the courtyard, Rebecca following.

Don Iago and the Captain exchanged glances.

'Ready,' Miguel said.

'Right,' said Thomas. He spoke to Simon. 'I won't be waking you later, Miguel is to be my host for the night.'

'Goodbye,' the Captain said and waved.

'Goodbye,' she called. 'Farewell and come back safely.'

Rebecca stood near the house, her arms wrapped around her body in the cold. She looked so vulnerable and sad, it was all he could do to walk away. Then the gate closed shut behind them, sealing him off from her.

Miguel felt someone clap him on the back. It was the Captain. 'Come on man. Don't look so miserable. She'll be there tomorrow. But I won't. It's my last night ashore and I want to enjoy myself.'

'Of course. Sorry.' Miguel forced a smile. 'Where do we go first?'

What had he said? She'll be there.....

'Let's begin at El Gallo.' Thomas started off along the street. 'They have some fine venison I hear.'

Miguel couldn't help but look back. The lantern was shining above the blue painted gate. Beyond it was she upon whom his heart was set. And he hadn't even told her.

7.

The Visitor

Rebecca hid a yawn behind her hand, as she sat at the table with her uncle, eating hot oatmeal and honey.

Her eyelids were heavy and she felt sluggish and slow. She had slept little the night before, going over and over in her mind the meeting with Miguel the previous day. He obviously wanted to speak with her alone, but, when he had the chance, he said nothing. What was going on?

She had been so sure of him – on the Teresa and afterwards. Had she been wrong?

Things were different now.

Her glance flitted around the little room. The solid wooden chairs, the iron poker and tongs in the hearth, the thick wool mat which her aunt had made before she died - comfortable, good things. But how would they look to a wealthy nobleman? Nathan had told her how sumptuously the Delgado house was furnished and appointed. He was a frequent visitor to Juan.

At least Miguel could find no fault with their ornament, she thought, Simon was a master craftsman. Her gaze settled on the fine silverwork, the lamps, the menorah.

Jewish. They might be fine objects, but they were all Jewish. The room was full of them - she'd never realised before - the tiled mizrach set into the wall, the folded prayer shawl on the chest. He must have noticed them, noticed another difference between them.

None of these things had mattered when they were at sea. But, since their return...? Maybe Miguel had had second thoughts, or had been persuaded that she wasn't for him.

Would he return this morning as he had promised?

She started, as Simon dropped his spoon into his empty bowl.

At least her uncle's mood seemed lighter - last night's visitors had pleased him. Two noblemen, one high in the King's favour, it was a great courtesy, though he'd never admit to being flattered.

'I've been thinking,' Simon said. 'About our visitors.'

What had he been thinking? Had he divined her feelings for Miguel?

'You told me the Captain saved your life.'

'Yes.'

'And that you slept in his cabin.'

'Alone, Uncle. He had moved elsewhere.'

'Yes, the man's a gentleman, I can see that.' He was working around to something. 'And now he comes to call on you.'

So that was it. He'd marked the Captain as her suitor - the wrong tack entirely.

'To collect Señor Thomas, Uncle.'

'Yes, yes, but I just wondered...?'

64

'It was an honour was it not, to meet Don Iago?'

'Undoubtedly. It will do us no harm to have friends at court. Especially now.'

He didn't need to say more. He meant now that she was ostracised.

Even so, Rebecca couldn't help but smile to herself. Her secret was still secret.

Simon got to his feet.

'One way or another I'll be back when the meeting finishes,' he said, his eyes sad, as he pulled on his coat. 'From what Thomas said last night they plan to set out today. If I'm going with them I will need the mare.'

The dishes clattered as she collected them up. Once she heard the gate close behind her uncle she relaxed. She wanted to be alone with her thoughts.

Yet she had tasks to perform. So she washed the dishes in the water pail, then carried the heavy bucket into the yard and poured its dirty contents down the drain at the pump.

What was that? A noise. Was someone at the gate? Had Miguel left the meeting to come to her?

Rebecca finished pouring and then turned.

The gate was closed. She could see that the latch was in place, yet she was certain she had heard the handle turn. Had Simon closed it properly?

Best to make sure.

She crossed the courtyard, raised the latch and looked out, this way and that, into the lane beyond.

Outside, all was quiet. She must have been mistaken.

Rebecca closed the gate and returned to the house, dumping the pail into its place. She began to put away the cleaned dishes.

But wait. Surely there was another sound, a noise from inside the house this time.

Her insides grew cold.

Someone had entered the yard when her back had been turned and now they were in the house.

All sleepiness banished, she scanned the kitchen and reached, silently, for a heavy iron skillet. She weighed it in her hand.

This would do some damage.

The kitchen door was opened wide, flat against the wall. She tiptoed over and pressed her back against it, hefting the skillet handle in two hands. Had the intruder got as far as the living room? Dare she look out?

A floorboard creaked.

She knew that creak - it was from the board just inside the living room door. Whoever it was had entered without knocking or calling. They were up to no good.

Rebecca raised the skillet above her head. She would leap out and...

She jumped.

A figure was silhouetted against the light. A little taller than she was, muffled up in a cloak and hat. He whirled around to face her, raising his arms to catch her wrists.

Nathan.

It was Nathan.

'Hey! What are you doing? Trying to brain me?'

66

'What am I doing! What are you doing, sneaking in like this?' Her arms dropped to her sides, skillet still clutched in one hand. She didn't know whether to hug him or hit him.

'I was waiting 'til the coast was clear,' Nathan answered. 'I saw father leave, but there was no sign of Thomas, so I wasn't sure.'

'You've been watching the house! Oh, you idiot!' The skillet crashed to the floor and she hugged her cousin. 'Where have you been? Simon's been half out of his mind with worry that harm had come to you. He's desperate for news of you.'

She stood back and appraised him, holding both his hands out wide. It had been five months since last she saw him, before she had run away. Such a long time ago.

He looked tanned and healthy enough, though there was stubble on his chin and shadows beneath his eyes, where the skin seemed bruised and thin, almost transparent. He seemed older, more grown up.

He was wearing clothes that she hadn't seen before, thick boots, a heavy sheepskin coat and a woollen cloak. At the back of her mind she wondered where and how he had come by them. They looked like travelling clothes. Was he going on a journey?

He smelled of animals and woodsmoke. Where had he been living?

'Are you hungry?' She drew him towards the table and they sat. 'Do you want food? We've got plenty and not just horse flesh either.'

'No,' Nathan smiled. 'I'm not hungry, I've plenty to eat.'

'Have you come home now?'

As soon as the words were spoken she knew what his answer would be. Why come creeping into the house if he planned to stay.

'No.' His smile disappeared. 'I can't.'

'Why not? Simon would be overjoyed to see you, he's been so worried.'

'Poor father. Always worrying. But then I wasn't the first to run away.'

Rebecca's cheeks flushed hot.

'I had to run,' she said, pushing her chair back from the table. 'What future was there here for me? All the young men were gone, or dead. I'd be married off to some old man I didn't want or love.'

'I know, I know,' Nathan reached over and took her hand. 'I'm not criticising. It was your going that made me think. It caused Father much pain, but I understood. Eventually.'

'Yes, but..'

'I do understand, I know it's not the same for me,' Nathan leant forward, his face serious and earnest. 'But things have changed. It's as if I've been asleep. It's been warm and comfortable, but suddenly I've woken up. I'm in the real world now.'

Rebecca studied her cousin's frowning face, his shock of short brown hair falling over his brow. She stroked it back from his forehead. She didn't really understand him. He had everything, he was the only son, he would inherit the house, the smithy and could make his own choices.

But he was still speaking.

'I - I've changed. I've seen too much pain and suffering. I can't go backwards to how I was before. And I have to find out for myself what I want to do in the world, what I want to be. I can't just fall asleep again, stay here, run the smithy, do what Father wants.'

Maybe it was all too much for him - the siege, Juan's death, Atta leaving. Who knows what had happened to him since. She forgot sometimes that he was younger than she, even if he no longer looked it. And it was partly her fault, she had abandoned him too.

She had handled her cousin since they were children, but he was right, he had changed. The young man in front of her looked roughly the same as the Nathan she had argued and bickered with, but he was different.

Be careful. If you insult his pride he will leave and you will lose him.

Change the subject.

'Atta's back,' she said.

'I know, I saw him.'

'Where? Didn't you speak to him?'

'No. I wanted to but...' Nathan cast down his eyes.

'I don't understand. He was – is – your friend? You and Juan and Atta, you used to be inseparable.'

'I know... it's hard to explain,' Nathan said. 'I will speak with him, if I get another chance. It's just difficult right now. Anyway, these days he's usually guarded, or with his uncle, the Ambassador.'

'That shouldn't make any difference!' So he knew about the Ambassador. 'Atta's at the hospital every day, if you really want to see him, he's not difficult to find – 'though you're well informed.'

'Not really, it's all over town, if you listen,' he answered.

'These days I try not to listen to what my neighbours say.'

Nathan grimaced. 'Is it bad?'

69

For a moment she was at a loss for words. To explain, unburden herself to her cousin was so appealing. But no, it wasn't fair.

'It's worse for Simon. He tries to protect me, but what do people say about him? First his niece runs away and now his son.' She paused. 'What we do reflects on him. It's his reputation, his good name.'

'The honour of the family. Father's favourite subject, he was always harping on about it.'

'No, not some abstract idea. You don't understand - it's real things that actually happen, how people talk to him, speak of him. No-one's buying anything from us now. You don't know...'

They mustn't argue. She mustn't antagonise him.

'No, I don't suppose I do,' Nathan sighed. 'Where is Don Reza?'

She was grateful for another change of subject.

'He was captured by bandits. They're camped on the way to the mountains. There's to be an expedition to rescue him.'

He was staring at her intently. 'When do they leave? How many men do they have?'

'I...'

'Where is Don Reza being held?'

'The bandits have a camp in the mountains.'

'Where?' He was insistent.

'Somewhere in the hills, before the high peaks, though they're not really sure.'

'So they don't know exactly where?'

Rebecca shook her head. Why all these questions? Was it just a way for her cousin to avoid answering hers?

'Stay and you could join them,' she said, then wished she hadn't as he turned away. 'Look, even if you won't talk to me, at least speak to Atta. He's worried about you. We're all worried about you.'

'What? Even you?' Nathan grinned and Rebecca cuffed him around the head. Laughing, he pushed back his chair and stood.

'I'll go now. I just wanted to see that you were alright.'

'Why not stay a while? At least until Simon gets back?' Rebecca rose.

'No. We'd only fight and I don't want to hurt him anymore,' Nathan shook his head. 'It's better that I go.'

'Then you hurt him anyway. What shall I say to him?'

'Don't say anything. It would only upset him.'

'I won't lie Nathan.'

'No. If he asks... but he won't. Why should he?'

'Where are you going now? Where are you living?'

'With some new friends,' Nathan replied. 'Don't worry, I'm alright. They'll look after me. I'm going away for a little while. I have something important to do.'

What could be so important?

'Nathan,' she flung her arms around his neck and held him close, as much a wrestling hold as an embrace. 'Don't do anything foolish or dangerous. Promise.'

'Promise not to be foolish,' his voice was light and mocking as he began to pull away, but then his smile faded and his expression grew serious. 'Very well, I promise.'

She let him go.

71

His ring. At least he should have something to remind him of home.

'Wait,' she said urgently. 'Just wait here for one minute.'

Rebecca took the stairs two at a time. In her bedroom she opened her jewellery box and drew out the ring upon its chain, together with a soft draw-string purse, which clinked as she picked it up.

Be quick, he might not wait.

She hurried back out on to the landing. Nathan was still below, wearing a puzzled expression.

'Here,' she said, descending the stairs and holding out the chain. 'I'm sorry I took it. I always meant to give it back.'

'My ring.' Nathan took the chain and ring from her out-stretched hand. 'I was so angry when I found out this was gone. But I had almost forgotten about it.'

Like you've forgotten your friends and your family, she thought. What has happened to you that you won't come home? That you run from Atta, who has a ring just like yours? And the memory of Juan.

'And here,' she handed him the little bag. 'Gold,' she said. 'Some of my bounty from the *Teresa*.'

Her cousin tipped out the contents of the purse into his palm.

'I can't take this,' he said, fingering the golden dinars and silver dirhams. 'It's yours, you earned it. Isn't it pirate gold?'

'So? What difference does that make? You might need money.'

'I have money,' Nathan re-filled the purse and held it out to her.

Reluctantly, she took it back as Nathan placed his chain over his head and thrust the ring beneath his shirt and jerkin. He patted it into place.

'Thank you,' he said.

She hugged him, her eyes closed tight. Then she let go.

'Take care,' she urged as they walked into the vestibule.

'I will.'

Nathan crossed the courtyard to the gate.

'How can I reach you, if I need to...? She called after him, but he shook his head and raised his hand in salute. 'Nathan....'

She hurried to the gate, to watch him slouch away along the cobbled street, pulling down his hat to shield his face.

Why was he so tormented? Why wouldn't he come home?

He might look little different from before, but he was right, he had changed in other, more profound ways. He had changed a lot.

8.

Unexpected Callers

'Pedro!'

Miguel shouted for the groom as he hastened across the hallway, sunlight from the high windows flooding the chequerboard tiles. Up the stone stairs, two at a time.

'Sir.'

Below him the man skidded to a halt at the foot of the stairs.

'Bring Evalina around to the front in fifteen minutes,' Miguel instructed, looking over the polished balustrade. 'Her saddle bags are ready and there's my pack too.'

'Yessir.' The groom hurried off in the direction of the stables.

Miguel strode on to his bedroom. He needed to change, to get out of his city clothes into something more serviceable. It would be colder in the mountains and wet.

There was so little time.

He should have proposed the previous evening, regardless of Don Iago's presence, he knew that now.

'Return tomorrow morning,' she had said.

He would. He had slipped out before the end of the meeting at the barracks so that he would have time to call at the Plateros house on his way to the Seville Gate. Even better, Simon Calamiel had been at the meeting and was joining the expedition. Once Rebecca had accepted, he could speak with her uncle about the details – the marriage settlement, the nuptials - on the journey.

Quickly Miguel changed his clothes, pulling on thick riding boots. He took his mother's ring from the drawer, grabbed a heavy cloak and a hat and hurried downstairs to his father's study. There was just one more thing he had to do.

Inside the room he closed the door carefully behind him. From the cabinet by the door he drew out a rolled parchment, laying it on the desk.

The document was his will.

No one else knew about it. He had a notary draw it up when he returned to the city after disembarking the *Teresa* and the man had been paid well for his silence. It was too soon to share its contents, which was known only to himself and the man who had compiled it.

He unrolled the parchment and cast an eye over the document. It was already signed and dated.

The bulk of the Delgado properties were bequeathed to family, distant cousins in Burgos; his personal goods he left to friends like the Captain, with small bequests to his old drinking pals. But a sizeable sum, together with title to the best of the Delgado farms, would go to Rebecca Calamiel and her descendants.

This was to be her marriage settlement when they wed, but it would stand anyway. If he didn't return from the rescue expedition she would be well looked after.

He had one item to add – the ring he would give to her now. If the worst befell him, there would be no claiming it back by the lawyers.

Miguel sat, dipped a quill into the inkpot and scribbled a sentence. He blew on the document to dry the ink.

'Mercedes!'

The serving maid came into the study.

'Come,' Miguel stood and gestured for her to come behind the desk. Time was of the essence if he was to call on Rebecca. 'Here.' He pointed to the document and put the quill into Mercedes' hand as she looked up at him, hesitating. 'I need you to sign this, to show that I have made an addition to this document, that it wasn't added later by someone else.'

She looked perplexed. It seemed she did not understand.

'To make your mark to say that this was written by me, not written by someone else. You're a witness that I wrote it.'

'Did you, Sir?'

'Yes, of course I did!'

Patient, be patient, Miguel told himself. It would only take longer if the girl was frightened.

'You sign your name or make your mark here.' He pointed to the foot of the document and, taking her hand in his own, dipped the quill into the ink.

'I can write my name Sir.' Mercedes was indignant.

'Good. That's good,' he said. 'Here, sit down at the desk.'

Mercedes looked askance at the heavy wooden chair.

'No, I'll sign it here, Sir.'

She pressed the quill to the parchment and slowly started to form the letters of her name.

Miguel fought the urge to march back and forth across the room, it would only fluster her. Instead he busied himself with melting a ball of wax in a metal dish. Second passed, then minutes.

'There Sir!' Mercedes looked up, beaming.

Miguel whipped the document from beneath her hand. Yes, she had signed it properly. Good.

He blotted the ink, rolled the document up and poured a globule of hot wax onto its end. From the drawer of the desk he drew the Delgado seal and pressed it into the wax.

There. It was witnessed, signed and sealed. He waited for the wax to cool and harden.

'In a moment,' he said to Mercedes. 'I want you to take this to Senor Mendez, the notary. He is to keep it safe for me, until my return. Or until my death is confirmed.'

Her face paled.

Of course, he thought, she might be able to sign her name but she couldn't read. She hadn't known what it was that she signed. Well, it would have to do.

Miguel placed the scroll inside a tubular leather holder, snapped closed its lid and tied it round with a leather tie. 'Don't stop on the way and don't lose it.'

Mercedes took it from him, gingerly, as if it was infected.

'Mercedes,' he said. 'Do it now.'

'Yessir.' She bobbed a curtsey and fled from the room, clutching the scroll box to her breast.

78

Right. Now for Plateros. He would just have time if he moved quickly.

He made for the door, but it opened before he reached it. Bonifaz the lawyer stepped through. What did he want?

'I'm in a hurry, Bonifaz,' he said. 'Is this urgent?'

'I, I fear so, Sir,' the lawyer looked uncomfortable. 'There are two visitors outside and I think you should see them.'

'I don't have time for visitors...' Miguel began to move towards the door.

Bonifaz stood his ground. This was unlike him.

'Please, Sir, I really think you should.'

This had better be important.

'Oh very well.'

Bonifaz opened the door and beckoned.

A tall woman entered. High black brows arched over heavy lidded eyes, her black hair was bound up into an elaborate turban above a whitened face. A younger woman followed behind her, a girl really, with a close resemblance to the older woman. Her gravid belly was thrust out before her.

Miguel looked at Bonifaz for an explanation.

'May I present Senora Verde, widow to the Jerez merchant of that name and her daughter...'

'Dolores.' The widow said and curtseyed. 'I am sorry to disturb you at this inopportune time, but our business cannot wait.'

Oh really.

'It concerns your family name and your dead brother's reputation.'

What? What had these people to do with Juan?

Miguel looked to Bonifaz, but the lawyer just shrugged.

'State your business. Quickly. Bonifaz, chairs for the ladies.'

'Thank you,' the older woman directed her daughter to sit. Miguel looked at her, stony faced.

She took the seat which Bonifaz provided and began. 'As your man explained, my name is Constanta Verde and this is my daughter, Dolores,' the woman indicated the girl, who was sitting, shoulders hunched. 'It is her... delicate condition which brings us here.'

What?

'Her condition brought about by your brother, Juan Delgado.'

What nonsense was this?

'Yes.' She nodded and compressed her lips. 'Your brother is the father, he who's now dead and unable to provide for his wife and child.'

Miguel heard her words but couldn't make sense of them.

'Any claim you make would have to be substantiated by evidence,' Bonifaz stated.

'Oh, we have evidence.' The woman snapped her fingers at the girl. 'Dolores, the ring.'

The girl fumbled at the neck of her gown and began to pull out a fine chain.

Even before he saw the ring Miguel had guessed. It had been Juan's, the chain on which he had kept his silver ring. He bumped into the desk as he took an involuntary step backwards. Could Juan have impregnated this child? And promised her marriage? Or undergone some sort of ceremony with her?

The woman grabbed the ring and chain from her daughter's hand, brandishing it in front of Bonifaz, before showing it to Miguel.

'Here is our evidence!'

The coloured light from the window behind him glinted on the silver. Miguel reached out, but the woman snatched the ring back.

'No, that is my daughter's property,' she said. 'Given to her by your brother. And she's keeping it. It is her proof.' The woman thrust the ring back towards her daughter, who took it, meekly, and replaced the chain around her neck. 'Now, what we want to know is what you're going to do about it?'

'If,' said Miguel, 'if, you can substantiate your claim then your daughter and her child will be provided for.'

'What more proof do you need? That is the ring he gave her. You recognised it well enough.'

Miguel sighed. Married in proper form or not, if the girl was carrying Juan's child she had to be looked after. If the child was a Delgado, he, as head of the family, had to acknowledge it as such. It was the right thing to do. In any case, many a child born out of wedlock grew up a credit to their begetters.

'Very well,' Miguel turned to Bonifaz, who was hovering at the side of the room, watching. 'Find out what form of ceremony Juan undertook, if any. I will want to meet the priest who married him to... Dolores.'

The woman raised her chin, a look of satisfaction on her face, though she clearly had more to say.

'But my girl needs a father for her child. We are a respectable family.'

81

'I'm sure one can be found,' Miguel said. 'Now...'

'Why not you?' The woman's eyes flashed. 'You're unmarried and his brother. It's common enough.'

Miguel felt his legs turn to water as he stood, barely able to keep upright. How could she imagine that he would marry this girl? But another part of his brain acknowledged that it was often done, for an unmarried man to marry his brother's widow, especially if there was a child involved.

Rebecca.

Ensure the girl and her child were cared for, yes. Even take her and her odious mother into his household. But marry her!

No.

'You get an heir out if it too,' the woman persisted. 'If the child is a boy. And if it's a girl, well, my daughter's proved herself capable of child-bearing...' She gave an unbecoming smile.

Before he could retort there was a knock at the door. A servant entered.

'The groom's at the door, Sir,' he said. 'He's waiting with Evalina, saddled and ready.'

'Thank you,' Miguel said, dismissing the servant. 'I'll be there directly. I must go.'

How much time had passed? He would have to go straight to the Seville Gate, no time to visit Plateros now.

Damn. What would she think if he didn't call?

Too late. And he couldn't offer marriage now, not with this other matter unresolved.

The woman was on her feet, seeming undecided about how to react to his departure.

82

'Madam,' Miguel forced out the words. 'When I return I will address your situation. I promise that I will do what is right.'

'You'll marry her then?'

'No. That is not what I said. I said that I'll do what is right.' There was no possibility of him agreeing to marriage, though, if the child was Juan's..... . 'Now, I have urgent business and must go.'

Miguel strode to the door, ignoring her protestations. The girl began to sob.

In the hall servants stood, looks of surprise and concern on their faces. Miguel ignored them. He had to get outside and away from these people. Everything was going wrong.

He strode through the front doors and down the three steps to the forecourt.

Evalina whinnied as she saw him, her metal hooves skittered on the cobbles. Miguel took the reins from the groom holding her and swung himself up into the saddle. He looked back at the Casa Delgado. People had spilled out on to its steps, Bonifaz, the woman and her daughter, the servants.

This couldn't be happening. It couldn't be.

Miguel kicked his horse's sides and they cantered through the gates into the street. As they rounded the first corner he felt the box holding the ring press into the flesh of his thigh.

9.

Left Behind

Rebecca stood at the gate, looking along the empty street. As suddenly as Nathan had arrived, he was gone. The sun was high overhead, it must be noon.

She wandered back into the empty house. Picking up a broom she half-heartedly swept out the house and then the yard.

Why wouldn't her cousin speak with his friend? What was going on in that head of his? And where was he going? To do what? Would she ever see him again?

Poor Simon. She stopped sweeping.

How could she keep Nathan's visit from him? Though it would only rub salt into his wounds for him to know. She hoped that he would go on the expedition and get away from here. It was even more important now.

Damn Nathan. It was typical of him to think only of himself. Didn't he realise she had problems enough of her own, without adding extra burdens on to her shoulders.

And where was Miguel?

The morning was over, the bells would be ringing soon.

He wasn't coming.

She had to face the truth, he didn't care for her. Perhaps he never had.

No, she wasn't going to wait around for someone who wasn't going to come. She would go up to the hospital. Anything to take her mind off things.

She seized her shawl, closed the house door and slipped out of the gate, locking it behind her. Striding through the streets of the Juderia, she tried to figure out what her cousin was up to and tried not to think about Miguel at all.

Two townswomen broke off their conversation as she passed and scowled at her. One began to scold, but Rebecca ignored her and carried on to the hospital.

She ducked beneath the awning into the shade beyond.

It was quiet within and seemed emptier than two days before, some of the pallet beds had been packed away. Only the badly hurt remained or those without a home to go to, including the former slaves whom she had been nursing. There was the distinctive smell of rose water and, cutting through it, pungent vinegar. Orderlies were tending to patients' needs, changing bandages and washing wounds.

Then suddenly there was noise. A group of men had entered, smiling and joking and shouting to their comrades. Wrapped in winter clothes they walked around her, smelling of fire and woodsmoke. They were freedmen come to collect their fellows. As they sauntered over Rebecca looked for Pablo's friends, Kasha and Luis, but couldn't see them.

Once the group had passed she noticed a richly dressed young woman sitting alone by the window. She had a long, refined face with pale skin and large lustrous dark eyes beneath perfectly arched brows. Her black hair shone in the sunlight, as did the blue-black silk of her gown. This must be the Lady Beatriz, still wearing mourning for her husband. Seated on an upright chair next to a large basket, she pulled out long lengths of torn cotton fabric and wound them into rolls of bandages. Tentative, Rebecca went closer.

'Good morning,' she said. 'Do you want some help?'

'Please,' the young woman flashed a warm smile. 'Here.' She passed over a fistful of cloth pieces.

Rebecca pulled up a chair on the other side of the basket and started winding.

'My name is Rebecca Calamiel,' she said.

'Pleased to meet you Rebecca Calamiel. I am Beatriz Vega y Montoya.'

'I had the pleasure of meeting your brother yesterday evening,' Rebecca continued. 'He called upon us, to collect our friend, Senor Thomas of Whelmstone.'

'Ah yes, Senor Thomas. He lives with you, does he not.'

Now the lady was looking her over.

Rebecca glanced down at her woollen skirt and heavy shoes. If only she had taken a comb to her hair and had worn her coat, not her old shawl.

Then the lady seemed to make a decision.

'I am new in this city,' she said. 'I know very few Jerezanos. Many of your fellow townspeople dislike us. My brother and I are followers of the King, we're newcomers here, interlopers.'

87

Rebecca knew that for many of the remaining townspeople the King, and his courtiers, would always be the enemy. Lady Beatriz and her brother would never be truly accepted. Yet the siege, the deaths, the occupation, none of it was the fault of this young woman, but she would bear the consequences of it. Another to blame. Just like herself.

'Times change and fortunes with it' Rebecca answered. 'I've lived here my whole life yet sometimes... it isn't welcoming.'

The lady raised an elegant eyebrow.

'It's a very traditional place,' Rebecca hesitated. It was her home town after all. She shouldn't criticise it to this outsider. 'People are set in their ways.'

How could she confide in this Lady, so rich and privileged, so unlike her? What interest could she have in her, Rebecca? And who was to say that she wouldn't be just as hostile and rejecting as the Juderia women?

But something told her that this young woman was different. She took a deep breath.

'I have been travelling. At sea and alone. My fellow citizens have made me less than welcome since my return. Especially,' she added, half under her breath 'the women.'

'At sea?' Beatriz' eyes sparkled, she leaned forward. 'And alone? Where did you go? What did you see?'

'South to the Pillars of Hercules,' Rebecca answered, reluctantly. 'I saw Ifriqa. Though we sailed no further than Algeciras before returning northwards again, along the coast to Tarif al Ghar, before the battle.'

'The battle! You took part in a battle!' Beatriz had stopped winding the cotton. She looked entranced. 'What excitement... and danger too, I'll wager. Tell me all about it,' she demanded.

This wasn't just a polite request. It seemed that she really wanted to know.

Why not tell her, what harm could it do?

'It was a cold, bright day and our ship, the *Teresa*, was at anchor in a small bay just north of the Cape of Caves....' she began.

As she told the tale Rebecca began to re-live it, feeling the sea-wind on her face, the gentle roll of the deck, all the sensations she had tried so hard to put behind her. There was the fear and the danger, stowing the weapons, hearing the alarm, the sword-play, Miguel, Baco.

'Was he a close friend?' The lady asked softly. 'Baco?'

Across the room the freedmen laughed loudly at some joke. She glared at them.

Then she felt a hand upon her own.

It was Beatriz. She had reached across to comfort her.

'Do you miss him?'

Rebecca didn't trust herself to speak. It wasn't really Baco she missed....

She nodded.

'I'm sorry.' Beatriz sat back in her seat and resumed her task. 'But it must have been thrilling. How I envy you.'

Rebecca looked at the young woman's fine clothes, her jewellery, the glittering hoops in her ears.

'You envy me?'

'Oh yes. To have such experiences and see new places,' Beatriz' face flushed pink and her lips parted. 'I envy you that.'

There was no artifice in the woman's voice, no irony.

'Well, my neighbours don't seem to envy me,' she explained. 'To them I'm a runaway, an ungrateful harlot.'

'Don't listen to them!' The silk of her skirts rustled as Beatriz thumped her fist onto her knee. 'I wish I had the courage to do as you have done.'

'I was lucky,' Rebecca said. And she had been. Very lucky. 'I found good companions and friends. It could all have gone very differently, very wrong.'

'Yes,' Beatriz nodded. 'But it didn't. And now you've seen and done things most women couldn't even imagine.'

But what happens now, Rebecca thought? What do I do now?

'Will you come and visit me?' Beartriz was asking. 'And tell me more about your adventures?'

'Yes, I would enjoy that,' Rebecca replied, and it was true. Already her heart felt lighter.

'Good,' Beatriz smiled. 'I'll look forward to it. I want for a companion and spend most of my days with servants or my brother. He is currently parading every eligible man in Jerez in front of me, so that I may choose another husband. But I have decided,' Beatriz gave Rebecca a conspiratorial look. 'I won't have any of them. Why should I? I have my own money and know my own mind. I've had enough of marriage.'

Rebecca's mouth almost fell open.

Even when she had run away, she had always assumed that she would marry. Not to marry at all, well, that meant a convent and no children. That was unthinkable. Beatriz' ideas were new and strange. And beguiling.

This young woman was fascinating. She seemed to have thought it all out and decided what she wanted.

'But you don't know, you might fall in love?'

'I might,' Beatriz conceded. 'If I do, well and good. If I don't, then that's alright too.'

Suddenly she smiled.

Rebecca smiled in response. Nathan wasn't the only one making new friends.

'You have been married. You know what it's like.'

'Yes, my late husband was a soldier of the King,' Beatriz answered. 'We travelled with the army. It was a life full of worry and anxiety. I never knew, from one day to the next, if I would become a widow by nightfall.'

'I know what that sort of worry is like. My cousin Nathan has left home and is missing. No one knows where he's gone, if he's dead or alive.'

'Oh my dear.' Beatriz grimaced in sympathy. 'Another burden.'

The hospital had suddenly become very quiet. The freedmen had fallen silent. Rebecca noticed them casting glances her way. Why?

It was when she had mentioned Nathan's name. That's when they had begun to watch and listen. Why would that be of interest to them? What did they know about her cousin?

Her mind raced. Could they know him? Were the freedmen Nathan's new friends?

It would make sense. He could have been living in their makeshift shanties, no-one would look for him there. The smell of woodsmoke..... And he had recognised her coins as pirate gold. The freedmen had received bounty, just as she had. Was that where he had seen such gold before?

She had to find out.

But the men were preparing to leave and she wouldn't get another chance to speak with them, to question them about Nathan.

'Excuse me.... I must..' She tossed the fabric back into the basket and hurried over.

Taking a deep breath she walked to stand in the middle of the group.

'Hello,' she said. 'I'm Rebecca Calamiel, Nathan's cousin.'

There were nods, but none of them spoke. Their faces were closed and wary.

'He came to see me this morning,' she persisted. 'Before he left. I am worried about him - he seems to seek out danger.'

Several of the men exchanged glances.

'Don't worry lady,' one answered. 'He's with Kasha and Luis. They'll look out for him.'

What? She had met them the other day, they were Pablo's friends. So, they had gone with Nathan. But where?

'I'm glad he's not alone,' she said.

'And Luis knows his way around,' another said, trying to reassure her. 'He'll find the bandit camp easily enough.'

The freedmen, the secret mission, it all fell into place.

This was why Nathan had been asking questions about the bandits and the expedition. He was going to the mountains with the two freedmen to get there first and infiltrate the gang. He was going to try and rescue Don Reza himself.

She had to know for sure.

'Joining the bandit gang will be dangerous,' she said.

One of the freedmen nodded. 'Yes, but he's got good company.'

Stupid, ridiculous, idiotic Nathan.

She had to tell her uncle and the soldiers had to know, they would be attacking the bandit camp. Who knew what might happen to Nathan in a battle.

With barely a quick backward glance, Rebecca darted towards the entrance, ignoring the shouts of the freedmen and the calls of the Lady Beatriz.

She sped across the paved square and down the hill, cutting across town into the road leading to Plaza Plateros. Townsfolk looked on open-mouthed as she ran past.

The large key to their gate caught in the lock.

She banged the flat of her hand on the gate and it opened. It wasn't locked. Her uncle must have returned.

But Simon's large sheepskin coat was no longer in its place on the hook by the door.

She dashed into the stables. Ruben the mule whinnied, but he was alone, the mare's stall was empty. So Simon had gone with the soldiers.

It was what she had been hoping for.

But now he was part of an expedition that was riding to destroy the bandit camp and, if Nathan's plan worked, her cousin would be in the camp when they attacked.

Had the expedition already set out? She had to find out.

Miguel was going with it, someone at Casa Delgado would know.

Rebecca rushed out, pulling the gate closed behind her.

Half walking, half running, through the streets she prayed that she might catch them. That they had not yet left.

She rounded a corner and found her way was barred. A group of young women took up the width of the narrow street. Rebecca jolted to a halt.

'It's the Calamiel slut.' One young woman, her long hair braided and covered, sneered at her, contempt in her voice.

'Where's your scarf today?' Sheba Barruch stood at her side, along with another young woman. All stared at her.

Rebecca put her hand to her head. She had come out without her headscarf. Quickly she pulled her shawl up over her head.

'Sailors like short-haired girls do they?' The first asked.

'Get back to the docks, where you belong.' This was the third. 'Keep out of our town.'

She wanted to argue. It was her town too. But she had no time if she was to catch the expedition before it departed. She put her head down and barged though them.

'Sailor's drab!' She heard them shout after her as she hurried away.

Then, at last, here was the Delgado house.

Its wide, high doors were open and people milled about around in the cobbled foreyard. She saw immediately that Miguel wasn't among them. Was she too late?

Gasping for breath, Rebecca addressed a red-headed man.

'Sir, I seek Don Miguel Delgado, is he here? It is a matter of some urgency.'

The man looked down his nose at her.

94

'He is a friend, Sir,' she persisted. 'Of Captain Morientes and myself.' The Captain's name might get his attention, even if this man wouldn't think of answering a breathless girl.

'Hmm,' the man looked shifty. He seemed disinclined to answer.

'Who's this?' A tall, be-turbaned woman demanded of the man, who hissed in exasperation.

'No-one. No-one of any concern,' he said. 'Come.'

Taking the woman by the arm, he steered her back to the house.

'Master's gone,' said a dark-haired young woman, wearing the apron of a servant. 'Gone to join the rescue party.'

Rebecca heaved a great sigh. She was too late.

'Are you all right miss?' The servant girl asked. 'You've gone all pale.'

'Yes, yes, thank you,' Rebecca replied, but she felt faint.

The girl turned away as people on the steps of Casa Delgado retreated inside.

The bells of the city began tolling. It was an hour after midday.

She'd best go home. No point in staying here.

When she reached Plaza Plateros she sat, listless, on the rim of the fountain, looking across at her home. The windows of her house were dark, it was empty.

Miguel was gone out of her reach, probably forever.

Nathan was off on a fool's errand to join the bandits.

Her Uncle, whom she had so encouraged, was riding, all unknowing, with the soldiers to attack the bandit camp.

Pray that he wouldn't be attacking his own son.

Rebecca slapped her hand down hard on to the stone, just to feel the cold, hard pain. What could she do now to prevent it?

Part Two

In the Mountains

10.

The Quest

An eagle floated high above the valley floor.

The huge bird hung in the air, its wings outstretched, black against the blue sky. Nathan raised a hand to shield his eyes from the afternoon sun as he watched it. He grasped the reins of his mount with his other hand.

From the ridge at the head of the valley a twittering flock of starlings flew down towards him, ten or fifteen birds. The eagle twitched its wing feathers and began to turn, tracking the progress of the small birds far beneath it. Its wings flapped.

Once.

Twice.

The eagle banked as it descended. Then it swooped.

Plummeting down, until, at the very last minute, its legs extended and hooked talons snatched a starling, quick as the blinking of an eye. The eagle flapped its great wings once more and rose, prize held in its claws, soaring back into the blue. Then it merged into the shadow as it flew towards the side of the valley.

The absolute perfection of the bird and the cold completeness of its swoop to kill took Nathan's breath away. It was so beautiful and so pure.

He turned in the saddle to tell his broken-nosed companion, Luis, who was riding along the trail behind him, hat pulled down over his brow.

'What?' Luis looked startled, peering suspiciously at the boulders and rocks.

'Nothing.'

No, Luis wouldn't understand. Nathan turned forward again, eyes searching the valley side for the bird.

It was the second day of their journey from Jerez and that morning they had entered the hill country. The terrain was wild, covered with shrubs and natural vines, which reached up to grey stone crags. Ahead dark clouds massed, shrouding the high mountains.

They rode in single file. Kasha led the way, a big man riding a big horse, then Nathan and finally Luis bringing up the rear.

It felt good, being with them on a shared mission. He could trust them. Better than any official rescue party. They were his true friends, willing to risk everything to come with him.

When first Nathan had explained that he wanted to find the bandit camp and smuggle Don Reza out before the raid, Kasha immediately offered to accompany him.

'Is this something you have to do?' The black-skinned man asked.

'I... yes,' Nathan answered.

100

How to explain? It was unfinished business. It was for Atta and friendship. But mostly it was because he wanted to help. As an outsider, maybe he could do what platoons of cavalry could not. How could he convey all this? He didn't have the words.

'It'll be dangerous,' he said, instead.

'Everything's dangerous, life's dangerous. If it wasn't for you, I'd be fish food,' Kasha had replied, referring to how Nathan had freed the oar-slaves from their chains and saved them from drowning. 'Anyway, it'll be good to move on. The townsfolk don't like us here and there'll be trouble, I can smell it coming.'

Where Kasha went, Luis went also. He, it was, who had discovered the location of the bandit camp, trawling the Jerez taverns to find someone who claimed to know it. The man had described it in detail and now they were following his directions.

Nathan hefted his bow higher up on his shoulder. Aside from the long hunting knife in his belt, it was his only weapon, though more for shooting game than for defence. Anyway, they didn't plan to fight, but to seek to join the bandit gang. It was an audacious plan, but probably their only chance of helping Don Reza. Kasha and Luis, former galley slaves, were the perfect cover. Ex-slaves were often shunned, ending up on the wrong side of the law and they wouldn't have been welcome in any official force, which should convince the bandits. At least, that's what they hoped.

Surely they must be getting close now.

Time was of the essence. The cavalry rescue party would be close behind them - a day or two maybe, but that was all. Atta would find the camp, nothing would deflect him from his search for his father, but by the time he did Nathan hoped to have spirited Don Reza away, before the fighting began.

Nathan looked at the track ahead. It climbed a steep ridge, forming switchbacks or hairpins, just as the man in the tavern had described.

'Keep your hands in plain sight now,' Kasha said, his voice urgent. 'There are look-outs. We're being watched.'

Nathan scanned the valley sides, but he could see no-one. Yet the hairs on the back of his neck rose as they reached the foot of the switchbacks.

'Top right of the ridge,' Luis said, sotto voce. 'Don't...'

Nathan turned.

'...let them know we've seen them...,' Luis' tone was flat. 'Oh well, I don't suppose it matters.'

'Sorry.'

Nathan cast his eyes down. How could he have been so stupid?

They were in the last of the sunlight now as they climbed upwards, his face felt its warmth. Behind them the valley was in purple semi-darkness. The sun would go down quickly and so would the temperature. Last night had been cold, they had shivered around a camp fire, but they were higher up now and it would be even colder.

His cloak was behind his saddle, inside his bedroll. He didn't dare reach for it, their watchers might think he was reaching for a weapon. Why hadn't he thought of it before? Had he left his brain behind in the city?

In front of him Kasha heeled his horse's sides to urge her up the final, steep gradient, on to the ridge. Nathan urged his horse to quicken her pace, trotting up the last turn and he heard Luis doing the same behind him. Once on the ridge Nathan followed Kasha's gaze.

In a natural hollow before them lay a settlement, almost a village. Its wooden palisade had large gates flanked by watch towers. The encampment was already in shadow, only the tops of the grey cliffs rearing up behind it glowed with the light of the setting sun.

Yet something didn't seem right about the scene.....

The gates were open wide.

'Keep your hands away from your weapons!'

Around them weapon-wielding fighters seemed to have sprung from the rocks. Swords clashed and men shouted.

Nathan's horse shied. He fought to control her, tightening his hold on the reins and gripping his horse's flanks with his knees, but still she skittered and snorted.

There were archers standing atop the boulders near the ridge's edge, arrows notched to bows, pointed in their direction.

The swordsmen surrounded them and grew quiet. With an effort Nathan calmed his mount. All were still.

'We are here to join you,' Kasha said, slowly holding up his horse's reins with his left hand while he raised his right.

'Dismount.' A red faced man sauntered out from behind a large boulder, thumbs tucked into his belt. 'Do it now if you want to keep your lives.'

Nathan kicked his feet from the stirrups, gripped the pommel of his saddle with trembling hands and slid to the ground. He felt his knife being drawn from his belt and a man took his bow. His horse was led away, cloak, bedroll and all, down into the camp.

A sword-point at his chest, he was forced backwards, stumbling, until he stood, back to back with his friends, hands raised.

'Who are you?' The red faced man demanded.

'We're galley-slaves,' Kasha said. 'Escaped. We've no-where else to go.'

'Escaped from where?' One of the archers demanded.

'The galley *Hebe*, attacked by the King's armada near the Cape of Caves,' Kasha replied. They had decided to tell as much of the truth as possible.

'Very lucky.' Another archer said as he stepped down from his vantage point, but he kept his arrow notched to his bow. 'How'd you get out?'

'I freed them,' Nathan spoke up, but his voice quivered.

The archers exchanged looks.

'These aren't the ones....'

'Bring them,' the red-faced man interrupted. 'El Zagal can decide what to do with them. You and you,' he indicated two of the men. 'Stay here. Keep watch for the others until the light goes. Come down after dark.'

He turned and led the way down the slope to the encampment.

Nathan was grabbed and got a shove in the back.

'Go on.'

One of the men tried to make Kasha move, but he stood, immobile as stone, looking down at the man. Then he began to walk down the slope to the camp. Nathan followed, with Luis.

They passed between the watch towers of the stockade, as torches were lit. One of their captors kicked out at what seemed to be a bundle of rags on the ground and, with a yelp, a grubby, malformed beggar scuttled away on his hands and knees into a lowly shelter leaning against the palisade. The high gates swung closed behind them with a thump.

It was difficult to see anything beyond the flames of the torches now carried by their captors, though Nathan sensed more men joining the procession, pacing alongside the little line of prisoners.

What was going on? What was going to happen to them?

'Stop,' one of their captors said, coming to an abrupt halt. 'Wait here.'

A semi-circle of men holding burning torches formed a ring of light around them, keeping just an arm's length away. There was a murmuring in the crowd and the occasional burst of harsh laughter. Nathan felt the rapid beat of his own heart.

He screwed his eyes up against the glare to try to see individuals in the crowd. One man picked at his fingernails with his dagger, looking up at the captives every now and again, another uncoiled a thick whip from around his waist.

There was no way they could break free or fight their way out, even with Kasha's huge strength. There would be no escaping, nor any mercy neither. These men looked like they were spoiling for a fight. They wanted violence.

Keep a clear head, he told himself. You have to be convincing.

He licked his dry lips and focussed on the building in front of them. It was raised on stone plinths, with a wide wooden veranda

105

and three steps down to the ground. Occasionally the men around them glanced up at its closed door.

When it opened everyone fell silent. A man emerged.

He was tall, his face seamed and pitted with scars and his dark eyes glittered in the flame light. He wore heavy boots, buckskins and a long leather coat. Was this the bandit leader?

The man stood at the edge of the veranda and observed the prisoners in silence.

Shouldn't they speak? Why didn't Kasha say something?

Nathan shot a look to one side. The big man stood to his right, feet apart. He appeared relaxed. Luis was on the far side of Kasha, hidden from sight.

The scar-faced man spoke, his voice guttural.

'Why are you here?'

'We've no-where else to go,' Kasha replied, in measured tones, matching the leader's stare. 'We're from the oar deck.' He sloughed off his coat, pulled his woollen shirt forwards over his head and turned around. There was more shuffling and muttering in the crowd. Nathan glanced across.

The skin on Kasha's back shone in the torchlight. It was criss-crossed by wheals and ridges of flesh, with stripes of pale tight skin where the wounds had been too deep to heal over cleanly. The marks of the overseer's lash.

The leader nodded.

'We heard about your band,' Kasha continued, after pulling back on his shirt and coat. 'We thought we'd come and join you. We could be useful to you.'

'How?'

'We can fight. And we have other skills.'

The leader studied them. His eyes came to rest on Nathan. 'You don't look like you pulled an oar.'

'I didn't,' Nathan spoke up. It was no use lying.

'So, what were you, boy?'

'I was the shipmaster's personal slave,' Nathan replied. 'I'm a smith. I welded the chain links, or broke them. I can be useful too.'

'That's why so many of us escaped,' Kasha said. 'He freed us. Now he's one of us.'

The leader slowly descended the steps and walked across to them. He stared at them of each in turn, ending with Nathan. He stepped forward to stand just inches away, Nathan could smell the sweat and leather of him. He was much the taller.

Hold the man's stare. Do as Kasha did.

Nathan raised his chin.

The man's eyes were flint hard and cold and Nathan felt a tremor of fear. He dropped his eyes.

'We already have a smith,' the man said. He tilted his head to one side and his thin lips extended into a smile, scars creasing his cheeks. 'Let's see what you can do.' He gestured to men in the crowd. 'Bring them,' he ordered and stalked away, beyond the circle of light.

11.

The First Test

Nathan's arms were grabbed from behind, his elbows pulled back. He was shoved forwards across the settlement, the way lit by men with torches. Oaths and curses from behind him suggested that his friends were being treated in the same way.

He tripped and almost fell, his arms wrenching, but then he was allowed to stop. In front of him was a stone building with a wide tiled canopy. A heavy anvil, a vice and a stone water trough stood beneath it beside a large hearth. He could see the red glow of the furnace within. It was a forge.

Nathan flexed his shoulders and rubbed his upper arms as his captor let him go. Men collected around him, the torchlight and the glow from the forge reflecting in their eyes. Aching arms might be the least of his worries. The crowd parted to allow the scar-faced leader passage.

'Here,' he said and tossed two shards of metal onto the large anvil, the metal ringing. 'Re-make it.'

They were the remains of a broken sword.

A sword. He had never made a sword before.

He couldn't do it. He didn't know how.

The crowd edged closer. The whip man, the man with the dagger and another, pale hair tied back into a long pony tail, were at the front. Kasha and Luis too, held at sword-point. The bandit leader leaned against one of the uprights, watching.

'I'm not a bladesmith,' Nathan said to him.

'Can you do it or not?'

He had no choice.

'Yes.'

He would just have to re-make the sword. Think. It's a metal item like any other, the principles are the same. Use the main pieces of the old sword.

'But I'll need men to pump the bellows.'

Kasha strode across, grasping the bellow handles to take the first turn. As he pumped, the fire beneath the forge chimney began to glow more brightly.

Nathan hefted the hilt end of the sword, it was heavy. But the weapon was crude, it didn't even have a fuller down the middle of the blade. The pommel, tang and cross guard were undamaged, though the blade edges were notched and rough. It had snapped half way along the blade.

So... hot forge the two pieces, hammer them together when the iron was malleable and then re-heat the whole of the blade to fix it and remove irregularities. And hope that that would be enough.

Gauntlets, tongs and hammers lay on a stone bench. The gauntlets, shiny and hard with long use, were too large for him but he pulled them on. They would have to do.

He lifted the pieces of the sword with the tongs, placing them into the fire, where the dull metal began to brown.

The watchers shuffled nearer. Their silence was unnerving. They were waiting for him to fail.

What would happen to him if he did?

Somewhere beyond the circle someone laughed.

Nathan blinked away the beads of sweat running into his eyes. It dripped from his face and ran down onto his chest as he looked around for the smith's hammer.

It lay propped against the smithy wall but it looked too heavy for him to wield.

'Finish your turn,' he said to Kasha and pointed to the hammer. 'I'll need your strength.'

As Kasha stepped away from the bellows Luis took his place.

'When I bring the pieces of the sword together on the anvil,' Nathan said. 'Hammer them while they're red hot. Keep going until I tell you to stop.'

The metal pieces were glowing red. Do it now.

He grasped the hilt of the sword with the tongs and placed it on to the anvil, securing it in the vice. Returning to the fire he lifted the other half of the blade and laid its broader edge atop the other.

'Now,' he said.

Sparks flew as Kasha crashed the hammer down again and again and, gradually, the two red shards merged.

'Stop!'

He began to shape the melded metal with a small hammer, making the edges of the blade anew.

That should be enough.

111

He picked up the remade sword with the tongs and placed it back into the forge fire, where it reddened once more. Then he withdrew it, placing the glowing blade on the anvil to cool. It faded to a dull grey.

Wiping a gauntlet across his brow Nathan spoke to the bandit leader.

'Its edges will need to be fullered and the whole thing tempered and quenched,' he said. The man's gaze shifted to the stone water trough.

'Do it,' he said.

'No, not yet. Otherwise the stresses will be sealed in the blade and it will break when it's used.'

The leader peered at the sword. The scars on his face creased as he sniffed.

'So, you can work metal,' he said. 'Maybe you're telling the truth.' He gestured to Kasha and Luis. 'You bunk in the main building. You,' he indicated Nathan, 'in the room behind the forge. Start work on our weapons at first light.' He addressed the crowd. 'That's all. There'll be no fun with them tonight.'

There was a disappointed murmuring as men began to disperse, taking their torches with them. Nathan, Kasha and Luis were left standing in the red light of the forge. The moon was rising above the ridge cast a silver light over the camp.

'Well done,' Kasha murmured as he came to stand by Nathan's side.

'I've never forged a sword before,' Nathan replied. He began to shiver.

'You did well. We're in,' Kasha said. 'But we'll have to watch out. They don't trust us.'

'We don't have much time,' Nathan began. 'The others...'

'I'll take a look around,' Kasha said, more loudly. Nathan followed his gaze and saw the outline of a figure standing just beyond the firelight. The big man lowered his voice. 'A shadow to ensure we do as we're told. We'll try and get our gear back, but there's not much we can do tonight. Look for your man before sun-up tomorrow, if you can. We'll meet you here later.'

'See you tomorrow,' Luis said. 'Take care.'

His friends walked away into the moonlit dark and Nathan lit a torch from the forge fire so as to light his way into the room behind the smithy.

The little room was dusty, but at least it was warm. It held two untidy pallet beds, a table, chairs and an iron stove set into the back of the forge's chimney. Someone had lived here once, but where were they now? He hung the torch in a sconce and set about pulling the thin blankets straight.

What was that smell?

He held a straw filled pillow to his nose. Fresh rosemary – what a place to find sweet-smelling herbs. How had that come here?

He was too tired to think and there was danger all around. He lay down, turning his back on the torchlight, and pulled the blankets over his shoulder. Tomorrow he would find Don Reza and they could get out of this place.

There was a howl of pain.

Nathan sat bolt upright.

What was that? Was it even human?

Shouts and jeers, a sobbing plea. Someone was being tortured.

Kasha, Luis!

No, this wasn't them. A name was repeated - Diego. Another unfortunate was being tormented.

Shouts, rising to a shriek and laughter.

What were they doing to him?

Nathan lay back down. He pulled the pillow around his head to stifle the sound. How could he sleep through this? How could anyone sleep?

Yet, despite everything, sleep came.

12.

The Surgeon

Frosty grass crunched under foot as Nathan left the warmth of the smithy and stepped out into the half-light of a very cold dawn. He rubbed his hands together, fingertips tingling and pulled his cloak tight around him. The sky had lost its inky blackness, yet one or two stars still twinkled faintly. He could see the settlement in the grey light.

The forge stood away from the other dwellings, rough wooden cabins mostly, temporary things, though the leader's stone-built house had a solid look. It and the forge must have been here before the bandits came. The camp spread across the floor of the vale and up the far slope to meet the encircling cliffs. It was big enough to hold a hundred or more. Yet it seemed almost empty.

Movement caught his eye. Sentinels walked atop the stockade. Within, people were stirring. None of them would be friendly. With a shudder, Nathan remembered the screams of the night before.

It hadn't been Kasha and Luis, of that he was certain. But nonetheless... and he'd feel safer if they were with him.

Pull yourself together, he told himself. Get on with the search for Don Reza.

High up the slope a large wooden building stood alone. If the settlement had a sick-house or hospital, that is where it would be, away from the others for fear of contagion. That was where he needed to go.

Nathan flitted from shack to shack, as noiselessly as he could. At the foot of the dirt track which climbed the side of the vale he stopped. If anyone was watching they would see him walk up the path.

Be purposeful, he told himself, stride out as if he had a task to perform. Don't look suspicious.

He started climbing the track.

Soon he was above many of the cabins. Once or twice he thought he saw someone following, some twenty paces or so behind him, but there was no one there when he turned to look. Should he stop, find out who it was? They drew no closer, so he went on.

The track ended at the large building he had identified from below. Was it the sick-house as he had surmised? There was nothing for it, he would just have to try the door and find out. He reached for the handle, but the door opened. A long, sinewy hand gripped his wrist and pulled him forwards into the building.

'Inside!' An urgent voice whispered. 'Quickly.'

Don Reza! Was it really him?

'Don....'

The surgeon put a long finger to his lips. He made fast the door behind them and beckoned to Nathan.

It was dark inside, with only one taper burning. Beds ranged along the walls of a long room. Nathan wrinkled his nose - it smelled of vinegar and of decay.

He followed Reza into a small side room. A heavy hide curtain across its door dropped closed, cutting off all light. Then he heard a flint strike and saw the pink flesh of Don Reza's palm, cupping a lighted taper. The blackness receded and he could see the surgeon's face, his large eyes and the grey hairs in his short pointed beard, illuminated from below as he lit a candle.

Nathan began to see the room. Don Reza pushed him, gently, towards a stool by the wall.

'Sit,' Don Reza said. 'Take a breath and then tell me how you got here.' He squatted beside Nathan. 'You're the last person I expected to see. Is Atta with you?'

'No, but he's coming. He and your brother and a raiding party.'

'A raiding party?' Don Reza looked thoughtful. 'I suspected something was afoot.'

'What do you mean? Do the bandits know about the raid?'

'Maybe,' Don Reza replied. 'People have been leaving the camp for days.'

That was why the rooms behind the forge were empty, whoever had lived there had already gone.

'Do you know where they went?'

'No.' Reza shook his head. 'I learn what I can, but... what's that?'

There was a loud drumming, reverberating, the sound of many hoof-beats, of horsemen riding down the slope into the camp.

It couldn't be the raiding party already, could it? They were at least a day behind.

'Open the gates!'

Nathan and Don Reza exchanged looks and stood. Outside the sky was lighter as they looked down into the vale below.

Dust rose over the gates as horsemen cantered in, shouting and milling. Archers and swordsmen on foot followed, like those who had waylaid him the day before. Was this who they had been waiting for then?

Men came to take the horses as the newcomers dismounted. All wore leather cuirasses and greaves and were heavily armed.

At the centre of melee a black-haired, black bearded rider remained mounted. He sat very still, gazing around him at the camp. He seemed to sniff the air and the others glanced up at him warily. He was the leader.

Nathan watched him dismount. He was led towards the stone house. Who was this man and why was he here, bringing his men to join the bandits?

There was no time to ponder. The raiding party would be arriving soon.

'We must get you out of here,' he said to Don Reza, turning away from the scene below. 'It'll be soon... they left Jerez only hours after I did.'

'Didn't you leave with them? With Atta and...?'

'No, I came on my own. That's to say, I came with others, but not the expedition.'

'Didn't Mustafa send you? Surely he knows you're here?'

'No. They don't know.' Nathan took a deep breath. 'I can't explain it all now. I got in to try and help you get out, before the raid.'

'This was your idea?' Don Reza looked astonished, but his expression grew grave. 'You've put yourself in danger on my account. These people are ruthless, Nathan. They.... you couldn't imagine their cruelty.'

Nathan thought of the oar slaves chained to their benches as the ship foundered. He remembered the pirates. How could the bandits be worse? Then again, he recalled the screams in the night.

Don Reza was frowning and listening.

Then Nathan heard it too.

It was only a slight noise, but someone was close by, just around the corner of the building, moving stealthily, taking care not to be heard. The figure he had seen following him earlier, maybe?

Don Reza signalled that he was going back inside to get a weapon.

Nathan crept towards the corner. Pressing his back against the wall he paused, heart thumping. He would leap out and surprise the eaves-dropper.

He took a deep breath and stepped forward.

There was no one there.

Yet he could have sworn.....

A heavy weight fell upon his shoulders and the earth came up to meet him as he was borne to the ground. His hands just broke his fall, his palms stinging.

He felt knees pushing down into the small of his back, pinning him to the earth, hurting. He couldn't move. His head was forced down, his face into the dirt. Nathan tensed, gathering his strength to push upwards with both hands and feet, and throw off his attacker.

'I wouldn't do that, if I were you,' a cold, dry voice said. 'I'm armed.'

His captor rocked back and forth on his knees. Nathan gasped in pain.

'I'm going to let you up now,' the voice was close to his ear. 'And you're going to answer my questions. Don't do anything stupid.'

The pressure of the knees reduced and then was gone.

Nathan rolled over and struggled to his feet. He looked into his adversary's pale blue-grey eyes in a pale-skinned, unshaven face. He'd seen this man before. He was one of the watchers at the forge the previous day, his fair hair tied back into a pony-tail.

'Who are you and why are you here?' The man demanded.

Stronger than he was, certainly, but probably not as quick. Over the man's shoulder Nathan could see the dirt track that ran down to the vale. If he could get past he'd be able to out-run him.

The man stepped closer, grasping the fabric of Nathan's coat in his fist and thrust him back hard against the log wall of the sick-house. The logs gouged into his shoulder blades and his head rang with the impact.

'I want answers,' he said. His face was close, Nathan could see the glinting stubble on the man's chin. His hand relaxed its grip.

Nathan tensed in anticipation of the next blow.

But his assailant had dropped his arms. He was staring at Nathan's chest, where his coat and shirt had opened.

'What's this?'

The man reached for the silver ring hanging on its chain around Nathan's neck.

'Mine.' Nathan closed his hand around the ring.

The man stepped back, frowning. 'Yet I recognise it,' he said. 'Save that the design is different, of a cup, not a bird.'

Nathan steadied himself, never taking his eyes from the man's face. Atta's ring had the symbol of a bird. How could this man know of that?

'Where did you see that?' Another voice demanded.

At the end of the alleyway stood Don Reza, brandishing a long lancet like a sword.

'Your son was wearing it, Don Reza,' the fair-haired man replied. 'For I assume that is who you are. My name is Jorge Garalon and I was sent to seek you by your brother, Don Mustafa.'

Don Reza didn't move.

'I arrived yesterday from El Endrinal, the bandit's fortress higher in the mountains. When you were not there I came to look for you here. Your brother told me to say that you will remember Miriam.'

Don Reza lowered the lancet.

Nathan looked at him, a question in his eyes. Why should he trust this man? Why should he trust anyone?

'My late wife,' the surgeon explained. 'Atta's mother. Her name is the password between my brother and I.' He addressed the man. 'Where did you see my son?'

'I travelled with him for many weeks through these mountains,' the man answered. 'Forgive me, but I can't explain everything now. The bandits are on the move, El Zagal was only waiting for his new allies before abandoning the camp. I'd guess there is a raiding party on its way.'

'It'll be here soon,' Nathan said and turned to Don Reza. 'We have to get you out.'

'No,' the man, Jorge, shook his head. 'Not now. We'd be cut down before we got far. The stockade is guarded and the cliffs are impassable, except for one gorge which is watched. And then, there is the question of what would happen to your friends.'

Did he mean Kasha and Luis? What did he know of them?

Jorge spoke to the surgeon. 'I'm sorry but you'll have to go with the bandits.'

'Yes,' Don Reza reached into his robes and drew out a cork foil, which he placed on the tip of the lancet. 'It's too dangerous to do anything else.'

'But...' Nathan began to protest. 'While the bandits are distracted....'

Who was this man to command them, even if he had been sent by Atta's Uncle?

'No,' Jorge cut him short. 'Plus, we need to know what's afoot down there. My money's on an ambush of the raiding party.'

An ambush. Was he serious?

What had all begun so well was starting to go horribly wrong.

'I'll wait for you both at El Endrinal,' Don Reza said, looking back over his shoulder as he returned to the sick-house. 'Keep safe.'

'Come.' Jorge started down the lane.

Nathan glowered at the man's back. He was much too ready to take command, even if he was on the same side. He hurried to catch up.

Cow bells clanged loudly from the encampment below. Men were gathering in the open space in front of the plinth house.

Nathan couldn't see Kasha and Luis anywhere. He turned to speak with Jorge before they joined the crowd, but he too seemed to have disappeared into thin air. There was no sign of him.

Where were his friends? He wove his way through the mass of men, but he couldn't even see Kasha, who towered above everyone else. Why weren't they here? What had Jorge meant when he asked what would happen to them?

The plinth-house door creaked open and the bandit leader emerged on to the veranda, followed by the black-haired, bearded rider so recently arrived.

The man wore the clothes of a nobleman, highly polished riding boots, a fine shirt and a doublet of what looked like black calfskin, in contrast to the leather and wool worn by the bandit leader. His long wild hair was now tied back but his face was still black-browed and hard. A sword hung at one side of an elaborate weapons belt and a long rapier-like blade at the other. Was he a two-handed swordsman then?

El Zagal leaned both his hands on the rail and considered the small crowd.

'There is a raiding party in the outer valley,' he said, raising his voice. Nathan looked around, no one seemed surprised. 'I want twelve men for an ambush. Arrows, a quick strike, then retreat. Slow them down enough to allow the rest of us to depart.'

A man stepped forward. Others followed. Nathan recognised some of the archers who had waylaid them on the ridge the evening before.

'Good....' El Zagal began. He looked directly at Nathan. 'Bring him,' he said.

Nathan was pulled and dragged to the front of the group, a space forming around him as men backed away. A the bandit leader gazed down at him from above a runnel of sweat trickled down Nathan's back bone.

'Where..,' he fought to keep his voice under control. 'Where are my friends?'

'Where I want them to be,' the leader replied. 'But you, you will join our ambush. Understood?' His eyes were cold.

Nathan swallowed hard. How could he agree? He couldn't shoot at his friends.

This was another test. He had no choice. He nodded agreement.

'Right, move out!'

The bandit leader turned on his heel and the gathering began to disperse.

An archer from the evening before walked up to Nathan.

'You're with us,' he said. 'And no tricks.' He smiled. 'Or you'll be our entertainment this evening. Remember, we'll be watching.'

13.

Dilemma

Low afternoon sun shone straight up the valley from the west. Nathan could see a long column of riders, forty men, maybe more, following the trail in middle of the valley floor, their elongated shadows advancing before them.

He lay on his belly on a large flat rock which protruded out over the valley. He was about thirty feet up, the height of the roof of a tall townhouse back in Jerez. Anyone approaching from the valley wouldn't be able to see him until they got very close. And by then it would be too late.

Focussing on the column he raised his hand to shield against the sun's glare. The scabbard of the sword at his waist snagged on the rough, rocky surface and he cursed.

It was just an encumbrance, he wasn't going to use it against his friends. Like the bow and quiver of arrows at his side, it had been given to him before they set out from the bandit camp.

The ride from the camp had been a nightmare. It had taken all his concentration just to stay in the saddle as his mount ran down the switchbacks with the others. Once they reached the valley floor they'd galloped even faster, the stony ground passing in a blur.

They halted just before the trail descended into a second valley and clustered around the archer in charge. He out-lined the plan to ambush the column.

'We'll surprise them,' he had said. 'First we disrupt their formation with arrows. Archers, pick your targets carefully, aim for the horses.' He drew his sword. 'No one fire until I give the signal. I'll raise my sword high and bring it down.' He demonstrated, causing his horse to shy. 'They'll probably ride for the valley sides, trying to find us. When they get close enough we'll attack those in front. Keep your horses close and ready for the charge. But remember, this isn't a battle, there are too many of them. We disrupt their advance, kill as many as we can, then we go.'

Kill as many.... Nathan couldn't imagine killing anyone, least of all his friends.

The archer brandished a whistle. 'When you hear this, it's back to the rocks and retreat. Ride back to the encampment and take the path through the cliffs. If you get isolated, head to El Endrinal.'

El Endrinal.

Jorge had mentioned the place. Already it carried a deadly allure.

'The bandit's fortress' Jorge had called it. This was where Don Reza was being taken and, he hoped, where Kasha and Luis had been taken too. He prayed that he would find them there. But he had no idea where it was. He'd have to stick closely to the bandits in the ambush group if he was to find it.

Bandits were hidden on both sides of the valley and some of them could see him. The archer had already warned him that he would be watched. Any suspicion of treachery, even if he did manage to keep himself alive, would condemn Kasha and Luis to who knows what fate. If he was shown to be a traitor, he didn't dare think of the ways in which they would be made to suffer.

They had chosen to come because of him, because of his hare-brained plan to mount a rescue and now they were in deadly danger.

Nathan adjusted his position to draw his bow and put an arrow to the notch. He scanned the scattered rocks and boulders and stunted trees on the opposite side of the valley, looking for the signal. Every bandit would be doing the same.

Along the valley the column rode nearer.

Now he could see individuals. At its head rode the curly-haired cavalry lieutenant with whom he had spoken at the Alcazar. By his side rode a lanky figure he would have recognised anywhere.

Atta.

Why was he up at the front of the column? Hadn't they thought about an ambush? Surely he should be further back, if Atta stayed at the front he was likely to be shot at, hurt, maybe killed.

Once the ambush began, he would also be in danger himself. His friends and allies in the column would be shooting at him, trying to kill him.

Something bright on the opposite side of the valley caught Nathan's eye. It was the sun flashing on the sword as the leading archer drew it from its scabbard. It wouldn't be long now.

But...of course!

That was it.

Nathan smiled.

Why hadn't he thought of it before?

He screwed up his eyes, peering into the low sun, then reached inside his jerkin and shirt.

14.

Ambush

Miguel stared at the column stretching out ahead of him along the stony trail.

Atta and Lieutenant Riccardo were leading, followed by Don Mustafa and a phalanx of soldiers, mostly Granadan guards. Then came Rebecca's uncle and a few cavalrymen. The silversmith had led them as far as the mountains but then had fallen back. Thomas followed, at Miguel's side, with more cavalry bringing up the rear. They were riding up a rocky valley, its sides dotted with grey boulders casting long shadows. Just the place for an ambush.

'We must be getting close now,' Senor Thomas said. 'Atta looks more confident of the direction.'

It was true. The column was no longer halting every so often to allow Atta to consult his map.

'Yes, but if we're getting close then Atta shouldn't be out front anymore,' Miguel said. 'He's too much of a target. I'm going up to tell him to fall back.'

Miguel kicked Evalina's flanks and she sprang forward into a trot passing the column on his right.

He frowned, screwing up his eyes against a sudden glare. Yet the shadows, including his own and Evalina's, were stretched out in front of him, the sun was going down in the west behind him.

So why was a light shining in his eyes?

In the rocks high on the valley's side the blinking light was a reflection, not the sun itself. What could be causing it?

Then the light was no longer in his eyes, but he could still see the reflection. Miguel looked down at his chest. A circlet of light danced on his leather surcoat. As he rode along beside the column, it was moving with him. This was no ordinary reflection, it was a signal.

A warning.

Miguel jerked hard on the reins and Evalina slid to an abrupt stop.

'Ambush!' He stood up in his stirrups and yelled as loudly as he could. 'Ambush!'

He felt a draught in the air and heard a zinging sound then a 'puck'. To his left an arrow struck the stony soil.

They were under attack.

Evalina snorted and pranced. She circled and he pulled hard on the reins to bring her back round. Crouching low over her neck, he kicked her sides and set her off at a gallop to the front of the column.

Arrows flew through the air around him. Horses screamed and fell as the iron arrow heads sliced into their flesh. Others jibbed and the cavalrymen fought to control their mounts at the same time as reaching for the round shields they carried on their backs.

The confusion was greater as he got closer to the front of the column. Here fallen riders called out for help as they lay trapped beneath their mounts. Horses' round bellies were exposed, their legs kicking out through the rising dust. Some of those still mounted raised their swords and charged, thundering towards the valley's side.

'Look out!'

He heard a shout and turned to see an armed rider bearing down on him only feet away. The man, his face tormented into a mask of rage, raised his sword.

Miguel tugged at the reins to turn Evalina. He had to meet the charge head on. He drew his sword from its scabbard, then the bandit was on him and his arm shuddered as he parried his assailant's blow.

Evalina skittered sideways and he fought to control her, but his attacker didn't return to deliver another blow but continued on and veered away. Miguel caught his breath.

He was in the middle of it all, amid the cries and shouts as horses snorted and swords clashed. A glance back down the valley showed him that the soldiers from the rear of the column had realised the danger and were coming up to help. But already the bandits were riding away, pursued by the Lieutenant and some of his troopers. The few on foot were disappearing into the rocks.

The attack seemed to be over almost as soon as it had begun.

Miguel sheathed his sword. He leaned forward to stroke Evalina's neck, speaking to her calmly as they walked on towards the head of the column. Along the trail men were on foot, soothing their horses as they ministered to those lying on the ground. Other troopers galloped after riderless horses which hurtled, across the valley floor.

At the head of the column a knot of guards had clustered around a figure lying on the ground. It was Don Mustafa, his huge form was unmistakeable. There was an arrow protruding from his chest, high up near the shoulder.

Miguel dismounted and, pulling Evalina behind him, forced his way through the little crowd. At its centre, watched by the Emiri major, a pale-faced Atta was kneeling at his uncle's side.

Mustafa's leather breastplate lay on the ground beside his long sword. The arrow had entered the side of his chest, beneath his arm. The young doctor's hands probed the flesh around the arrow head. Mustafa's breath was quick and shallow, but his lips were not blood-flecked.

'It's not too deep,' Atta said to his uncle. 'Senor Thomas can extract it. Look, here he comes.'

Mustafa turned his head to follow his nephew's out-stretched hand and, at that very second, Atta wrenched the barb from his uncle's flesh.

The Ambassador's body arched upwards as he shouted in agony, then relaxed back on to the ground.

Miguel winced.

Blood welled from the gash in Mustafa's shoulder and Atta began to staunch the flow with his uncle's cloak, packing the fabric into the wound.

'Here, let me help you.' It was Thomas, pushing his way through the men, pulling bandages from his medical bag.

He knelt and began to reassure with the fallen man. 'The arrow entered at a shallow angle, your vitals should be intact... that's good.'

Atta sat back on his heels and Miguel noticed that the young man's hands were shaking. It had taken courage to do what he had done and nerves of iron.

Yet now the young doctor seemed distracted, speaking with Thomas, in low, urgent tones. What was he saying?

'Did you see? Did you see who it was?'

'I... no,' Thomas replied. With the help of a guard he had manoeuvred the Ambassador into a sitting position and was cutting off his clothes so that he might bandage his chest. 'What do you mean?'

Atta stood, rigid.

'It was Nathan Calamiel. I swear I saw Nathan in the melee.'

Surely that couldn't be. What on earth would Rebecca's cousin be doing with the bandit gang?

'Are you sure?' Miguel asked. 'Could you have been mistaken?'

Atta shook his head vehemently. 'No, it was Nathan alright. I...'

'How is the Ambassador?' Lieutenant Riccardo pushed his way through the guards and was peering anxiously at Mustafa. He and the troopers had returned from pursuing the bandits.

'He should recover,' Thomas answered, 'as long as the arrow wasn't poisoned.'

The Lieutenant heaved a sigh of relief and Miguel caught the glance he exchanged with the Emiri Major. Neither officer would come out of this skirmish well. They should not have allowed the bandits to surprise them and the Ambassador had been badly hurt.

'He'll have to go back to Jerez,' Thomas continued. 'He won't be able to ride and he needs better medical attention than I can give him here.'

The Lieutenant nodded in assent.

'Other casualties?' He asked his sergeant.

'One dead, sir,' the man replied. 'At least two wounded so as you'd notice and there'll be others.'

The Lieutenant cursed. 'We can't afford to lose any more men, we are too few already.'

'But we are going to continue, aren't we?' Atta asked. 'We are going on?'

'Is that all?' The Lieutenant asked the Sergeant.

'Yes Sir,' the man replied. 'Aside from our other guide.'

Simon Calamiel. Rebecca's uncle.

'Simon?' Atta swung round toward the Sergeant. He seemed to have forgotten his question.

'Aye, the smith.'

'I must go to him,' Atta said. 'Where is he?'

'Further down the column,' the sergeant said and summoned a trooper, who lead Atta away.

Miguel almost followed. If her uncle was badly hurt Rebecca would be distraught. But he wanted to know what was going to happen next. Was the mission going on? Or were they to give up and return to the city, after just one reversal?

'I'm afraid I can only give you a couple of outriders to take you back to town, Doctor,' the Lieutenant said. 'We've no more to spare. But I don't think the bandits will trouble you further. We start out at first light tomorrow, I suggest that you do too.'

That was the answer to his question - the mission was going to continue.

'Don Mustafa will need a sledge of some kind,' Thomas replied. 'We won't be travelling quickly.'

The Lieutenant called to two troopers. 'Martinez, Suarez, you'll accompany the doctor tomorrow.' He turned to Miguel, his face grim. 'Will you return with them, or are you coming with us?'

'Do you have enough men to attack? We must be close to the camp now.'

'We are, but it's not the camp which worries me,' the Lieutenant said. 'We caught up with one of the bandits after the attack and questioned him. Before he died he claimed that they have retreated further into the mountains, the camp is abandoned. We must follow them,' the Lieutenant sounded careworn. 'Though what we'll do when we find them I don't know. We may not, as you say, have enough men to attack their mountain stronghold.'

So the Lieutenant needed every man.

Yet Rebecca might need him back in Jerez, now that her uncle was hurt. What was he to do? Should he return?

No. He wasn't ready to do so. There was a mission to perform.

'I'll go with you,' Miguel replied.

'Thank you.'

'What about Atta?' Thomas asked.

'We couldn't dissuade him even if we wanted to and his medical skills will be useful, now that you're going back to Jerez,' the Lieutenant said. He sighed. 'For now, we'll camp here, in what cover there is at the side of the valley. Sergeant,' he addressed his officer. 'Set watchmen just in case, there's an hour 'til sun-down.'

With a nod the Lieutenant strode away, his sergeant following and calling out to his men. Troopers came for the horses and Miguel unsaddled Evalina.

'I'll come and see you,' he said, stroking her as he handed over her reins. 'Look after her.' She whinnied as she was led off to the makeshift corral.

Miguel stood with Thomas, Don Mustafa lying between them. By the valley side soldiers were making camp, gathering dry kindling for cook fires, picking places to bivouac for the night.

'So our ways part here,' Thomas said, wiping his hands on an already bloodied bandage.

'So it seems,' Miguel said. 'Take care going home.'

'I will, but I think you are riding into the greater danger.' For a heartbeat Thomas hesitated, then continued. 'Do me a favour would you? Keep an eye on Atta. He's set on finding his father, but he might have some ideas of his own on how to go about it. He might not say much, but he's an independent sort.'

'Yes. Of course.' Miguel gripped the doctor's proffered hand. 'He is, was, my brother's good friend. I'll make sure he's alright.'

'Thanks.' Thomas turned back to his patient. 'Now, let's get you ready to travel.'

Already Miguel felt the deflation which was the aftermath of battle. He should keep occupied, do something useful.

'I'll go and organise your sledge,' he said and strode towards the side of the valley.

136

15.

Atta makes a decision

Atta followed the cavalryman along the column.

Around them men and horses were scattered across the valley floor. They passed a young trooper, who was trying hard not to weep as he cradled his fallen horse's head and spoke gently to her. He would cut her throat rather than leave her to be eaten alive by the wolves and the vultures, which were already circling above.

Men nursed minor injuries, a slashed arm or a crushed leg. They needed medical attention, but Atta walked on.

He would deal with them later. Right now he had to find Simon. If the smith was mortally hurt, how would he tell Nathan and Rebecca the news?

'Is he badly wounded?' Atta asked. 'The smith...?'

The man shrugged his shoulders.

And what was going to happen to the expedition? How many horses had they lost? Would they be able to continue? Or would they all have to return to Jerez?

Whatever happened, he wasn't going to go back. He would continue, somehow, and find his father. Even if he had to do so alone.

'Here,' the cavalryman's voice broke into his thoughts.

Simon lay at the side of the trail, propped up against a saddle, his eyes closed. The right side of his head was red with blood, a large flap of skin falling over his ear.

'Simon,' he called, kneeling at his side. 'Simon. It's me, Atta. Can you hear me?'

The smith's eyes opened and Simon's mouth moved, but at first no sound emerged. He licked his lips.

'Yes,' he said. 'I'm all right.'

'No, you're not.' Atta examined the scalp wound. 'You're lucky to be alive.'

A sword swipe had sliced across the top of his skull. Simon must have ducked at just the right moment. 'But, if we can keep the wound clean, you might mend.'

He felt around in his bag for a metal mug. 'I need water,' he said as he handed it to a soldier. 'And can someone make a fire please. I need a cleansing flame.'

The soldier filled the mug from his canteen while another made a ring of grey pebbles and, within minutes, a small fire burned.

Atta checked Simon over for other injuries. There seemed to be none.

Taking the mug of water he wetted Simon's lips, then gently bathed his head wound with a piece of soft cotton. It looked ugly, there was a lot of blood, but, as he cleaned it, he saw that it was only shallow. Simon's skull was still intact. Nathan still had a father.

Nathan.

It was Nathan he had seen. He was sure of it. Standing amid the rocks, bow raised in his hands. But then, he seemed to be seeing Nathan everywhere - first in the shanty town, then here.

No, he wasn't imagining it. He had seen Nathan. It was as if he wanted to be seen.

Simon groaned.

'Keep your head still,' he said. 'I'm going to have to sew you up.'

He took a spool of cat gut and a fine needle from his pack, threaded the needle and held it in the flame. He winced as it grew hot to hold.

'This is going to hurt,' he said to Simon. 'You must stay as still as you can.'

'I'll try,' Simon said as he levered himself up.

As he made the first incision in the scalp Simon flinched, pulling back. Atta stopped. Then Simon steadied himself, holding himself rigid.

'Go on,' he said, eyes open, staring but seeing nothing.

At the next incision Simon didn't move. Glancing down Atta saw that his brow was furrowed and his eyes were closed. He was concentrating on keeping still.

Atta pulled through the twine and brought up the flap of skin, his fingers sticking to the bloodied hair. He plied the needle as quickly as he could until the skin was sewn back across Simon's pate. Then he wrapped the cotton fabric around Simon's head, careful to pull it taunt, but not so much that it hurt. He knotted it to hold it in place.

'That'll do for now,' Atta said, sitting back on his heels to survey his handiwork. It looked tidy enough. 'It will get you back into town and, as long as the wound doesn't putrefy the skin should re-knit.'

Simon exhaled. The tension seemed to leave him.

'Will I be able to ride?' He asked, looking up.

'I doubt it.' Simon would have problems simply getting to his feet, he looked very weak. 'Lie back for now. You'll feel better if you relax and stay still.'

The smith lay back against the saddle his eyes closing. Then he opened them once more.

'Thank you, Atta,' he said. 'Your father would be proud of you.'

'You're welcome,' he said. 'But how could I ever face Nathan again if I hadn't fixed you up. And Rebecca would have flayed me alive.'

As he packed his things away, Atta beckoned a soldier aside.

'We'll need two sledges, not one,' he said. 'Tell them.'

The trooper nodded. Atta watched him hurry off to the valley side where the company was now making camp among the boulders. Fires were already alight and horses were being corralled together.

There was Thomas, overseeing the placing of Uncle Taf onto a sledge, a robust frame of logs covered with brushwood, sheepskins and cavalry blankets.

Uncle Taf.

He had been the first to react to Miguel's shouted warning, riding forward to the front of the column. In no time, it seemed, the arrows were flying and the horses falling or panicked. Taf saw the bandits coming and drew his sword to engage the first rider who

140

reached them. That was when he'd been struck by the arrow, a much more serious wound than Simon's. Maybe a deadly one.

Taf had ridden forward so as to protect him, Atta. And he had fallen.

Atta remembered scrambling from his horse to give him aid. It was then that he had glimpsed Nathan.

Metal struck rock and someone swore.

Startled, Atta turned. There was a burial party at work nearby. A body lay, awaiting interment beneath a cairn. How many more would there be if they carried on to the mountains?

The trooper who was scratching a shallow hole in the hard earth stopped, wiped his arm across his brow and leant on his spade. Even in the chill of the approaching night sweat ran freely down his face.

'Hey, Martinez! Take a turn,' he called to his comrade.

'I'm glad we're going home tomorrow,' the other trooper grumbled as he picked up a spade. 'Abandoning this fool's errand.'

So the expedition was over. The Lieutenant had given the order. They were returning to Jerez.

Atta turned away.

Well, their numbers were fewer now and the bandits would be ready for any pursuit. Perhaps it was for the best. He didn't want more men to die. But he would go on. He had to.

Perhaps...? Perhaps he could slip away alone? As a lone rider, he wouldn't attract much attention and he knew the way from here.

Atta looked around for his horse. He had handed her reins to one of the guards when he dismounted, thinking only of his uncle. Where was she?

141

Tethered to the other mounts, grazing on what little grass she could find.

Atta walked over and released her. Taking up the reins, he threaded their way through the encampment. No-one took any notice of him. Everyone was concentrating on their own tasks.

If Nathan was with the bandits, the two of them might be able to spirit his father away. He would go on and find Nathan. His feet turned towards the valley head.

'Where are you going? The camp's back there.'

A voice rang out.

Leaning against a large rock, up ahead, arms folded, was Miguel Delgado. The young man looked relaxed, but his sword protruded slightly from its sheath.

'They'll be cooking soon. We ought to go and find some food'

What was he doing there? Had Miguel divined his intention? It wasn't possible, he had only just made up his own mind. Miguel couldn't possibly know.

He said nothing.

'It's dangerous to be wandering around alone,' Miguel said 'Best stay close to the camp.' He levered himself upright and sauntered over. 'Come on, let's go and eat.'

Who was Miguel Delgado to tell him what to do? The Delgados had always had a high opinion of themselves, even Juan......

But there was no point in starting a confrontation now. He led his horse round in a circle and started back to the bivouac. For the moment, he had no choice.

Yet he knew the terrain better than Miguel Delgado did, probably better than anyone in this band. A chance to get away was bound to present itself and, he determined, that was just what he was going to do.

Tonight, perhaps, while the others slept. Yes, that was it.

Atta smiled to himself. He would wait for darkness and no one, including Juan's brother, would be able to stop him.

16.

Asunder

Miguel flexed his shoulders. His back hurt.

There was a pain between his shoulder blades. Something sharp was digging into him. He turned over, but whatever it was pressed into his upper arm.

It was his sword hilt.

Miguel sat up, abruptly.

He had placed it there, so as to prevent himself from dozing. Alot of good that had done.

He shook his head to force himself awake and shivered.

It was icily cold. The embers of the fire were ashes now. He must have been asleep for some time.

Around him he saw recumbent forms huddled under blankets and heard snores and wheezes. Skeins of thin cloud whipped across the face of the three-quarter moon lighting all in shades of grey.

High atop one of the boulders stood a still, silent figure.

As Miguel watched the man blew on his hands, rubbing them together. The sentry was alert, the camp was well guarded.

So why did he feel uneasy?

He stretched, his limbs cracking, and got to his feet. Stepping lightly around and between his sleeping comrades, he walked over to where Rebecca's uncle and the Ambassador lay on their cushioned beds. Thomas was there, breathing evenly in sleep. But where was Atta? He had bedded down here, beside his uncle, but now there was no sign of him.

Exactly what he had feared - the young man was planning to go it alone. Just as Thomas had thought; just like Juan would have done.

Cursing under his breath, he retraced his steps.

He ought to rouse the camp, or at least wake the Lieutenant.

But Atta wouldn't be able to get far. The bandit camp, if the captured bandit was to be believed, was empty and the way onwards was a path through the cliffs which circled the camp, but that wouldn't be passable by night. Atta would have to wait until sun-up before going on.

By then he would have caught up with the young man and brought him back. He didn't need to bother the Lieutenant with this. The man had enough on his mind.

As quickly and quietly as he could, he picked up his saddle, pack and weapons.

The sentry had spotted him moving around and Miguel raised his hand in salute, pointing towards the pickets where the horses were held. There would be another guard on duty there.

Had Atta taken a horse from among the others, under the guard's nose?

Miguel was plunged into darkness as cloud crossed the moon. He stood still.

146

His eyes would become accustomed to the starlight, if it was enough to see by. Gradually grey shapes resolved into boulders. He could hear every little noise, the grunt of a sleeper, the whinny of a horse. Where was the guard?

'Hsst.' He tried a sound. There was a low whistle in answer from his left. Miguel turned and stumbled over a sleeper. The man groaned a curse, but did not wake.

Then the moonlight returned. He could see again.

The guard, a Granadan soldier, was looking his way. 'What's afoot?' He asked in low tones as Miguel drew near.

'One of our physicians has decided to wander off,' Miguel replied

'Who?'

'The Ambassador's nephew.'

The soldier swore. 'There'll be trouble if he's not found.'

'I know, I'm going to find him. Has he taken his horse?'

The horses were gathered in a hastily made corral within the boulder field. He could see them in the moonlight as they grazed and snorted gently.

The guard clambered atop a rock and proceeded to count the horses. Some of them looked up and snickered. He jumped back down.

'The big bay mare with the white blaze has gone,' the soldier said.

'As I thought,' Miguel said. 'I'm going after him. We can't let him go off on his own and if we wait until daybreak he'll be long gone.' He moved a picket aside and slipped through the fence, into the corral. 'I'll get my mount.'

147

'But you won't be able to track him at night.'

'I think I know where he's going. As long as there's moonlight I'll be alright.'

Miguel whistled softly and listened for Evalina's answering neigh. When it came he made his way over to untether her, leading her out of the corral to saddle her as quietly as he could. He buckled his weapons belt around his waist and placed a throwing knife in his boot.

'If I'm not back by dawn tell the Lieutenant I've gone after Atta and I'll bring him back. But I hope we'll both be back before sun up.'

Miguel mounted and, without waiting for a response, urged his horse forward to walk through the boulder field. The first look-out waved.

As he gained the trail he urged Evalina into a trot and then a canter. Soon he reached the top of the valley and saw another opening up before him, the wide trackway running along its centre, going ever higher.

Moonlight reflected on a pool to his right as the thudding of Evalina's hooves reverberated from the valley sides. Then, up ahead, Miguel saw the path begin to wind, back and forth up the ever steepening gradient to a ridge. The bandit camp was just beyond it. He reined in his horse.

If the captured bandit had lied, the bandits would be waiting and he'd be riding into danger – best to tether his horse here and approach cautiously, on foot. On the other hand, if the camp was empty he would lose valuable time.

No, he had to press on. It would be dawn soon and Atta would have slipped away.

Miguel urged Evalina forward and listened for any half-sound as he climbed the switchbacks. All he heard was the calling of an owl and the creaking of the leather of his own saddle. He rode on the grass at the side of the track whenever he could to reduce the noise of Evalina's hooves.

If the bandits were still here, their look-outs would have spotted him by now. A single, silent arrow would be all it took. As he neared the final turn Miguel tensed, ready to spur his mount into a gallop if need be.

Then he was on the ridge, gazing down at the encampment, still and silent in the cold moonlight. Cabin doors stood ajar, the stockade gates were open and there was no movement anywhere. It was abandoned.

Miguel slowly scrutinised the high grey cliff wall which circled the camp.

There.

There was a dark gash in the striated rock on the far left. Was this the path?

He walked Evalina around the ridge towards it.

Yes, it was a chasm in the cliffs. Within was deep in darkness, the moonlight didn't penetrate the shadows.

Where was Atta, he must be here somewhere? Surely he hadn't tried to pass through in darkness? That would be courting disaster. He had to be close by.

At the mouth of the gorge Miguel dismounted. He would lead the horse just a little way in, but it would be dangerous to go further without being able to see. He started forwards into the blackness.

Then he stood stock still, his senses straining.

Was that the sound of breathing? Of a man or a beast? Or both?

Evalina snuffled and whinnied.

An answering whinny came from the darkness, away to Miguel's right. Seconds later he heard a voice.

'Why are you following me?' It was Atta.

Miguel called back into the shadows. 'To prevent you from getting hurt,'

'Someone else protecting me.' Atta's tone was hostile. 'I can look after myself.'

Miguel frowned and looked towards the voice. Was that a movement? There was a change in the density of the darkness. Could he get to Atta?

'I believe you, but you're no fighter, if I'm any judge. And you'll need to fight if you want to help your father.'

'You saw the abandoned camp. The bandits have retreated, further up into the mountains I'd say. I know these peaks, I've crossed them before.' Atta went on. 'And I know mountain people who will help me.'

Silence.

'I know this path, too.'

What! The voice now came from Miguel's left. Silently, he cursed. This wasn't working out as he'd hoped.

'Not that well,' he said. 'Otherwise you would be far ahead of me by now.'

He took a step to the left and kicked a large stone. Ow!

'But better than you, that's plain.' The voice had a smile in it.

'You can't go on alone.' Miguel shuffled his foot along the ground, anxious not to trip. 'Come back with me to the expedition, if you want pursue the bandits.'

'The expedition's going back to Jerez.'

'No, it's not. It's going on. We can search the mountains together.'

Again, silence.

Was Atta considering it? Or didn't he believe him? How to persuade him?

'We could find your friends and they could help our soldiers scout the area.' He prompted, sensing Atta's resolve was weakening.

Then Atta spoke again.

'Come with me.'

What? An invitation. The last thing he'd expected.

'I'll make a deal with you.' It might work. Better that he accompany Atta than he should go on alone. 'I'll come with you to find the bandits' hide-out, but then we get a message back to the Lieutenant – tell him where it is.'

He waited. There was no response.

'What do you say?'

'Very well.'

Miguel almost jumped out of his skin. The voice came from right next to him.

There was a touch on his arm.

'It'll soon be light enough to see our way, even if sun-up isn't for an hour yet.'

Atta was right, already the darkness seemed less black.

'So then we go on, until we find the bandits' lair.'

'I agree.'

Not what he'd had in mind when he left the camp, but preferable to allowing Atta to go off on his own. He felt responsible for the young man and he had promised Thomas....

So all they had to do was find the bandit hide-out. Then, somehow, he had to send word to the Lieutenant and stop Atta from trying to get into it. That was all.

17.

The Followers

Rebecca's hat shaded her eyes from the high sun as she peered ahead.

Yes, she hadn't been mistaken, there was movement on the trail which ran down the stony valley. Someone was coming towards them, to the greener, undulating plain.

'We've got company,' she said to her companion.

Ben reined in his horse and stood in his stirrups. He looked to the hills.

'Three riders,' he said. 'They're dragging something along behind them.' He sat down in the saddle. 'Come on, let's meet them.' He urged his horse into a trot.

Rebecca did the same, kicking her horse's flanks. She held on to the pommel of the saddle with both hands, not trusting herself with the jerking motion, which bounced her up and down. She gripped the sides of her mount with her knees and tried to adjust to the flow of the horse's steps as Ben had shown her, but her legs were already strained and tired and she couldn't find the rhythm. This wasn't like plodding along on old Ruben the mule.

Gradually the figures became clearer and she could see two sledges being drawn behind the horses. One rider had spurred on his mount, he was approaching rapidly.

'Looks like they're bringing wounded back to town,' Ben said.

'Wounded...?'

Please, please don't let it be Miguel.

Please don't let it be Simon.

Two of the riders were soldiers, wearing the uniform of the King's cavalry, but Rebecca recognised the other, coming closer. It was Senor Thomas.

'Hello! What are you doing here?' Thomas reined in his mount.

'We have news,' Ben replied. He said no more.

'It's important,' Rebecca said, words spilling out. 'Nathan's gone to join the bandits. He and two friends, former galley slaves, plan to rescue Don Reza. Nathan freed the oar slaves during the sea battle. I tricked them into telling me about his plan, in the hospital back in Jerez.'

Thomas stared at her.

'We thought the Lieutenant and the soldiers should know that they have allies in the bandit band.' Ben said. 'And to watch out for Nathan. She would have set out by herself. So I insisted on coming along.'

Insisted? It had taken her two days to persuade Ben to accompany her and he'd only agreed when she had threatened to set out alone.

She glared at Ben.

At least he had the grace to look away.

'I must tell Atta and my uncle,' she continued.

Thomas eyes slid sideways as the sledges came abreast of him.

'What is it?' Rebecca sensed that there was bad news coming.

'Rebecca...? Is that you?'

It was Simon's voice. He was one of the wounded men.

She kicked her feet from the stirrups and slid to the ground, almost toppling as she hit the hard dirt of the road. She ran to the stretchers.

'Uncle!'

Lying there her uncle looked forlorn, his head swathed in bandages, his one eye bruised purple and almost closed. What had befallen him? Was he going to be alright?

She knelt at his side and grasped his hand.

'What happened? Are you alright? Did you find the bandits?'

'They found us,' Simon said as he patted her hand.

'Ambush,' Senor Thomas walked over to them. 'He'll mend, though he'll need some nursing. I'm more concerned...'

He looked at the other stretcher. On it lay Atta's uncle, the Ambassador. His head lolled to one side and his eyes were closed. Beneath the pelt which covered him she saw bandages, with blood upon them.

'Is he...?'

Thomas shook his head. 'Opium,' he said. 'Otherwise the pain would be too great to bear.'

'How was he hurt?' Ben said, leading forward both the horses.

'An arrow. Luckily Atta prised it out quickly and staunched the wound.'

Atta, where was Atta? But of course, he would go on to find his father.

155

'Atta stayed with the raiding party?' Rebecca said.

'No. It was strange. He left the camp during the night,' Thomas' mouth tightened into a thin line. 'Miguel Delgado too.'

What? Why should Miguel leave with Atta?

'Why?' Ben asked, glancing at Rebecca sidelong.

'I'm not sure,' said Thomas. 'I think Atta went on alone to try and find his father, one of the soldiers says that Miguel followed him. Atta said he'd seen Nathan during the bandit attack. They ambushed us in the valley.'

'Nathan!' Simon gasped with pain – he had turned his head sharply when Thomas said his son's name.

Should she tell her uncle about Nathan? Yes. She had to.

'Atta was right,' she said. 'Nathan's joined the bandits. He and two friends, former galley slaves, plan to rescue Don Reza.'

'He's what?' Simon struggled to sit up.

'No, lie back,' Thomas instructed, easing the smith back down onto the blankets. He raised his eyes to Rebecca.

'He saved the oar slaves, in the battle,' she said. 'They've been sheltering him, I think. He came to see me when you were out at the barracks.'

Simon sighed and closed his eyes.

'He came when I wasn't there.'

'Yes,' Thomas said. 'The Lieutenant needs to know that Nathan and his friends may have infiltrated the enemy camp.'

'Ben,' Simon called. 'Thank you. Thank you for looking after her.'

'I'm here, uncle,' she said. 'You don't need to talk about me as if I wasn't.'

156

'Is the expedition far ahead?' Ben asked.

'We started out at first light so it's several hours' ride to where we left them,' Thomas replied. 'They'll have moved on, but the Lieutenant will be more careful now, for fear of another ambush. If you ride hard you should catch them up in a day or so.'

Ben said nothing, but he looked at the two soldiers.

'I'm sorry, but I can't spare them, they're here to protect the Ambassador. I can direct you,' Thomas continued. 'You'll have no difficulty following our back trail. Go up the valley until you reach the abandoned bandit camp....'

'Abandoned?' Rebecca asked.

'Yes, it's empty now, the bandits have withdrawn to higher ground. There's a passageway through the cliffs behind the camp. Through that and you bear north east...,' he paused, waiting for Ben to respond.

'I can find north east,' Rebecca said.

'I doubt you'll be able to see the stars.' Thomas pointed up the trail, where black clouds were massing over the mountains. He looked from her to Ben.

'North east,' Rebecca prompted.

'Keep the peak of Torreon on your left and you'll hit the track. Beyond that, who knows. But... won't you be returning with us, Rebecca, with your uncle?'

Simon protested. 'You'll come home with us, Rebecca. It's no place for you up in the mountains.'

'It was no place for me at sea either,' she answered. 'But I managed well enough.'

157

'Be reasonable...' Simon began to lever himself up. He stopped and grimaced.

Thomas leaned over and gripped the smith's shoulder. 'Lie back,' he said. Simon subsided. Thomas shot a concerned look at Rebecca.

She swallowed hard. She had encouraged her uncle to come on the raid and now he was hurt and in pain. She should help and comfort him, but Nathan was out there somewhere with a company of soldiers on his trail.

She looked across at Ben. Could she trust him to get the message to the soldiers?

Ben and Thomas were both watching her.

They both want me to go back, she thought. That's what good girls do, look after their family, stay at home. Know their place. Do as they're told.

She thought of Lady Beatriz and her determination to direct her own fate.

'I'm going on, Uncle,' she said, raising her chin. She wouldn't show weakness, however much anxiety she felt. Thomas would look after him.

Simon gave a shuddering sigh and closed his eyes.

Almost she wished her words unsaid, but no, she would go on.

'Then I suggest that you get going,' Thomas said, as he rose. 'The gorge through the cliffs is narrow. You need to get through it before sundown today if you're going to have any chance of reaching them. You'll need to ride hard.'

'Thank you,' Rebecca said. She looked at her uncle. His eyes were still closed.

Thomas followed Rebecca over to her horse and bent down to lace his fingers together and boost her into the saddle.

'He'll heal better if he's not worrying,' he said in a low voice.

'I know,' she replied. 'But Nathan's the best medicine for that.'

'Will he come?'

'I think, if he can, he'll come when he knows his father is injured.'

Thomas' eyebrows rose.

'How do you know he doesn't know already?'

'I don't,' she said as she swung into the saddle.

'Very well,' Thomas said. 'I'll look for your return. As, I am sure, will he.'

Rebecca saw that Ben was ready, though he looked unhappy. She wasn't that happy about pressing on at a gallop herself, but it was what they had to do.

She clicked her tongue to her mount and kicked the horse's sides.

18.

Higher Up

Nathan pulled his hood as far down over his face as he could.

Gusts of driving rain swept across the line of horsemen ahead of him as they plodded along in single file. No-one spoke. Hunching his shoulders, his teeth chattering, Nathan just followed the horse in front.

He flexed his toes. His feet were wet and numb with cold. His boots were leaking. It didn't matter. Nothing mattered now.

Was Atta dead?

He replayed the ambush, over and over in his head.

Juan's brother racing up the line of the column and yelling a warning for all he was worth, he'd been pleased with that. Then there was the general melee, with flights of arrows and milling horses. But, clearest of all, once the first volley had been fired, was the sight of the empty saddle of Atta's horse.

Then the fury came.

Fury at the cannon which had killed Juan, fury at the desperate straits of the galley slaves, fury at the needless waste of life and, most of all, fury for Atta. He ran, screaming and unthinking, following those bandits on horseback, down the boulder strewn valley side, determined to get to his friend.

As the heavy cavalry horses from the column thundered down on them he slashed and spun, exultant at the squeal of pain from the horse and the clatter and thud as the rider fell to the earth. He revelled in destruction. All he had wanted to do was to hurt and kill.

He would have run on, across the valley floor if it hadn't been for a bandit rider who had grabbed him and pulled him across his horse as they headed back to cover.

This whole endeavour seemed so pointless if Atta died.

If only he had not run from his friend, back in Jerez. Friendship was too important to waste it. All that they had done together, all that they endured since the siege. It should bring them closer, not drive them apart.

I will make things right, Nathan made a silent promise. If Atta is alive. If only Atta is alive.

He would make things up with his father too. If he got back to Jerez he would go home and talk with him. Explain and ask for forgiveness.

If he ever got back home.

They were climbing a wooded trail now, along the side of a slope, the forest protecting them from the wind. Here the rain was merely a softness drifting mist-like in the air. The thick trunks of the pine trees stood black above the ruddy earth amid scattered rocks of startling whiteness.

The column slowed and Nathan looked ahead. Something was happening.

162

Through the rain he saw a group of mounted men waiting on the trail ahead. One of them was Jorge, water dripping from his wide brimmed leather hat on to the worn and shiny surface of his sheepskin coat.

It was good to see him again. He was a dubious ally, maybe, but still an ally.

As Nathan drew level, Jorge swung his horse alongside him. Nathan felt the older man's scrutiny.

'The ambush was a success,' Jorge prompted.

Nathan said nothing.

'I'm told you fought well and bravely.'

Nathan gave him a sidelong glance.

'Ye gods, you're as close-mouthed as that friend of yours.'

'Atta,' said Nathan. It was difficult to talk about him. 'He was there. In the column we ambushed. I don't know what happened to him. His horse was riderless.'

'I see,' Jorge looked as if was going to speak further, but the trail narrowed and he was forced to fall back to walk behind.

How could Jorge understand? He hadn't been in the siege, among people hurt and broken by months of hunger, their homes destroyed by the siege machines. Or seen men fight each other for a few extra seconds of precious life as the water rose around them.

After a half a mile or so the trail widened again. Nathan looked around for the Granadan.

'Where are we now?'

'We've just crossed a pass,' Jorge replied, drawing level. 'We're approaching the Sierra El Pinar.'

'What is El Endrinal?'

163

'Another mountain range,' Jorge cast a glance at Nathan and, apparently satisfied that he had his attention, continued. 'It has its own peaks, called Simancon and Reloj. 'No-one lives there. It's a desolate place.'

'You said before that you'd been to the bandit hide-out there.'

'I have' Jorge replied. 'It's an old fortress and well defended, built into the rock.'

He said nothing more, for the trail narrowed and began to descend. The sound of water grew louder as they approached the valley floor, where a swollen stream rushed past.

Nathan heeled his horse's flanks to urge her into the water after the others. Once across they began to climb, zig-zagging up the other side of the gorge. Nathan's horse jibbed and tossed her head. He pulled on the reins and spoke to calm her. She was nervous and twitchy, but then, so was he.

The rain had finally stopped, but the pine trees dripped. When the mist cleared, he could see the heavy white clouds above.

Great birds of prey circled above him. Nathan remembered the eagle in the foothills, against the bright blue of the sky, as he rode with Kasha and Luis. How long ago that seemed. Were his friends already at the bandit stronghold?

Nothing more was said until the encroaching darkness forced the group to stop and make camp. Barely had they turned into the forest and unsaddled their horses, than a starless night descended. They set a fire, using the dry kindling they carried and the spluttering glow of the flames gave the only light. Beyond the small circle of brightness the blackness was complete. Sentries were set to protect the makeshift camp and all within it.

164

Nathan took his turn. He stood just beyond the ring of light, a torch of pine pitch in his hand. The rain had finally stopped, but occasional thunder rumbled far off. Ghostly flashes lit the underside of the clouds, castling shadows blacker than black and making the drifts of mist in the forest seem like solid, wraithlike forms.

The sentry's torch on the other side of the camp was a small light in the darkness. A horse whinnied softly. The horses would warn them if wolves came near, or the great cats that were said to roam the mountains. But the one enemy they might not sense until too late was man.

As he peered into the darkness of the forest a twig snapped behind him. He spun around.

A figure had left the fireside. It was Jorge.

'See anything?' He whispered.

Nathan shook his head. 'I wanted to ask you...about Kasha and Luis, my friends.'

'Garalon,' hissed a figure, striding over to them from the camp. 'I want a word with you. Keep your watch, lad.' He beckoned Jorge to return to the fire.

Damn. It would have to wait.

Now he must keep awake and keep alert.

So he walked back and forth, back and forth, until grey pre-dawn light filtered down between the trees. Then the smell of roasting meat drew him to the fire and, taking a stick from the flames, he burned his fingers as he pulled pieces of rabbit from the wood upon which they had been cooked.

19.

Old Friends

Atta heard sounds of water all around.

Soft rain pattered on moss and leaves, it slipped and dripped from the needles of the pine trees. Streams tumbled and raced, released from winter's freeze to run across the path and down the slopes into the forest below. The clouds overhead was heavy, pregnant with more rain.

His hood scattered droplets as he glanced at his companion. Riding by his side, Miguel peered up at the cloud shrouded peaks from beneath the wide brim of his hat. Rain ran in rivulets down his greased cloak.

They were travelling along the northern side of a high range of mountains. The grey cliffs and outcrops were hard and stony. It was late afternoon on the second day since they had entered the gorge behind the bandit camp.

This was the right route, he was almost certain, though it looked very different from when he had last seen it, covered with snow. They had been climbing steadily for hours and should soon reach a pass. From there he could find the village where he had been sheltered by the shepherd, Antonio and his wife, Carmen.

He sensed that Miguel wasn't convinced that he knew the way. Already he was looking sceptical and his impatience was growing. Ever since they had ridden out of the ravine together, as the sun had risen, the atmosphere had been tense. Miguel didn't trust him, indeed, he was anxious not to let him out of his sight, watching his every movement.

It was hard not to think of Juan when he looked at Miguel. Sometimes his face wore that expression, one eyebrow raised, with his head tilted to one side, which made him look so much like his brother that it hurt.

'We should find my shepherd's village before sundown,' Atta said.

Miguel only grunted in response.

Sometimes he wasn't like his brother at all. Juan would have had a stream of questions. There was a greater introspection in Miguel or maybe it was just that Juan hadn't had a chance to grow up.

Atta also sensed that Miguel was uncomfortable in his company. Maybe it worked both ways? Perhaps he reminded Miguel of his dead brother?

Either way, together they had a task to perform.

'If I'm right,' Atta ventured. 'There is a pass close by. From there it's not far.'

Miguel said nothing.

Their horses plodded on, stepping around the jagged outcrops on the trail. They passed into cold, wet cloud and out again. Finally, they rounded a turn and the cloud parted. There it was, the saddle of the pass.

'So you were right,' Miguel said, his eyes smiling, mocking. 'I suspected that you were making it all up, back there in the canyon. That it was all a story to trick me and you'd slip off by yourself the first chance you got. But I was wrong.'

Juan wouldn't have admitted he was wrong like that, or given ground so easily.

'Come on,' Atta urged his mount forwards with his heels. 'We only have a couple of hours left before nightfall.' He crossed the pass and headed down into a valley as goat bells rang. Already the *campesinos* were bringing their herds up into the high pastures.

It was dusk when they finally saw lights and smelled chimney smoke. Houses and cabins clustered, clinging on to the sloping sides of the mountain. It was the village.

'We'll call at the forge first,' Atta said. 'I would like to say hello to an old friend.'

'Lead on.'

Atta encouraged his mount into a trot and they were soon entering the smithy yard.

'Hallo!' He called out as they dismounted. Atta handed his horse's reins to Miguel and poked his head around the door to the forge. 'Hallo.'

A stocky figure turned, silhouetted by the red glow of the furnace.

'Atta!' He strode towards him, wiping his hands on a cloth.

'Hello Felipe,' Atta smiled broadly and pumped the hand held out to him. 'This is my friend, Miguel, from Jerez.'

169

He and Felipe acknowledged each other with a nod.

'We're going to Antonio and Carmen,' Atta said. 'We're tracking a band of riders, *bandeleros*, we were on their trail but we've lost them.'

Felipe's face took on a knowing expression. 'Things are happening in the peaks. You'd best speak with Antonio, the shepherds always know what's going on.'

'We will. See you later.' Atta raised his hand in salute as they led their horses out of the yard and up a sloping path behind the forge.

'I stayed with Antonio and Carmen last year,' he explained, looking behind him at Miguel. 'He was in a bad way, he'd fallen into a crevasse higher up. Here we are.'

There it was - the familiar cabin, its external shutters closed against the coming night and smoke rising from its chimney stack. Before Atta could pound on the door it opened.

'Atta!' It was Carmen, a beaming smile on her face.

She was just as Atta remembered, black hair tinged with grey and pulled back from her round face.

'Come in, come in. 'Tonio!' She called back into the cabin. 'It's Atta, he's back! And with a friend. Come and take their horses.'

'Atta,' Antonio stepped past his wife and Atta was engulfed in a warm embrace. Then the shepherd stood back and appraised him, his lined and bearded face split by a broad grin. He slapped his leg.

'The leg's holding up well, good as new.' He jerked his thumb over his shoulder. 'She's been worrying about what happened to you.' Carmen pursed her lips. 'Let me take your mounts.'

'This is my friend,' Atta indicated Miguel. 'Miguel Delgado.'

'Any friend of Atta's is welcome here.' The shepherd shook the hand offered to him and took the horses' reins. 'Go in, please. Out of the cold.'

Inside the cabin was the same too – the large bed in the corner, the big hearth and fire with its iron pot hanging from a hook, the tall settle and the table and chairs. The lamps were lit, it was warm and cosy and he could smell cooking.

'Sit, sit,' Carmen drew chairs back from the table. 'Are you hungry? You'll eat with us tonight. How long are you staying?'

'Miguel and I are tracking bandits,' Atta explained as Carmen took their cloaks. 'We'd be grateful for your hospitality for a night or so, while we search.'

'These are soaking,' she said, placing them on a frame by the side of the hearth. 'How long has it been since you were in shelter? You're tracking bandits, you say? Are they the ones who took your father? '

Atta relaxed and let her words flow over him.

He felt at home here. More at home than he did in the fine palace in Jerez.

The cabin door opened and Antonio entered, sloughing off his hooded cape, which he hung on a hook on the back of the door.

'This time he's hunting *bandeleros*,' Carmen said to her husband as she carried the cooking pot over to the table, holding its handle with a folded cloth.

'We think there's some sort of fortified hide-out up here,' Atta said, turning his chair to face the fire. 'That's probably where my father is and I believe my friend Nathan has gone ahead of us to find him.'

171

'Do you know where it is?' Antonio took his place at the table. His wife spooned a thick and unctuous stew into bowls.

Atta sat back and let Miguel explain how they had come there, describing the raiding party, while he savoured Carmen's cooking once more.

'Soldiers, you say?' Antonio looked sharply at his wife, his spoon half way to his mouth. 'Whose soldiers? Is there to be war in the mountains now?'

'I don't know,' Miguel's eyes flicked to Atta and then back to Antonio. 'But I know our expedition won't start it. It includes people from both sides, King's cavalry and Emir's guards.'

'My uncle, Mustafa, of whom you know, is now the Emir's Ambassador to the King,' Atta explained. 'Both monarchs want the bandits dealt with.'

It was stretching things a little, but it was broadly true. He was becoming a diplomat, Uncle Taf would be pleased.

'Hmmm,' Antonio began to eat again. 'We don't want war here.'

No, that would destroy these villages and their people, Atta thought. Their lives were precarious enough as it was, dependant on weather and good fortune. So far the war had left the mountain people largely alone, but neither side could allow the other to occupy the peaks.

'There are already rumours of armed men in the mountains,' Antonio continued. 'Shepherds have seen war bands. I'll go into the village tonight to find out what's been seen up in the peaks. Some of the *campesinos* will have come down. Everyone will be wary of any soldiers, even if there isn't to be war.'

'You and your friend can dry out in front of our fire while he's gone,' Carmen added. 'And you must tell me what happened after you left us. Was that man you went with a wrong 'un?'

'No,' Atta smiled. Carmen had been so suspicious of Jorge, she hadn't trusted him at all. 'He turned out to be an ally, working for my uncle. He was a good friend.'

'You tell Carmen all about it,' Antonio said, as he stood. 'I'd best go down now. I'll be back later.'

*

'Atta. Atta!'

Someone was shaking his arm, insistently.

Atta opened his eyes to see the wooden beams above him. He was lying on the bed. The warmth and shelter of the cabin must have lulled him to sleep.

Miguel was at the bedside.

'Antonio's back,' he said. 'Get up.'

Beyond Miguel, Antonio was sitting by the fireside and taking off his wet boots. Atta looked down at his own feet. His boots had been removed too, probably by Carmen. His right big toe protruded through a hole in his thick sock.

Atta sat up and swung round. He shook his head to throw off sleep. Better have a clear head, what Antonio said might be important.

He drew a chair closer to the hearth and Antonio began to talk.

'There's more than one set of interlopers in the mountains,' he said. 'There was a small group riding on Torreon only this morning, *bandeleros*, heading for the flats.'

'That may be the group which ambushed us,' Miguel said.

173

'They headed for El Endrinal. But there's something else.... Soldiers have been seen, from Ronda to the east. Nico heard it from a *campesino* who lives that way.'

'Not King's men, surely' Miguel said. 'Not from that direction.'

'No,' Antonio agreed. 'Though there's a big company travelling from the north-west including King's men. Would that be the group you were with?'

'Probably,' Miguel answered. 'We need to bring them up here. Are they far?'

'A day's ride maybe,' Antonio replied. 'Maybe a little more.'

He looked reluctant, unwilling to bring the soldiers higher into the mountains.

'The *bandeleros* won't be good neighbours to anyone,' Miguel said. Carmen bit her lip and laced her fingers together, nervously.

Antonio sighed. 'No, you're right.'

'And, if the *bandeleros* went to El Endrinal, that's where Atta and I need to go.'

'They won't be easy to find,' Antonio's laugh was mirthless. 'El Endrinal is a labyrinth, riddled with deep caves and treacherous with flash floods right now.'

'But you know it?' Atta asked. Without Antonio and his friends they would have little chance of finding his father.

'I do, though not as well as others,' Antonio looked at him. 'If you're determined to search there I can ask them to take you.'

'Tonio.'

'We can't stop him, Carmen...'

'But it's dangerous.' She looked from her husband to Atta. 'Why don't you wait for the soldiers?'

'We will,' Miguel said. 'Once we find the hide-out. Won't we Atta?'

All three of them were watching him. Carmen's face was anxious, Antonio's wary and Miguel...? Miguel was studying him closely, leaning forward, waiting for his answer. Atta didn't want to lie.

'Antonio, if you ride back to tell the expedition where we are, Miguel and I will go with your friends to search El Endrinal,' he said. 'If we find the hide-out we can take the soldiers straight there when they arrive. As for me, I want to see where they're keeping my father before I decide what to do.'

Carmen looked at her husband, who nodded his agreement.

Miguel sat back in his chair. 'Very well,' he said. But the look in his eyes was guarded.

Atta was convinced Miguel would try to prevent him from entering the bandit lair alone. But that was tomorrow's problem. There was nothing he could do about it now and first they had to find the hide-out.

20.

El Endrinal

Nathan was riding third in line, with a breakfast of rabbit meat in his belly. He was bone weary.

They were riding through a noiseless landscape of white crags and jagged cliffs. All sound was deadened by cloud lying heavy above, save for the whistling of the wind. Nathan had no idea where they were. He wanted only to arrive at the bandit hide-out, to find stone walls and a solid roof under which to shelter and get dry.

The mist parted for a moment and Nathan caught sight of cliffs and a tower up ahead. That must be it. It vanished as the cloud wrapped around them again. He rose in his stirrups and strained to see it again, but could not. From behind him he heard a rider chuckle.

'Yes, that's where we're headed,' the man said. 'I'll be glad when we get there.'

So he was close, now, to Kasha and Luis and to Don Reza.

Then the bandit fortress came fully into view.

Tall cliffs of grey-white stone reached up behind the tower, which looked as if it was hewn out of the mountain itself. The crenulations of the battlements mirrored the teeth of the limestone crags above, thrusting sharply into the grey sky. It looked old, as if it had been there almost as long as the rock.

On each side the cliffs curved, forming protective arms around the fortress. Stone battlements continued out from the rock face. The old outer defences of the fortress were patched and low in places, yet they still formed a formidable obstacle.

Even from so far away, Nathan could see figures on them, guards keeping watch.

About thirty feet in front of the battlements a stockade, like the one he'd seen at the previous bandit camp, stretched around to complete a wider circle. Here log and stone cabins clustered. Black smoke floated from some of the chimney holes.

Oh, for the hot room at the baths and a roaring fire. Nathan's skin tingled.

No, there'd be no baths here.

Still, he felt the mood of his companions lighten as they heeled their horses into a trot. Soon they were through the gates to be met by stablemen.

'Get your pack and follow me,' said Jorge as he and Nathan dismounted.

Nathan followed him into a long hut beneath the encircling cliffs. It was a kind of bunkhouse, with a vaguely familiar feel. What did it remind him of? The new barracks near Plaza Mercado back in Jerez, but built of wood not brick.

A group of men lounged around by the door. Their high boots and leather cuirasses marked them out as part of the mounted group which had recently joined the *bandeleros*. Inside a few bandits sat around playing cards. It seemed that the two groups did not mix.

Jorge acknowledged grunted greetings as he walked between the rows of bunks to the one end of the long room.

'Leave your things here,' he said, pointing to a lower bunk. He lowered his voice. 'Now let's go where we can talk.'

One or two of the men watched them, eyes narrowed, as they left. This was no place to relax.

He followed Jorge up a goat's path. When it became too narrow for any but goats, they sat, backs against the rock, looking out across the camp. Here they would not be overheard or surprised.

Nathan surveyed the stronghold. It had a permanence about it which contrasted with the rough and ready nature of the other camp.

There were men out in the mist and rain and the stockade and battlement walls were well-guarded, with archers on both. The working buildings, forge, stables, cook-house, were all outside the wall, but inside the stockade. There were three bunkhouses like the one they had just left, which meant there was room for several hundred men. Why so many?

'I think Don Reza is in there,' Jorge said, indicating the tower. 'He's valuable to them. They'll want to keep him and the tower is very secure.'

Nathan's heat sank. It would be difficult to get into and even harder to smuggle the surgeon out.

'The gateway to the inner compound is guarded. I doubt you'll be able to spirit Don Reza away,' Jorge said, echoing his thought. 'Your best chance might be to barricade yourself inside the tower

179

when the attack comes. You'll have to think of some excuse to get in.'

'You're talking as if you won't be here.'

Jorge took a deep breath, his face grim. 'Nathan, there are even more men here than when I left, as well as those riders from the other camp. Their commander is Don Raul Ramirez, a warlord, it is said, who has more men to come. Allied with El Zagal they will have a small army. This will be more than just a bandit gang.'

'Then you have to warn the expedition.'

'Yes,' Jorge's voice was resigned. 'I've come to the same conclusion, but...'

'Don't worry about me. You got me here, from now on I'll manage on my own - find Kasha and Luis.'

'Take care Nathan, this is a dangerous place,' Jorge shifted his position. 'I'm going to try and leave right away. If I can get into a scouting party I should be able to slip away from the others in this mist.'

'Yes, I understand.'

Jorge nodded. 'Try to get into the tower. It'll be the safest place once the fighting starts.'

'I'll try. And I'll collect the others.'

Jorge held out his hand and Nathan took it in his own. The man's grip was firm.

'Take care of yourself,' Jorge said, pushing himself to his feet. 'I'll return if I can, but if I can't, look for me when the fighting starts.'

Nathan watched Jorge go down into the camp. Despite his earlier longing for warmth and a bath he stayed on the goat path, his back to the rock. There was a lot happening and he wanted to think, to absorb it all.

Time passed.

He saw Jorge depart, leaving the camp with three other scouts. He watched the gate in the wall, it was manned at all times. He noted the changing of the guard.

Now it was up to him. He had to get inside the tower and speak with Don Reza, but first he had to find Kasha and Luis. He scanned the cabins and other buildings in the outer bailey.

There. That looked like the forge. He'd start looking there.

Within minutes he was striding across the outer compound, trying to look purposeful.

'Nathan!'

That was a familiar voice.

It was Luis, advancing on him, a wide smile on his face.

'You're finally here,' he said, giving Nathan a huge clap on the back. His moved closer and lowered his voice. 'We were worried, Kasha and me, wondering what had happened to you.'

'I was worried too. About what happened to you?'

It was good to see him again.

'At the other camp - we heard El Zagal call for volunteers, but we were held at sword point, there was nothing we could do,' he muttered, checking to see if they could be overheard. 'Then everything moved very quickly and we were brought here. Now we work the smithy but aren't allowed out of the outer compound and we're closely watched. But what happened to you?'

As they walked towards the forge Nathan answered Luis' questions, about the ambush and how the expedition from Jerez had fared.

'And your friend – what's his name? Atta?'

Nathan was silent for a moment.

'I don't know,' he said. 'His horse was riderless.'

Luis glanced at him, a sympathetic grimace on his face.

'Nothing's certain, he may not be hurt, or.....' he looked down at his feet.

They approached a three-sided building lit by the glow from a small, roaring fire. Sparks flew as a man hammered metal on an anvil, his back to Nathan. Short and stocky, with wide, strong shoulders and arms, he was sweat-shiny and wore a heavy leather apron and gauntlets. Beyond him Nathan glimpsed Kasha working the bellows and, at the same moment, Kasha caught sight of him.

'Nathan!'

The smith turned to follow Kasha' gaze. He had a short brown beard and thinning hair, plastered to his skull.

Then Nathan was engulfed in Kasha's hug.

'Eh? Who's this?' The smith asked, putting down his hammer. He took off his gauntlets and wiped his hand across his brow.

'The young smith we told you about.' Kasha said.

'The one who worked on the sword?' The smith gave Nathan a fierce look.

'Er, yes, but... I'm not a bladesmith.'

'I could tell.' The man seemed to make a decision. He moved forward, hand out-stretched. 'Fabio Gomer.'

182

'Nathan Calamiel.' He shook the man's hand. Its palm was calloused and hard.

'Could we have a moment to talk?' Kasha asked.

Fabio began to wipe his hands on the cloth which lay besides the anvil. 'I'll be back in five minutes.' He stalked off across the compound.

Once the smith had left Nathan spoke quickly. In short order he told them about Jorge, the arrival of the cavalrymen and why Jorge had left.

'I don't know how we can get Don Reza out of here,' Nathan said. 'Jorge thinks the assault will come soon and, once it begins, the tower will be the safest place. That's where he will look for us.' He paused. 'He's managed to get into a scouting party,' he explained. 'The bandits seem to trust him.'

'Do you?' Kasha asked.

'Yes,' he said. And he did. Jorge had turned into a trusted ally. 'Anyway, I have to get into the inner compound and the tower.'

Luis and Kasha exchanged glances.

'There may be a way,' Luis said.

'Fabio's daughter, Anna – Johanna - assists the surgeon,' Kasha explained.

'He brought his daughter here?'

'I don't think he had much choice,' Kasha replied. 'They like to have a hold over the people who work for them. Anna's safety depends on her father's co-operation.'

Their conversation was curtailed as the smith returned with a girl at his elbow.

Barely as tall as Nathan, she had glossy dark brown hair which fell, curling, to her shoulders. Her nose turned upwards at its end, above a wide mouth. Wearing male garb, she stood with feet slightly apart and her arms folded, a watchful look in her large, dark eyes.

He felt her glance flit over him. Her gaze was cool, appraising and intelligent.

Why did it make him feel uncomfortable?

'My daughter, Johanna,' Fabio said.

'Anna,' the girl added, offering her hand. 'Everyone calls me Anna.'

'That was my mother's name,' Nathan said as he took her hand. He was surprised at its softness. He shook it, awkwardly.

'Was?'

'She died.'

'Mine too.'

'I'm sorry.'

'Show him around, Anna,' Fabio said, reaching for his gauntlets. 'He'll have work soon enough.' With a nod Kasha returned to the bellows.

'I'll take over soon,' Luis said. 'I'll collect more weapons for sharpening first.' He looked at Nathan, sliding his glance to the girl and back. 'Leave you to it.'

'Come on,' Anna said and strode off, arms swinging, her chin tilted upwards. She was neat, her movements were precise and she looked very pretty indeed as she led him out of the forge, into the centre of the outer compound.

She pointed out the bakery and the stables that he had spotted earlier, as well as a small lime kiln for leatherworking.

'This isn't so much a camp, more like a town,' Anna said, her mouth twisting into a scowl. 'The baker is new, he was taken from Ronda. Father and I have been here from the start, they brought us here when they first began to fortify this place.'

'When was that?'

'About a year ago.' They were walking towards the gatehouse. 'The place has grown since then. Runaway slaves, criminals, those displaced by war, they all come. Then there's this new man - he's been closeted away with El Zagal since he arrived. Some survive, some don't. You have to be hard to live here, a town whose business is plunder and robbery. It's true,' she said and shrugged. 'But then I suppose you'd know.'

What? She must think he was a bandit, a thief and a robber. After all, why should she think otherwise?

It wasn't like that, he wanted to tell her. He wasn't like that at all.

'El Zagal's planning something,' she continued. 'We're well supplied. We even have a doctor here.'

'A doctor? I used to work in a hospital,' Nathan said. 'Maybe I could be of some use? It's easier than working the forge. Where is the sick-house?'

'You won't get off so lightly. They're always wanting more weapons. It'll be better for you if you work hard, show them you're useful,' Anna said. 'The doctor is kept in the tower, where I was headed, but they won't let you through the gatehouse.'

They walked over to the massive iron-bound gates.

'Father made them,' Johanna said.

185

The gates were closed, but there was a narrow archway to one side of them, a postern. It had two guards.

Anna gave Nathan a sidelong look.

'Have you really worked in a hospital?' Anna asked, her lips pinched.

'Yes,' Nathan answered. 'I have. When Jerez was besieged.' He sensed her relax at his side. 'Though I wouldn't say that I had any skill. I just did as I was told.'

'Like me,' she said. 'If they let you in Don Reza will tell you what to do. He was from Jerez too.'

As she said Don Reza's name, she kept her eyes on his face, trying to read his expression. Had she guessed something? Maybe he wasn't very good at lying?

Perhaps he should tell her that he knew Don Reza? Instinctively he wanted to.

Their eyes met. He couldn't pull his gaze away.

Take care, he told himself. He wanted to trust this girl, but in El Endrinal, aside from Kasha and Luis, he couldn't trust anybody.

21.

Eagle's Crag

For the first time in months Atta felt he was getting close to his father.

The horses picked their way along the trail, around thorn bushes and through the pine trees. They rode with two *campesinos*, friends of Antonio and Carmen, who had collected him and Miguel at the cabin that morning, after Antonio has gone to find the expedition.

His father was almost within reach. Maybe today they might find him.

To their right a massive wall of grey rock reached up vertically into the cloud. To their left the ground sloped first down then upwards, a carpet of green grass, studded with pine trees, until it too disappeared.

All sound was muffled, the keening calls of a bird of prey echoed dully from the rocks, but Atta could see none.

Pepe the *campesino* led the way. He had eyes like pieces of jet in a weathered, lined face. Mounted on a stocky pony, he carried a large bundle of skins and rope tied at the back of his saddle. Atta followed close behind him, then Miguel, with Nico, the other *campesino*, bringing up the rear.

'What sort of place do we seek?' Pepe had asked when they started out.

'We're not sure,' Miguel answered. 'Somewhere they could survive the winter and defend against attack.'

'And hold at least fifty men,' Atta added.

'There are caves in the sierras that could hide a hundred or more,' said Nico. He was younger than his companion, bigger too, with a round, bearded face. Like Pepe he wore sheepskin and carried a similar bundle.

'Yes, Antonio told us about them. But I don't think they'll be hiding in caves,' Atta said. 'They have horses and livestock'

'The livestock could have been slaughtered and salted,' Pepe said. 'They can steal more come Spring.'

'But not the horses.' Atta had spoken with Miguel about this on the trail. 'They're bandits, they live by raiding and ambushing. They won't want to give up their horses.'

'Let's say you're right. We'll rule out the caves. But there's still a lot of ground to cover,' Pepe continued. 'Plenty of hiding places in El Endrinal.'

Now they had been riding for several hours and conversation had ceased. Pepe drew rein and the others came up alongside him.

Miguel tilted back his head to view the sheer cliff face. 'I wouldn't fancy climbing that without a rope,' he said.

'No.'

Atta felt a looming sense of foreboding. Just the thought of climbing set his pulse racing and made his palms sweaty.

'We're going to leave the trail now,' Pepe said. 'Enter the Sierra del Endrinal. It's going to get harder from now on.'

So saying, he steered his horse onto a rough mountain trackway leading up the green slope.

Atta exchanged a glance with Miguel and prodded his horse to follow Pepe's.

The grass ended and trees grew fewer. Atta concentrated hard on not losing his seat as they crossed a field of scree, the horses slithering and sliding, battling to keep their balance. Once across Pepe dismounted and the others did the same.

'From here we lead the horses,' said the *campesino*. 'The path is narrow and it's safer on foot.'

Atta was grateful for the gathering white-grey of the cloud, it masked the drop which he knew was there, falling away from the path. They were in a world of wet mist and no sound, moving onwards at Pepe's behest.

'How will we find anything in this mist?' Miguel asked.

There was no reply.

After a time they began to descend, back below the cloud, into a valley. So far they had seen nothing. Was this all a fool's errand?

Then Pepe reined in his horse sharply and raised his hand to signal them to stop. He had heard or seen something. The shepherd turned and put his finger to his lips. Seconds later he heeled his horse up the slope at the side of the path, waving to the others to follow.

What was going on?

Atta urged his horse upwards towards a small copse, where Pepe and Nico had dismounted, their horses tethered further back.

189

'*Bandeleros*,' Nico said in a low voice. 'Take the horses downwind, away from the trail.'

Atta did so. He dropped to his knees to crawl back to Pepe and Nico, who were hiding amidst the bushes, the scrub screening them from the valley. Miguel had done likewise.

Along the trail a group of four riders was approaching in single file. Dressed for the mountains, the men wore sheepskins, cloaks and hats, they were armed with bows and swords.

So these were the *bandeleros*.

At his side, Atta felt Miguel reach for the pommel of his sword.

But there was something about the fourth rider in line which drew his eye. The sloping shoulders beneath his cloak and the way he rolled with the horse's gait was familiar. He'd seen that man before, Atta was certain. The riders drew nearer.

It was Jorge.

Jorge was riding as one of the *bandeleros*.

'Ouch!' Miguel hissed.

Atta realised that he had gripped Miguel's arm hard.

Pepe glared at them both.

The horsemen trotted past, oblivious to their presence.

As they disappeared into the mist Atta exhaled. He realised he had been holding his breath.

'What was that about?' Miguel asked. They were all looking at him now.

'One of those men works for my uncle,' Atta explained, his mind racing. 'I've seen him before. I think he's a spy in the *bandeleros*' camp.'

190

So, all along, there had been an agent on the inside. Uncle Taf had arranged it. Yet, when he had pleaded with his uncle to let him go, or to send someone else into the bandit camp, Taf had not trusted him enough to tell him about Jorge.

He'd been kept in the dark. Like a child. It was mortifying.

'Can you follow their back trail?' Atta realised that Miguel was speaking. 'It'll lead us to where they came from.'

'Yes, I think so,' Pepe answered as he stood, limbs cracking, and they all proceeded back to the trail.

Their progress now was slower, with Pepe on foot. Every so often he crouched or knelt to examine the ground.

Atta strained to see ahead through the mist. There was something beyond the next ridge. It was a tower.

Surely this was the bandit fortress. His father was close by.

'How can we get nearer without being seen?' Atta asked.

'There'll be look-outs...,' Pepe muttered.

'What about up by Eagle's Crag?' Nico said.

'It could be done.' Pepe seemed unwilling to say more.

'Someone should tell Antonio and the soldiers where we are,' Miguel said.

'You go,' Pepe said to Nico. 'I'll take them up to the Crag. We'll take a look then head back.'

Nico re-mounted and, with a wave, he set off back along the way they had come.

'Follow me,' Pepe said, as he too re-mounted. 'If they have look-outs, we need to get above them.'

As they set out the shepherd began to unwind the bundle attached to his saddle. He slung a thick rope over his shoulder and

191

wound it loosely across his chest, diagonally, so that eventually he carried a multi-stranded hoop of rope over one shoulder.

Atta's sense of foreboding returned.

Pepe turned off along a narrow path, scarcely a path at all, sending a pair of mountain deer springing away across the rocks in surprise. The little trail climbed sharply up the mountainside and soon they were in the cloud again.

Were they above the height of the tower yet?

Pepe stopped when they reached in a small depression in the mountain side, in front of a cliff face. Shrubs and trees grew from the cliff's crevices as it continued round the mountain.

'Leave the horses here,' he said, as he dismounted. He tethered his pony to a stunted tree and hobbled her. 'Now we have to climb.'

To climb. Again. Somehow he'd known this was coming.

Atta breathed deeply, hoping that the others wouldn't notice his reaction.

Miguel was asking Pepe about what was ahead.

'We'll work our way around the cliff until we're above the bandit's hideout, so keep quiet,' Pepe was saying. 'Be careful, the mountain drops away soon and the path narrows.'

Atta saw Miguel's jaw drop slightly. There wasn't much of a path to begin with.

'Only for about ten feet, then it widens onto Eagle's Crag. Face the rock and hold on with your hands. Feel your way with your feet and try not to look down.'

Atta's stomach clenched. He couldn't do it. But he had to, if they were to see the bandit fortress and find his father.

'Atta?' It was Miguel. 'Are you ready?'

192

Not trusting his voice, Atta nodded.

Pepe walked on and Miguel strode after him, his form becoming indistinct in the mist. It was getting thicker. That would help.

Atta hurried after. At the edge of the little dell he stepped onto the path along the cliff. For a few yards it was as before, but then it seemed to end with swirling whiteness beyond.

Immediately ahead, Miguel was holding on to the cliff as he stepped sideways and down. For a moment he met Atta's gaze, then he was gone. At the edge Atta saw that the path continued, but it was little more than a ledge, clinging to the mountain side.

Courage! Remember the ledge above the bandit encampment. Remember the roofs above the Juderia back in Jerez.

Heart thumping, Atta faced the mountain and did as Miguel had done. He inched down and along the ledge, his limbs shaking, all the time aware of the emptiness at his back. Loose fragments of rock fell into milky space.

He closed his eyes and rested his forehead onto the rock. It was cold and rough and bit into his skin.

But he had to keep going. Ten feet, Pepe said. It was just ten feet.

He slid his feet along the ledge, heels hanging over the void and grabbed at sharp rocky projections for handholds. Was it going to vanish altogether? His fingers and palms were wet and slippery with his own blood, where the sharp rock had pierced his skin, but he felt nothing.

Keep going. Miguel would be on the other side now, on Eagle's Crag.

Sweat dripped from his brow on to his cheeks, despite the cold, as he reached for more handholds and shuffled his feet along once more.

Then the ledge widened, ahead was a wide rocky terrace. Atta almost cried with relief. Miguel and Pepe were watching him with anxious looks on their faces.

He fell forwards into Miguel's waiting arms and closed his eyes.

'We've got you. You're all right.'

Then he leaned back against the cliff face, panting, his mouth open, gasping for air. He was safe, at least for now.

'You're scared of heights!' Miguel said. 'Why didn't you say?'

'Let him be,' Atta heard the shepherd's voice. 'He's got to go back the same way.'

Atta opened his eyes wide. He couldn't do that again.

They were standing on a flattened terrace. It was littered with branches, twigs and detritus and reached out into airy nothingness. There was no way beyond it.

'The cloud is clearing,' the shepherd said. 'If you want to see what you've come here to see, best to lie on your belly. But first, tie this around your waist.'

He handed the end of the rope he carried to Atta.

'You too,' he said, as he gave the other end to Miguel. 'Then loop it around that spur of rock there. Just in case.'

Atta secured the rope around his waist with a knot, as he slid his back down the rock face, ignoring the jags and juttings, and lay on the floor to look over the edge.

He saw dark patches in the thinning whiteness, pieces of ground far below. Gradually the camp was revealed.

194

The crag was about sixty feet above the bandit stronghold, as high as a tall minaret. Immediately below him was a walled enclosure and beyond that the ground sloped away to a stockade. He could see people moving, oblivious to being observed and hear shouted orders. Men were practising a battle manoeuvre, running and dropping to their knees, then running again. Horses grazed in a corral, cows and goats in pens.

Closer to him, a little way to his left, was the top of the tower, its battlements and flat roof about thirty feet below.

A rushing sound and a high-pitched screeching broke in upon his thoughts and he turned to look whence it came.

Hovering above them was the largest bird he had ever seen, its black eyes, golden rimmed, focussed on the terrace, its curved beak opened to emit the hideous cry. He ducked down, raising his arms to cover his head as it dived at him.

Sharp talons raked fiery pain across his back.

At the edge of his vision he saw Miguel waving his arms.

'Get back against the cliff face!' He heard Pepe's shout, but he couldn't move.

Then the bird swooped once again. He rolled over to avoid the vicious talons.

Onto the edge.

The edge!

He scrabbled at the rock surface, but his own momentum carried him forward.

Out into the void.

22.

The Tower

What was that noise?

Nathan looked up from his scrutiny of the postern gate.

A pair of great birds, eagles, were flying high up around the cliffs above the tower. They were shrieking and diving at a ledge.

Around him people began to watch them, the guards on the battlements pointing upwards.

'There are people up there,' a man just behind them said. 'That's what's got them excited. Look. You can see them through the mist. On the ledge!'

'That's their nest,' Anna said. 'I've watched them build it, flying up with sticks and branches. They're a mating pair.' She looked at Nathan.

'Archers!'

A shout came from the battlements above. It was El Zagal, accompanied by the richly dressed man who had been at the other camp, Raul Ramirez, Jorge had called him. Both stared up at the cliffs.

The two guards from the postern gate ran into the inner compound, arrows notched and bows at the ready.

'Come on,' Anna hissed and his hand was grabbed as she darted through the postern gate, pulling him behind her.

That was quick thinking.

Beyond the thick wall the inner compound rose up to the tower and the encircling cliffs, the ground criss-crossed by walkways and steps.

The eagles screeched, their calls echoing around the crags as they dived through the mist. The birds were killers. The archers were firing arrows, at the birds or at the figures he couldn't tell. All fell short. Nathan was transfixed by the aerial drama, like everyone else.

A shout came from the ledge and a figure plummeted down.

Nathan gasped.

The falling figure jolted to a halt, arms and legs flailing, a full fifteen feet below the ledge. He swung out from the rock face and then back towards it, grabbing a jutting rock. He wound his arms and legs around it, and what rope he could, clinging on for grim death.

It was Atta! He was sure it was. He would know him anywhere.

So he was alive! But what the hell was he doing up there?

There was someone else up on the ledge too. Had he and Jorge misjudged things? Was the raiding party already here? No. This was no assault on the fortress. So what was going on?

'Stop shooting!'

198

Atop the battlements the dark haired man, Ramirez, bellowed an order. He turned to El Zagal. 'Get them down, don't kill them. Let's find out what they're doing here.'

El Zagal hesitated then signalled to the archers. 'Do as he says.'

The men hesitated, looking unenthusiastic about climbing the sheer rock face.

'Get to it!' El Zagal shouted and they ran towards the foot of the cliff.

Still the eagles shrieked and dived. Then they rose, circling higher.

Someone was leaning out from the ledge over the edge of the precipice, waving and shouting to Atta.

'They're coming back!' Anna gripped his arm, staring upwards.

The eagles were stooping, falling out of the sky, talons outstretched, their hooked beaks open, shrieking.

The figure on the ledge raised his arms to defend himself but the birds were too big and had too much force. He plunged earthward.

Nathan ran forward, peering up to see what was happening.

The figure crashed past Atta, ricocheting from outcrop to spar, not falling free as Atta had done. Then the rope around his waist pulled him up short about forty feet above the ground. Slowly, his body rotated in mid-air, his limbs dangling like those of a broken doll.

Nathan caught his breath. It looked like Miguel Delgado, Juan's brother.

How came he here? And with Atta?

Nathan stood, rooted to the spot. He felt a shiver run down his spine.

Above Miguel, Atta clung to his rock.

The archers were close to Miguel now, reaching out to grasp the straining rope and pull his body towards them. One shouldered his limp form while the other sawed at the rope with his knife. The first man sagged as the rope broke and he took Miguel's weight. A third had already begun to climb, so as to help bring him down.

Higher up Atta had relinquished his hold and was climbing down.

At the foot of the cliff men waited with a crude stretcher and Miguel was placed upon it. White-faced and shaking Atta was led across the camp at his side.

Nathan shrank back. He dared not approach to comfort his friend, or even let Atta see him. In his distress Atta might give him away.

El Zagal and Ramirez strode past to meet the stretcher bearers.

'Ye gods,' Ramirez stared at the stretcher, an incredulous look on his face. 'You! Delivered into my power and helpless.' His grin widened and he laughed. 'An old enemy,' the man explained to El Zagal. 'One who thought he had escaped my vengeance, I'll wager.'

His expression was exultant as he bent down, bringing his face close to Miguel's.

'You thought you'd seen the last of Don Raul Ramirez, maybe that he was dead?' He said, his voice silky smooth. 'You owe me a death. Believe me, you'll be begging me to kill you before you die.' He straightened up. 'Do you have a dungeon, a cell? Somewhere where I can question them?'

'We do.' El Zagal nodded. 'Take them to the tower and get the surgeon,' he ordered.

200

'Yes. I don't want them dead. Not yet. And post a look-out on those cliffs,' Ramirez said as he turned on his heel.

Nathan sensed uneasiness in the bandits around him. Who was this man to give them orders? They all looked to El Zagal.

The bandit leader frowned, his scars twisting his face, but he gestured that they should do as Ramirez said and strode over to the tower.

'I wouldn't be in their shoes.' It was Johanna's voice. She stood at his side looking up at him, observing his face.

Nathan took a deep breath. He had to trust her.

'I have to get into the tower,' he said.

Johanna nodded. 'You know these people, don't you? They mean something to you.'

'Yes,' Nathan answered. His eyes met hers. 'They are my friends and.... I think they may have come looking for me and Don Reza. Please Johanna, there's no time. I promise I'll explain later, but it's important that I get into the tower now.'

She seemed to make a decision. 'Very well.'

To trust him, or at least to help him, he wasn't sure, but, either way, he was glad.

Up close he could see that the tower was hewn out of massive blocks of dark grey stone, protruding from the bare rock of the mountain-side, with deep stone steps going around its sides. To the left these reached up to a solid-looking metal door, about four feet from the ground, to the right they descended.

The prisoners had been taken down the steps.

'There's usually a guard there, but he must have gone down with them,' Johanna said. 'Quick, before he comes back.'

201

She started up the steps, reaching behind her for Nathan's hand. Together they climbed to the metal door. Johanna rapped on it hard.

It opened a crack.

'It's me,' she hissed. 'Anna.'

The door opened and Nathan was pulled after her, her body warm next to his as she stepped inside.

'Who's this?' A large youth demanded, pointing at Nathan as he closed the door and turned to Johanna. He stood very close, looking down at her with an angry, disappointed look on his face.

Instinctively, Nathan disliked him.

'He's here to help the surgeon,' she said, smiling as she looked up at the young man. 'And, Carlo, there's no guard on the steps, you'd better go down.'

'Why, my post is here.'

'But El Zagal is bound to notice,' Johanna said. 'He won't be pleased.'

Carlo grunted, non-commital, then he relented.

'I'll get my sword.' The muscles on his arms bulged as Carlo strapped on a sword belt, which had been lying on a chair beside him, but he didn't stop looking at Nathan. Fair-headed, with light, almost colourless eyes, he was at least a head taller than him and broader too. 'Stay here. You,' he glared at Nathan. 'Remember I'm just outside.'

With a malevolent backwards glance at Nathan, Carlo let himself out of the door, slamming it closed and locking it behind him.

Nathan exhaled. He smiled at Johanna. She had got him in.

'Thank you,' he said. 'For trusting me.'

'I'll probably regret it,' she said, looking into his eyes.

202

Nathan looked around the chamber. The room had a number of narrow windows spaced at regular intervals in the curving walls. A hearth and mantelpiece was on the left, set into the wall, with a table and chairs to the right. Old shields hung upon the stone walls, their designs faded. Cupboards stood against a flat partition wall running across the back of the room. It had one doorway.

The door opened and Don Reza came towards him.

'Nathan! I feared the worst,' he said and gripped Nathan by the shoulders.

'I'm alright.' Nathan sensed Johanna watching closely.

'What's happening?' Don Reza asked. 'I swear I saw Atta from the window. Is he here too?'

Nathan hesitated. What else dare he say, in front of Johanna? She had helped him, trusted him, but he couldn't talk about the raiding party and the troops.

'You're right, he is here,' Nathan said. 'He's a prisoner, in the cellar.'

They were interrupted by a loud cry of pain. There was shouting from the cellar below, it was Atta's voice, raised in protest. A rapid exchange of words ended with the sound of a blow.

Don Reza's face lost all colour. Johanna reached out her hand towards the surgeon. She shot a puzzled look in Nathan's direction.

He couldn't begin to explain everything, but....

'One of the newcomers is Don Reza's son, Atta,' he said.

The cry sounded again.

Nathan shuddered. He tried not to think of what might be taking place.

203

'There were two people on the crag above the tower.' Johanna was explaining. 'One was already half way down, but the other fell. The chief's new friend seemed to recognise one of them.'

'That was Miguel,' Nathan added. 'Miguel Delgado.'

'Delgado. What's he doing here?'

'I don't know,' Nathan replied. He stopped and waited for any further sound from below, but there was none.

The key sounded in the lock of the door.

'Quick, Anna, take Nathan inside,' the surgeon said. 'In case it's El Zagal.'

'Come on.' She grabbed his hand and hurried him through the inner door.

Beyond was a small storeroom, with a pallet bed close to the straight wall. The leather pouch lying on the bed belonged to Don Reza, Nathan guessed.

'Stay here until I come to get you,' she said and closed the door behind her.

The sound of voices came from the outer room, but Nathan couldn't hear what was being said. Then the heavy tower door slammed. Was that Don Reza leaving?

Low voices and laughter, were Johanna and Carlo alone together? Nathan bristled.

But there were also noises coming from below. He lay down and tried to listen. First a harsh, discordant voice, then Don Reza's even tones, but strained. The cellar door clanged shut.

He heard Atta's voice. Then the voices grew softer and Nathan sat up.

So Atta was finally re-united with his father. But now what was to be done? They couldn't just wait for the attack to come - that might be too late for Miguel and Atta.

He began looking at the room around him. The rear wall was the white rock of the mountains and there was only one thin side window, looking out onto the mountain and the inner bailey below. Rough hewn shelves filled with boxes lined all the walls save where the bed lay.

The cellar door clanged shut again. Was Don Reza returning?

Nathan listened for the tower door. Yes, there it was. He heard Don Reza's voice soon after. Seconds later the door opened and Johanna's face appeared around it.

'Carlo's gone,' she said. 'You can come out now.'

'Carlo.' Nathan got to his feet. 'Sweet on you is he?'

Johanna flushed pink. It made her look even prettier. Before she could leave he blocked her path, standing close.

'I do trust you, it's just....' he whispered.

'What?' She hissed.

He realised that he would have to explain. Begin at the beginning.

'Atta and I have been friends for a long time,' he said in a low voice. 'From Jerez. When the town fell Atta and Don Reza fled.'

'Yes, that much I had learned from Don Reza,' Johanna said. 'But how do you come to be here with the *bandeleros*?'

'It's a long story,' Nathan said. Her hair smelled of rosemary. 'I'll tell it to you sometime. I came to try and rescue Don Reza.'

'On your own, just like that. Into a bandit fortress?' Her eyebrows arched and she sashayed around him into the other room.

She might at least have thought he was brave.

On re-entering the outer room one glance at Don Reza brought him back to reality. The surgeon was staring at the wood of the table top, a look of blind despair on his face.

'How... how are they?' Nathan asked. 'Is Atta all right?'

'Yes, bruised and shocked, but Atta is well enough.'

'And Miguel? Is he badly hurt?' Nathan asked.

'A broken rib or two that's certain,' Don Reza's voice grew grave. 'There may be other injuries I cannot tell yet.'

'Have they told about the....?'

Don Reza shook his head. 'El Zagal knows there are soldiers in the mountains. Miguel passed out before he was forced to say more. The other man, whoever he is, will be back, with more inventive ways to make them talk. He hasn't questioned Atta yet – he's too busy taking pleasure in Miguel's pain – but he will.'

'So we have to get them out,' Nathan said.

'Yes, but Miguel isn't fit to go anywhere,' Don Reza replied. 'And there's nowhere to go. Nowhere any of us can go.'

'The floor in the back room is above the cellar. We could prise up some boards and at least give them some light,' Nathan said. 'It would be a start.'

He scanned the room for anything they could use to lift the floor. Johanna was already rummaging through cupboards.

'Here,' she said and passed Nathan a metal hammer. 'And here.'

She handed him an iron bar.

'You came to help your friend,' she said, her eyes shining. 'Let's go and do it.'

206

23.

Cavalry

Muddy ground squelched beneath her boots. Her cloak caught beads of wet mist and the water in the brim of her hat ran off on to her back every time she turned her head. Although it wasn't raining any more, the air itself seemed soaked. She had never been so wet and cold, even when at sea.

Around her cavalrymen were feeding their horses and eating the cold rations they carried.

She and Ben had ridden hard. Their horses were exhausted, but they had finally caught up with the expedition. She rubbed her hands to stop them trembling, the strain of clinging on to the pommel of her saddle for much of the ride had left them weak. The chafing on her thighs hurt with every step as they were led to Lieutenant Riccardo's tent.

Two cavalry men stood guard outside, but they raised the tent flap and indicated that she and Ben should enter.

Inside, the Lieutenant sat on a canvas chair at a small table upon which a large map lay, unrolled. By his side sat a tall, dark man wearing the uniform of a Granadan guard. Both looked forbidding, official.

Rebecca stood half a pace behind Ben, who spoke.

'My name is Benjamin Isaacs and this is Rebecca Calamiel. We come from Jerez with news about your mission,' he said.

'What news?'

Ben hesitated.

'My cousin, Nathan Calamiel and two companions have joined the bandit gang in an attempt to rescue Don Reza al Mansuri,' Rebecca said.

The Lieutenant raised an eyebrow.

'We understand that the Ambassador's nephew has followed Nathan,' Ben interjected. 'Senor Thomas told us that Atta thought he'd seen Nathan during the ambush. It turns out he was right.'

The Lieutenant ground his teeth.

'That young man was supposed to be our guide.' He glanced down at the map before him. 'Now we must make our way as best we can.'

'And Miguel Delgado?' Rebecca couldn't forbear to ask.

'Followed the Ambassador's nephew. Civilians.' The Lieutenant almost spat the word. 'I've had more than enough of them. This is a military expedition. And every man we lose makes our task harder.'

'How many are you now, Sir?' Ben asked.

The Lieutenant didn't answer immediately, but gave Ben an appraising look.

'You're the townsman who led the rescue party on to the ship *Hebe*?' He said.

'I – I am.... but...'

'We'll be glad to have you join us,' the Lieutenant said.

'Sir.' One of the guards entered the tent. 'There's someone else demanding to see you. Says he comes from the Ambassador's nephew.'

'The devil he does,' the Lieutenant looked exasperated. 'Bring him in.'

The guard hurried away, within moments returning with a man of the mountains. The *campesino* wore thick sheepskins and a wide-brimmed leather hat which he removed as he stood before the Lieutenant and the Granadan. There was a wary look on his weathered face.

'My name is Antonio Vellos, shepherd of these mountains,' he said. 'I come from Attalah Al-Mansuri, nephew of the Ambassador to find Lieutenant Riccardo and bring him up into the Sierras.'

The Lieutenant said nothing, but the man next to him, who had remained silent thus far, now spoke.

'What sign did he send to show that you spoke the truth?'

'He said that you would ask and that I was to ask for you by name, Major Rashid. And I have this.' The shepherd drew an item from inside his coat. It was a silver circlet, a ring, upon a chain.

Rebecca gasped.

'That's Atta's,' she said. 'My cousin has one similar.'

'Well?' The Lieutenant said to the *campesino*. 'You've found me.'

'Atta and his friend, Miguel, have gone in search of the bandit fortress,' the shepherd continued. 'Into the Sierra El Endrinal.'

So Miguel was alive and with Atta.

'Are they alone?' The Lieutenant asked.

'Two *campesinos*, friends of mine, are guiding them,' the man answered. 'If anyone can find the bandit stronghold, Pepe and Nico can.'

'Do you have any news of my cousin, Nathan Calamiel?' Rebecca asked.

The shepherd paused before he answered. 'No,' he said. 'I don't know that name. But Atta said that a friend of his was already in the mountains, hoping to rescue Atta's father. Might that be your cousin?'

'Yes. Yes. It must be.'

Thank heaven.

The Lieutenant questioned the shepherd. 'Can you lead us up into El Endrinal?'

'It's what I came here to do,' the man answered, then hesitated before continuing. 'But you should know....yours isn't the only group of soldiery hereabouts. There's said to be another group, from the east. I haven't seen them, but there have been rumours...'

'What!' The Lieutenant's eyes fixed on the shepherd's face. 'From the east - Granadans?' He turned to the guardsman on his left, eyes sharp with suspicion.

'I know of no such force from the Emir,' the man said. 'Truly. Though that doesn't mean there isn't one. It's been weeks since we left Malaga.'

Lieutenant Riccardo gave the shepherd a long stare. He seemed to consider things and then reach a decision.

'Very well,' he said. 'We'll be more careful, just in case. I want a scouting party up ahead. Will you go with it?' He raised his eyebrows at the shepherd.

'Yes, if you send out scouts I'll go with them.'

'Good. And, Major Rashid, one of your guards, just in case they run across any Granadans.'

The guardsman gave a curt nod.

I'll go too,' Ben said.

Rebecca swivelled her head in Ben's direction. Why was he volunteering? It seemed very unlike Ben to do something like that.

'Get yourselves some food,' the Lieutenant said. 'Then start out. We've a few more hours of daylight left, we can make some progress before making camp.'

'It'll be a moonless night and no starlight will get through that cloud,' the shepherd added. 'We'll have to bivouac before dark.'

'Ride as wide an arc as you can in the time that we have. If there are any enemies in the vicinity, I want to know about it before we make camp for the night.'

The shepherd left with a guard and the others rose to their feet. As the Lieutenant and the Major ducked beneath the open tent flap, Ben made to follow.

Rebecca put her hand on his arm. 'Ben, why...?'

'Why not?' He cut her off. 'And don't pretend that you care very much. You just concentrate on worrying about your precious Miguel Delgado.'

Ben turned on his heel and stalked off

Oh.

Rebecca shut her mouth with a click as she stood in the empty tent.

24.

Scouts

So it was true.

The gossip hadn't been so wide of the mark after all.

He'd never imagined that anything could be more painful than when she had refused him, but he'd been wrong. This was far worse.

That Rebecca loved someone else was torture.

'Hey!' The soldier in front of Ben gave a cry as Ben's horse almost walked into his. 'Be careful where you're going!'

'Sorry.'

He pulled at the reins to slow his horse.

There were four of them. Antonio the shepherd led the way, followed by a cavalryman, then the Granadan soldier, with Ben bringing up the rear. The shepherd led them higher into the mountains, through pine forests and across rocky scree, travelling in a broad arc from where the soldiers had stopped for their meal.

So far they had seen no-one. Not a hut or any other sign of habitation. Every so often the shepherd would dismount and collect stones to make a marker by the side of the path, so that their trail could be followed by the main party.

The valley they were plodding into looked just like the valley they had plodded out of. The roots of holm oak and pine spread across the stony trail which occasionally widened into a clearing.

A thin mist was forming, hanging in the air and distorting the landscape, making distances hard to judge.

Surely the shepherd wouldn't carry on for much longer. They could wait for the others to catch up and then make camp. Dusk would be falling soon.

Not that it mattered.

Nothing mattered any more.

He might as well just ride off the next cliff. That would show her.

He heard a zinging sound, then a thud to his left. The horse in front of him reared and there was a cry, as its rider dropped from the saddle.

They were under attack!

'Arrows!' Ben yelled.

He kicked his stirrups away and jumped to the ground, running, bent double, to the side of the fallen soldier. His horse's harness jangled as it cantered away into the trees.

The soldier was clutching at an arrow protruding from his upper arm. His face contorted, his breath coming in sharp spurts as he fought the pain. Ben knelt at the man's side.

What should he do? He looked along the trail for Antonio, the shepherd.

From both sides of the valley, helmeted soldiers emerged from the trees. Mounted cavalry rode up, arrows notched to their bows.

All wore the red and black insignia of Granada and carried scimitars at their belts.

Two foot soldiers ran to Antonio the shepherd and two to the King's cavalryman, grabbing the reins of their horses. The riders were made to dismount.

Ben raised his hands.

A tall, straight-backed cavalryman walked his horse through the others to the front. His mount was a high-stepping Arab, its harness finer than those of the other horses. His uniform, too, looked richer and his scimitar was still sheathed at his side, though his hand rested upon the pommel. He had a long face with a pointed beard and he wore a jewelled earring. This must be the leader.

'As-salamu salaykum!' The stricken soldier called out from beside Ben, levering himself up on his elbow.

'Wa-alaykumu s-salam,' the rider responded, peering at the soldier. 'Are you a true soldier of the Emir? You ride with the King's man?' He pointed at the cavalryman, upon whose coat the escutcheon of the King was clearly to be seen.

'We ride together against a common enemy,' the soldier answered, from his position on the ground. 'My master is Mustafa Al-Mansuri, Emir's Ambassador to the court of Alfonso of Castile.'

Ben noted that the leader moved his hand away from his sword hilt at these words and the others lowered their bows a little. So, were they friends? Or foe?

Encouraged, the soldier continued. 'We're searching the Sierras for bandeleros who have kidnapped my master's brother. Our main group...'

That was a mistake. The officer's demeanour changed in a flash. He leaned forward.

'How many and where?' When the soldier on the ground did not answer immediately he continued in a harsher voice. 'It is your duty to tell me, if you are a true Granadan and not a renegade.'

'I am a guard of his Excellency the Ambassador, I don't answer to you,' the soldier said, though his face was pale and blood was now flowing around the arrow shaft. Ben began to lower his hands to help the man, but he raised them again as a Granadan pointed his bow in his direction.

'You won't be answering to anyone when you're dead,' the officer replied. He raised his right hand and his archers tensed their bows, the scimitars rose.

'Nor will you!'

He knew that voice.

Ben turned to look. Further back up the trail Lieutenant Riccardo was walking his horse forwards towards them, with the Emiri Major alongside him. Mounted cavalrymen followed, some with swords drawn, others with arrows notched. They edged their way towards Ben.

He relaxed. Help was at hand. They would sort things out.

'The question is, who are you?' The Lieutenant asked the Granadan officer. 'And why are Granadan soldiers in the territory of his most Christian Majesty King Alfonso?'

'This is not Christian territory,' the ear-ringed officer answered, eyes flicking from side to side. At a signal from him his soldiers edged closer to Ben and the others. 'What master do you serve?' He snarled at the Emiri Major. 'Or are you a renegade like your trooper?'

The Major began to walk his horse forward.

'Stay back! He comes any closer and your scouts die,' he said, looking the Lieutenant in the face.

Your scouts...?

Us, he means us.

'Your men would be cut down before they moved, long before you could get to my scouts' the Lieutenant replied.

'Try it and see,' the Granadan replied, his voice dry and hard.

The Lieutenant didn't reply.

Surely they weren't going to fight here? The bandits were the enemy.

But neither man looked ready to back down.

He could hear his blood pounding. When the arrows flew, he would be sure to be caught in the crossfire, he would surely fall.

To die here.

No. He wasn't ready to leave the world after all, however he had felt an hour before.

The cavalry archers raised their bows.

25.

Allies

'Stop!'

The shout came from among the pine trees.

Ben turned to look. As did everyone else.

For a moment he could see nothing but tendrils of mist between the trees. Then a horse appeared, carrying a hooded figure. The rider held his horse's reins high in his left hand and raised his right aloft.

Ben glanced at the men around him. All had fixed their gaze on the newcomer, but he sensed their uncertainty amid the tension. One noise or a sudden movement would start a full scale fight.

The Granadan officer's horse neighed and shimmied. The Lieutenant looked on suspiciously.

Then the newcomer spoke.

'My name is Jorge Garalon, servant of his most high the Emir Mohamed of Granada and of his Ambassador, Don Musafa Al-Mansuri,' the man called out. 'Don't shoot. I bring news for soldiers of both the Emir and of the King.'

The man's horse continued out of the trees onto the trail, halting mid-way between the Granadan and the King's officers.

'I come direct from the *bandelero* fortress. Put up your weapons.'

There was a low murmuring, as men exchanged comments and looks with their comrades.

'The bandits are commanded by a man named El Zagal. He collects more men every day. Their fortress is well defended and they have a new ally, the brigand and pirate Raul Ramirez...'

A picture flashed into Ben's mind, of a vicious pirate captain cleaning his nails with a stiletto, in front of a growing pile of human bodies. This was the stuff of his nightmares. He shivered. Would he never be free of them?

'Ramirez!' The Lieutenant exclaimed, his horse shying. 'But Ramirez died in the sea battle.'

'No. He's alive and so are many of his followers,' the newcomer said. 'Put up your weapons, I say. The bandits and the pirates have joined forces. They threaten both your masters' lands. Already you will need all your men to overcome them.'

There was silence.

Ben looked first at the Granadan officer and then at the Lieutenant. Both looked uncertain, unwilling to back down.

'Raul Ramirez!' A female voice sounded.

It was Rebecca.

She paced her horse forward along the side of the path, past the Lieutenant, stopping when she had almost reached the newcomer. Everyone was staring at her in surprise.

What was she doing? Couldn't she see the danger?

220

Why was she drawing such attention to herself?

Her hat hung down her back and her damp hair was stuck to her skull. It made her seem vulnerable and childlike. Her face was white and her chin was jutting out in the way it did when she was determined to do something which was unpleasant.

He recognized that look.

'I can attest to who he is, I almost died at his hand,' she said. 'He kills and tortures without conscience. I saw him slit open his own man's stomach and leave him to bleed to death, his guts on the floor.' She paused. 'He fancies himself a lord of war and has soldiers, horses and ships. He is the avowed enemy of the King and will baulk at nothing. If he has joined forces with the bandits no-where is safe. You must act together, now, to stop them before they grow too strong.'

The Lieutenant looked at the Granadan officer.

The Granadan gave him a curt nod.

'Very well,' he said. 'Sheathe your weapons.'

As his men un-notched arrows or sheathed scimitars he dismounted.

Ben exhaled in relief, blowing out his cheeks.

'Archers, arrows down.' The Lieutenant commanded and he too dismounted.

The two men approached each other warily.

Rebecca was speaking to the newcomer. 'Can you tell me anything of my cousin? His name is Nathan Calamiel.'

'I can, lady,' the man replied. 'He is in the bandit fortress, with Don Reza.'

Nathan. He hadn't given Nathan much thought for a while, but Ben was pleased that no harm had come to him. But what was going to happen now?

'I suggest we camp for the night and agree our plan of action for tomorrow.' the Lieutenant said.

'There is a good place to camp up ahead,' Antonio the shepherd spoke. Ben had almost forgotten that he was there. 'Let's get out of this valley.'

'Our guide,' the Lieutenant explained to the Granadan.

The Granadan officer nodded and returned to his horse.

The soldier who had been wounded was helped back into the saddle, the arrow still in his arm. Someone brought Ben's horse back to him. Both groups started out along the trail, following the shepherd, the opposing soldiers eyeing each other with unease.

Ben heeled his horse's sides to urge her forward, to catch up with Rebecca, who was riding alongside the man who called himself Jorge. He was almost level when she spoke.

'And did you hear anything of a Miguel Delgado?'

Ben reined back his horse.

There was an empty feeling in his chest, a hole where his heart had been. He wanted to scream and shout and sob at the same time. But he couldn't do anything, especially when the Granadan officer trotted to his side.

'You are not a soldier,' he said. 'Why do you ride with them?'

'I came looking for my friend's cousin,' Ben replied, indicating Rebecca with his hand.

'Ah,' the man nodded and smiled. 'An unusual young woman.'

Say nothing. Look straight ahead.

At that moment, Rebecca turned in the saddle and smiled at him, her eyes shining. She hauled on her reins and fell back to join him.

Laughing, the Granada officer urged his horse forward to take her place beside the newcomer.

Ben concentrated hard on what was in front of him, the rear of the horses, the drooping tree branches, the dripping water. His mind seemed white and blank. After a while, he realised that Rebecca was no longer by his side and he began to hear snatches of the conversation taking place just ahead of him.

'You would do well to ally your company with these men.' The man, Jorge, spoke with the Granadan officer. 'They have the authority of both the King and the Emir's Ambassador.'

'Authority? There is no authority. This is war.'

'Not yet it isn't. And it won't come to that if the treaty is signed?'

'Treaty? I know nothing about a treaty. My lord prepares for war.'

'Preparing for a war is not the same as starting one.' Jorge sounded angry. 'Your men shot needlessly and you've wounded an Emiri guard.'

'An accident,' the Granadan replied. 'We didn't shoot to kill. The man couldn't control his horse.'

The sound of rushing water had been growing louder. Now it drowned out their voices as the valley opened out into a clearing, a stream tumbling down into it.

At the front of the column Antonio signalled that they should cross the stream and make camp for the night on a grassy terrace which lay beyond it, the mountain against their backs. The

223

Lieutenant rode up alongside Ben, looking grim-faced but purposeful.

'We plan the joint attack tonight. With Garalon's knowledge and the extra men we might just succeed,' he said. 'Your - the lady has done us a service. Could she do another? Has she skill in nursing?'

'Yes, I believe so...'

'Will you ask her to help the wounded man? There's an arrow to remove before he's made comfortable.'

'Er.., yes, yes of course.'

Rebecca would want to help, he was certain. He reined in his horse and waited for her on the bank of the stream as the Lieutenant rode on.

Beyond him the soldiers and guardsmen began to bivouac, fires were started, tents erected. But the men segregated themselves, they were in separate groups. They might have decided to co-operate for now, but both sides understood that they were enemies. The truce was a fragile one and Ben prayed that it would hold.

224

26.

Preparations

It was morning. Nathan's eyelids were pink with light.

So warm and comfortable.

He turned away from the daylight. Beneath the blanket another clothed form lay close to him. A breathing body like his own, but so unlike. Johanna murmured as he snuggled up to her back, left hand slipping around her waist. Her soft, wavy hair lay on the pillow.

Events of the previous day came back to him.

They had opened up the floor in the rear room, always on the look-out in case they were heard or interrupted. Medicines had been lowered into the cellar. He had been overjoyed to see Atta again, but the sight of Miguel Delgado and his injuries had turned his stomach.

Through it all, the shared danger, the exultation of success, Johanna had been at his side, brave and quick-thinking. He remembered the evening which followed, as they sat by the hearth while Don Reza was down below. She had told him how unhappy she was at El Endrinal, where cruelty triumphed over kindness. She was badgered and beset by men, only able to keep them at bay because of her father's usefulness to El Zagal.

Nathan had promised her that he was different. He would not impose.

He moved closer, folding his body around hers, feeling a pleasurable tingling in his blood. He could wait until they were out of this place. Until she felt the time was right.

There was a sharp rapping at the door.

Nathan froze.

A split second later he rolled on to his back, eyes snapping open.

Who could that be? Carlo? A guard? Someone for Don Reza? Perhaps Johanna's father, looking for his daughter?

Beside him, Johanna stirred.

The stone walls of the tower room were mouse grey with light, the window slits paler. Last night's fire has burned out in the hearth by which they lay, though there was still warmth in the hearthstones.

The knock came again.

Johanna got to her feet, re-arranging dishevelled clothing as she flitted, barefoot, to the window to look out over the steps.

'I can't see anyone,' she said.

Nathan flailed around for his shoes. Where was his sword?

There, leaning against the table. He stood at the side of the tower door and raised the blade, hilt held in both hands.

'Ready?' Johanna whispered.

He nodded.

She drew back the bolt and opened the door a crack.

'Yes?'

'I've come to find Nathan.'

It was Jorge's voice

226

'It's alright,' Nathan let his sword drop. 'Let him in. He's a friend.'

Johanna stepped back from the door and Jorge entered, quickly closing the door behind him. Johanna slid the bolt home.

'I'm glad to find you here,' he said, reaching to take Nathan's hand in his own. He glanced at the crumpled blankets and pillows beside the fire and his eyebrows rose.

Johanna shot him a sidelong glance, pursing her lips.

'Did you find...?' Nathan only just stopped himself from saying more.

Johanna knew nothing about the expeditionary force - he hadn't told her about it. Not because he didn't trust her. It simply hadn't arisen. Now he should tell her, he must trust her as she had trusted him. Whatever the future, he realised, his was with her.

But there were others' futures at stake too. He hesitated.

She was standing with her arms folded across her chest, watching him. The cool, detached look in her eyes made him feel uneasy. What was she thinking?

'Come,' he said to Jorge, leading him towards the back room. 'We've had visitors in your absence.'

Johanna didn't try to follow. With more than a twinge of guilt, Nathan closed the door behind them.

Lying on the pallet bed Don Reza jolted awake. He looked as if he hadn't slept much at all.

'Did you find the soldiers?' Nathan asked.

'I did. They will be here within hours. We need to prepare.' Jorge was eyeing the boxes and shelves in the small room. 'We'll need a barricade.'

'There is a complication,' Don Reza said, rising to his feet. 'My son and his friend have arrived.'

'What?'

'They're imprisoned in the cellar of the tower,' Nathan said, pointing to the newly re-laid floorboards. 'We lifted the planks to give them medicine and food.'

'You need to get them out of there,' Jorge said, immediately. 'Their lives won't be worth much when the fighting starts.'

'My son's friend was badly injured coming down the cliff,' Don Reza said. 'He shouldn't be moved.'

Jorge stared at Don Reza. 'What do you mean, coming down the cliff?'

'Atta and Miguel came down from Eagle's Crag,' Nathan explained. 'Above the...'

'I know where it is.' Jorge began to walk back and forward, tension in every stride. 'A party of soldiers are going to attack the camp from those very cliffs, to surprise the bandits once the main assault begins. But now....?'

Nathan and Don Reza exchanged looks.

'They're walking straight into a trap.' Jorge banged his fist against the stone of the wall. 'Damn it. With so few men we need the element of surprise.'

'Could we warn them?' Don Reza suggested.

'I can't leave again,' Jorge replied.

'We could find the look-outs and prevent them from raising the alarm' Nathan said. 'Kasha and Luis would help, as long as they can get into the inner compound.'

Again he felt guilty. He hadn't thought about his friends since coming to the tower.

'Yes, that's what we must do,' Jorge sighed heavily. 'But the lookouts will be picked men, ones El Zagal trusts and tough. It will be dangerous.'

Nathan reached for the door handle, as if to leave, but Jorge caught his arm.

'No,' he said. 'You should remain here to help Reza with his son. Have you told Kasha and Luis about me and who I am?'

Nathan nodded.

'Then I'll go.' Jorge crossed to the door. He hesitated before leaving and lowered his voice. 'About Anna - she's a fine woman, a good ally, but who knows that her father will do to keep her safe. He's probably wondering where she is right now.'

He hadn't thought about how her father might react to Johanna's absence. It had all happened too fast, been too overwhelming. Fabio must be worried. He hoped, when he discovered where she had been, that Kasha and Luis could persuade the smith of his trustworthiness.

The three of them returned to the larger tower room.

It was empty. There was no sign of Johanna.

Nathan was dumbstruck. Had she overheard their plans, listening at the door? No, the door was too thick, he knew that from yesterday. She had gone because he had disappointed her, because he had not repaid her trust with his own.

Nathan took a deep breath.

'I'm not going to leave Johanna out there when the fighting begins,' he said. 'I trust her and I think Fabio's a good man too.'

229

If need be he would go and get her himself.

Jorge opened his mouth to speak, but Nathan continued.

'She and her father know their way around the camp better than anyone,' he said. 'They've been here from the beginning. Fabio helped fortify this place. If there are ways to escape they'll know them.'

'And we could use some extra help,' Don Reza said. 'Especially with two wounded.'

Jorge looked from one to another.

'Very well,' he said. 'I'll find her and send her and her father here. But let's hope she, or her father, hasn't already betrayed us.'

With that he opened the door and was gone.

27.

On the Heights

The only sound was the whistling of the wind among the rocks.

There were no trees, just a few bushes. Everything was wrapped in a blanket of white mist, giving his journey a dream-like quality. Ben could see the corporal walking in front of him, his sword strapped diagonally across his back distorting his form. Beyond him, he could just make out their guide, a *campesino*, through the fog.

All were roped together, front and back, making a chain. Five more men followed Ben. There had been more, but another group had split off about an hour before, aiming for the cliffs at Eagle's Crag. His group was to climb down the nearer escarpment, unseen in the mist. At the signal of a horn blast, they were to rush down on the bandits from behind.

They had travelled along goat tracks since dawn, ascending the mountain behind the fortress. Ben was grateful for his heavy boots, as the track was stony. Beneath his thick cloak, he wore a sword and a small pick dangled from his belt.

It was cold and unpleasant and would be very dangerous.

Just the thing for him then.

He hadn't really had a choice, he had to get away from Rebecca before he made a fool of himself. It was too painful to see her face light up whenever Miguel Delgado's name was mentioned. Anyway, he had to help, he couldn't just do nothing and the alternative was to go with Rebecca, Antonio and the wounded guard, to sit in a *campesino* hut and await what befell.

His foot turned on a shard of rock and he stumbled. The rope between him and the soldier in front grew taut.

Concentrate on what you're doing.

The corporal had explained it all. They would climb down the cliffs as far as an outcrop, within a rope's length of the ground, where they would wait for the signal.

Three notes on a horn would launch the attack. The main party would assault the front walls of the fortress and they would surprise the bandits from behind. If Jorge Garalon had been successful, Don Reza, Nathan and his friends would know what was afoot and would be barricaded inside the tower.

Up ahead their guide was waiting for them all to join him. Ben drew level and stood by his side, stamping his feet in the cold. Nothing was said until all eight men were clustered together.

'We are almost there,' the *campesino* said.

'What then?' A soldier asked as he blew upon his hands.

'You'll be climbing down,' the guide replied. 'The first part is the most difficult. There's a rock chimney, a fissure in the rock, for about the first twenty feet. You'll have to brace yourselves between the sides of the chimney. It's the most dangerous part of the descent.'

Ben's companions exchanged grim looks. Some of them were mountain born, like the corporal. Others, like Ben, had no experience of manoeuvring their bodies safely among the rocky heights.

Yet no-one even considered turning back. They were all prepared to do whatever had to be done.

Ben was proud to be with them. They were fine and brave men.

'There's a terrace at the bottom,' the *campesino* continued. 'That's where you wait for the signal. You won't be visible to anyone in the encampment below, at least not until you start to rope down the rest of the way.'

'Right,' another soldier said, as he handed around a spirit flask.

Ben took a draught from it. The liquid was fiery and warmed him as it passed down his gullet.

The flask returned to its owner, was stoppered and thrust back beneath his cloak. His companions took out what tools they had brought with them and Ben untied the pickaxe from his belt and wrapped its cord around his wrist.

'Ready then?' The *campesino* asked. 'We don't have much time.'

There were nods and grunts of assent and he started off, leading the way. Soon they reached the top of the escarpment.

Ben joined the corporal, who was kneeling at the cliff edge, his sword on the ground next to him.

'The chimney's just below here,' the corporal patted the ground to their left. 'Though this ledge overhangs, so you can't see it until you're over the lip. It's only a few feet below, like a funnel but open on one side to the air. Have you climbed one of these before?'

233

Ben shook his head. 'I haven't climbed anywhere before.'

The man looked Ben over.

'Well, you're young and strong, you shouldn't find it too hard,' he said. 'Position yourself against one side, bracing your legs and feet against the opposite side. Then work your way down. You'll have to leave your sword here. I'll go over first – you and the others will have to lower me – here.' He pointed to the smoothest part of the rock lip. 'Watch what I do.'

'What about me – the last man?' A voice asked. The whole of their group was now standing ready.

'I'll let you down,' the *campesino* said. 'I'll let your swords down after you too?'

Ben began to remove his sword belt. The others did likewise, handing their weapons over.

'Ready?' The corporal asked Ben.

Ben nodded. He stood as far back from the edge as the rope around his waist would allow and, setting his feet slightly apart, gripped the rope which tied them together.

'Ready,' he replied.

The corporal sat on the lip of the rock then turned, lowering himself on his forearms, then his hands, until he disappeared below the edge. Ben braced his legs as the rope went taut, being pulled, slowly towards the edge.

Then the rope slackened. The corporal had found support.

'He's working his way into the chimney.' A soldier was leaning far out, watching the corporal descend. 'You need to go now.'

There wasn't much slack left in the rope.

Ben crouched near the edge then sat with his legs dangling. When he stretched out he could see movement below, but the mist made it difficult to see what was happening.

How had the corporal done it?

Ben swung himself around, his torso lying on the rock, then he inched backwards until his forearms were holding him in place. He couldn't hold that position for long, his muscles burning.

Ben glanced upward, briefly, to see the next soldier was taking the strain of the rope.

He had to go over now.

For a moment Ben swung free, the rope riding up his chest. He began to rotate.

Then his feet made contact with the rock below the overhanging lip and he reached out to grab it. He pulled himself into the chimney, wedging himself between the two sides, back pushed against the rock. The rope slackened.

Move down now, to let the next man come.

Ben ran his hands over the rock face, feeling for handholds and protrusions. The gritty rock pressed into his flesh as he took his weight on his hands for a moment and moved his back inches down the wall. Then he walked his feet down, so as to keep himself poised between the walls of the chimney. Slowly he inched his way down.

Brace your legs, the corporal had said. Keep the tension or fall.

He concentrated on doing so, though his hands became slippery with blood, cut by the sharp rock. Gloves or gauntlets would have helped, but it was too late now.

Inch by inch. Down he went.

235

The chimney was growing narrower, his knees bending. What must he do? Should he turn around and try to climb down the rock face?

'Keep going.' He heard a strained whisper from beneath him. It was the corporal. 'It widens out again. You're over half-way now.'

Ben slid himself down further, gradually moving his feet.

Yes, it was widening again.

But he didn't know how much longer he could keep this up. His arms and hands were shaking, weakening and pained, especially his left arm, where he'd been hurt before. His legs were numb with tension.

Then he felt hands on his body - it was the corporal reaching for him.

He'd done it.

Ben relaxed.

And tumbled downwards.

He was shoved up against the back of the chimney and, scrabbling, his feet found the floor. The corporal, who had broken his fall, swore quietly and laughed.

'Hey - are you all right down there?' A hushed cry came from above.

'Yes, I'm down,' Ben answered.

'Thanks,' he murmured to the corporal.

'You did well,' the man said, quietly. 'Let's hope we can get the rest down with as little mishap. Take a rest.' He indicated the wide terrace on which they now stood.

Untying the rope from around his waist Ben stumbled across to sit, his back to the cliff wall, while his comrades descended to the

236

ledge. The man who had come down after him dropped down at his side.

'I'm glad that's over,' he confided and gave a weak smile.

Ben smiled in return. 'Me too.'

'Here.' The corporal threw a coil of heavy rope to Ben, who caught it, clumsily, as he sat. 'Fix that securely to something. We need about fifteen feet of it.'

Ben stood. A sharp scrunching pain in his legs caused him to gasp. The tension of the descent had taken its toll on his body.

There was a spur of rock bending back towards the cliff face. That would do.

Ben wound the rope around the spur, securing the end in a knot and pulling at the rope to test it. Other soldiers were doing the same at different points along the wide ledge. After the last man was down, a bundle of weaponry descended on a long rope. The *campesino* was doing as he had promised.

Two soldiers caught the weapons, making sure they didn't crash to earth and loosed the rope. It snaked upwards, disappearing into the mist. Men passed weapons around, handling them with care.

Ben took his sword, slinging the belt around his neck.

Now all they had to do was wait.

He sat with his back to the cliff as fine rain began to fall.

28.

In the Cellar

Black darkness. Absolute.

The only light came from under the door, a sliver of greyness penetrating but a tiny way inside.

Atta shivered as he sat on the uneven floor. The bruised skin across his chest hurt when he pushed his hands beneath his armpits for warmth. The only sound in the cellar was Miguel's regular breathing as he slept a drugged sleep.

The shivering was not just because of the cold. It was a symptom, he knew, a reaction to all that had happened.

When he closed his eyes, eagles swooped. Harsh, discordant cries echoed as he rolled into the white nothingness, the fall to certain death.

He had to keep in control.

He needed a light, that would help. There was a candle stub and tinder box inside his pocket given to him by his father. His hands trembled as he reached for them.

Concentrate. Keep your hands steady. Just like in surgery.

With an effort of will he forced his hands to stop shuddering. He rested the candle on the floor and struck sparks to light its wick. It glowed a cindery orange, then the flame took and the light grew.

Cupping his lacerated palm around the flame to protect it, he stood, holding the candle high. The warm light reflected on the damp rock of the walls, part hidden behind wooden crates. Above were the planks of the floor, back in place now, so as to prevent discovery.

The prone form of Miguel lay at his feet, his bruised cheek resting on Atta's rolled up cloak, his mouth slightly open.

It was good that he slept, it meant he was free from pain.

How could someone be as full of evil and malice as the man Ramirez? That he hated Miguel was clear, but how could Miguel have attracted such enmity? It was all bound up with what happened on the *Teresa* somehow.

No sooner had they entered the cellar and the stretcher carrying Miguel been placed down on its floor than Ramirez had kicked out at Miguel's broken body. Vainly Atta tried to intervene, but the guard held him back.

Miguel tried to roll away from the vicious booted feet, but to no avail. Ramirez then crouched over his victim, his face inches away from Miguel's as he poured out his venom, threats of greater tortures, more punishment and questions, always questions.

Where are the King's soldiers? How many were there? When would they be here? How could he really think he had escaped his, Don Raul's, vengeance? He levered himself up by leaning on Miguel's chest and Miguel screamed in pain.

Atta had broken free then, but Ramirez dealt him a heavy back-handed blow.

He touched his forehead with his finger tips, then looked at them in the light from the candle. They were unmarked, the bleeding had stopped.

To deliberately cause such agony and take pleasure in it – it was beyond understanding. Miguel had lost consciousness. It was a mercy.

Then they had called for the surgeon.

Pretending not to know his father had been hard, but he had done it. Ramirez suspected nothing and he and his henchman had left them in the cellar together. Then he had been able to greet his father properly.

Yet now that euphoria had seeped away.

What would befall them all? Ramirez had not yet returned. But he would. Their questioning was not over.

Atta carried the candle over to the crates against the rear wall of the cellar. He sat with his back propped against one of them. It was uncomfortable, but it afforded some support. Above him the floor boards creaked, someone was walking over them.

At least there were friends close by. It was good to know that he wasn't alone. And he'd been right, Nathan was here. It was so good to see him again.

Maybe he could try to sleep. His chest ached, his ribs were bruised. He remembered the jolt and the harsh pain of the rope cutting into him. He felt so tired....he would just rest his eyes, for a moment only.

241

When he opened them all was blackness. Time had passed, the candle had burnt down.

A noise had awoken him. Were they coming back?

His insides grew cold.

No, the noise came from above.

He shielded his eyes as light flooded in and struggled to his feet.

'Atta?' Nathan's voice.

'Still here,' he answered.

'Take this.'

A wooden box was lowered down through the hole.

'Poppy juice, bandages and salve,' his father said, his anxious face looking over Nathan's shoulder. 'Do you want me to take a look at Miguel?'

'No. He's sleeping.'

'Not for long,' Nathan said. 'Stand back, I'm coming down with some things.'

Atta stepped away from the hole, as Nathan was lowered into the chamber, clutching a bundle of planks and tools. He was wearing a sword belt and a sword.

Another figure followed him. Was it...? Yes, it was a young woman, though she was wearing trousers and carrying a bow. She had a long hunting knife at her hip.

'This,' Nathan said, reaching to catch her around the waist, 'is Johanna.'

'Anna,' the girl said, as she reached the ground. 'Everyone calls me Anna. Bar the door, I'll look for the passageway.' She lit two tallow candles.

242

Nathan crossed to the door of the cellar and felt around the door and its frame.

'You're right,' he said, taking tools from the pouch at his waist. 'It opens inwards. The frame's solid, I can nail the boards over it.'

So, he was going to barricade them inside. But then how would they get out?

'Nathan...?'

'Is there anyone near to the tower?' Nathan looked up at the hole above and Atta saw his father move away. 'We have a plan.' Nathan's glance flicked beyond Atta. 'Have you found it?'

'Give me a chance.'

The girl was on her knees, crawling, pushing the crates out of her way. The floor was wooden there. She was knocking on its planks.

'There are supposed to be caves in the cliffs behind the tower,' Nathan said, as he stood poised with hammer raised against a plank of wood held across the door frame. 'The way into them is from the cellar.'

'Covered over years ago,' the girl said without looking up. 'So I've heard tell. Yes, here it is.' There was a hollow sound as she knocked against the boards.

Above him his father reappeared at the edge of the hole.

'All clear,' he said. 'Bar the door.'

Nathan swung the hammer, driving nails into the planks.

'That should do it,' Nathan stepped back, inviting Atta to admire his handiwork. Two stout planks were nailed across the doorway. Only a great deal of force would open the door now.

In the rear of the cellar the wooden boards had been raised.

Through it all, Miguel lay, oblivious to the noise and activity.

'Atta!'

It was his father's voice. He was leaning over the gap handing down a pouch. 'Take this. Be careful or it'll break. You'll need it to bring your patient round.'

Atta caught as it dropped.

'Use it now,' Nathan said, coming to join him beneath the hole. 'We're getting out through Johanna's caves and we can't carry him. Miguel must be awoken.'

'But...?' Atta looked up.

'Yes, do it now. I'll be following you,' his father said. 'Do you have the markers, Anna?'

'Yes.' The girl replied, patting a leather bag hanging at her waist. 'I'll leave a trail.'

'Good. We won't be far behind.'

'Father, I....'

'No. No discussion... it's the only way to get Miguel out of here. I wouldn't give much for his chances otherwise.'

Atta looked down at Miguel, then up at his father.

To come all this way, through everything, just to leave his father behind? He'd done that once before. Now, it seemed, he was to do it again.

'Go now, Atta,' his father repeated. 'Anna's father is here and Nathan's friends will join us as soon as they can. We'll barricade the doors, like the one below and climb down to follow you. The camp will be under attack then, the bandits will have other things to worry about.'

'No, father, I can't...'

A sound from outside echoed faintly in the tower and the cellar. All fell silent.

A single note, repeated. How loud it must be outside.

It was a horn.

Someone was blowing a horn with all their might.

29.

Battle

The note of the horn reverberated around the mountains, rebounding from rock to rock, echoing through the mist and rain.

The signal.

It was time.

Ben looked at the corporal.

'Yes,' the man said. He lifted one of the ropes tied to the mountain and wound it around his waist. 'Come on.'

He slowly walked backwards to the edge of the ledge, testing the rope's ability to hold his weight. Water sprayed and ran from his helmet.

'Twenty feet down to the foot of the cliff,' he said. 'The ground's rocky with boulders, good cover if we need it. Most of the bandits should be looking the other way, manning the wall, or the stockade. Come on lads.'

With that he stepped over the lip and began to let himself down the cliff face.

There was a second's hesitation, then, in a rush, everyone reached for the ropes.

Ben was ready. He wrapped his rope around his waist and over his right shoulder then stepped back towards the cliff edge. As he leaned back the rope tightened, flexed, then held his weight. He stepped out over the edge, out into the mist.

His scratched palms hurt as he slowly let out the rope and walked down the cliff face.

From the whiteness came disembodied shouts and the clash of weapons. The frontal assault on the fortress had begun.

A dark mass loomed to his left. Was that part of the cliff? Or the tower?

Where was the corporal? Was he on the ground yet? It was difficult to see very much of anything.

A low rumble of thunder rolled around the valley. The rain increased in intensity, bouncing from the rock face. The mist would soon disperse if this kept up.

Where was the ground? He must be almost there.

Keep going.

His arms and shoulders hurt, they wouldn't take the strain for much longer.

Then his feet hit rock and he toppled sideways.

'Steady lad,' it was the corporal. 'Get down, here, behind this rock.'

Ben uncoiled the rope and crept over to join him, crouched behind a boulder. Further along another man reached the ground and ran over.

'Right, when everyone's here we'll move off, head for the tower...'

There was a long despairing cry and Ben heard the familiar sound of arrows zinging through the air.

'Archers,' he said, as he buckled his sword-belt around his waist.

'Aye,' the first soldier said.

Two more men joined them, strapping on weapons as rain ran down their faces.

'The other group's been spotted,' one said. 'There must have been look-outs.'

'We must move quickly.' The corporal nodded towards the base of a round stone tower to the right, hewn out of an outcrop of the rock face. 'Over there.'

A bright flash of electric-white lit up their hiding place amid the rocks, followed by a deafening crash of thunder.

'Stay close together.'

Rain drummed on the ground and Ben could hardly hear him above the noise of the storm. The mist had almost gone and the water was coming down in silvery white sheets.

Ben followed the corporal through the boulder field. As the thunder rolled again, two armed figures appeared, seemingly from nowhere, or from the rocks themselves. One of them was huge.

Ben halted so abruptly that he slipped on the wet ground.

There was the ring of metal as swords were drawn and the corporal charged. But the giant swatted his sword aside with only the flat of his blade, sending the corporal tumbling.

'Stop!' He shouted. 'We're friends.'

'Nathan sent us!' The second figure shouted. 'Nathan Calamiel.'

What?

Peering through the rain, Ben studied the big man. Yes, he looked familiar. Where had seen him before?

On the deck of the galley *Hebe*.

'Stop!' Ben yelled, standing with his back to the giant man. 'I know them.'

The corporal was on his feet again, looking determined, but he hesitated.

'From the *Hebe*,' Ben said. 'They fought the pirates – in the sea-battle.'

The soldiers lowered their weapons.

'We have to get to the tower,' the corporal said. 'To meet our comrades from Eagle's Crag and then to attack.'

'Not all of your comrades made it.' The big man's companion said.

His face seemed familiar too.

'We heard,' the soldier's voice was grim.

'Come, we'll take you there,' the big man said. 'I'm Kasha and this is Luis. Quickly, the wall is holding. You need to attack, to draw off some of the archers.'

The thunder rumbled on, never ceasing, and lightning flashed across a black sky every few seconds, lighting their path through the boulders. Sounds of the battle grew louder, the cries and crashes more distinct, although always some distance away.

They skirted the cliff face, around the spur of the mountain. When the rain curtain shifted Ben saw an open space in front of them, then a high stone wall. Atop it archers were shooting arrows which vanished high into the rain.

Kasha was right, they needed to distract the archers to give the assault a chance of success.

'Where's Nathan?' Ben asked Luis.

'In the tower, with the others,' the smaller man answered. 'That's where Kash and I are going.'

He stopped and pressed himself against the rock, gesturing for Ben and the others to do likewise. Crouching, Kasha went onwards and disappeared from view.

'Be ready to run,' Luis said, over his shoulder.

A piercing whistle cut through the noise.

'Now,' Luis yelled and sprang forward. Ben followed. They were running across an open space, criss-crossed by wooden walkways towards a stone tower. More King's soldiers awaited them there.

'Come on,' the corporal shouted, raising his sword in the air. 'Bowmen, give us cover. The rest, follow me.' He started off at a trot towards the battlements.

Ben went to draw his sword, but he found his arms pinioned to his body.

'You'll be more useful where we're going,' Kasha said in his ear.

He was propelled up worn stone steps to a door. Luis hammered on it.

Within seconds the door slammed behind them. Ben was inside the tower.

'Isaacs,' a voice called. It was Jorge. 'Glad to see you safe and sound.'

'Jorge, I.....'

Ben caught sight of a tall, black robed figure beyond the pony-tailed horseman. It was Don Reza Al Mansuri, the Jerezano surgeon.

'Barricade!' Jorge looked over at Kasha.

Thunderclaps reverberated as rapid flashes of blue-white light lit the room. A stocky, red-faced man began pulling crates and items of furniture across the door. Kasha bent at the knees, wrapped his arms around an enormous chest and dragged it over. He grunted as he let it go.

Everyone seemed to know what they had to do – except him. But what could he do to help?

Ben turned to ask Jorge, but he was speaking with the surgeon.

'Is the bottom door impassable?'

'My son says no one can get in that way,' Don Reza replied. 'It's boarded up.'

So Atta was here too.

'Right. Into the back room,' Jorge said. 'It's time to go. Isaacs....' He gestured for Ben to follow.

Beyond the door Ben halted abruptly. There was a gaping hole in the floor. He had almost plunged downwards.

'Careful where you step,' Jorge said.

The red-faced man closed the door and heavy items were piled against it. By the far wall Don Reza was lighting lanterns.

Through the sounds of the storm, Ben could hear a thumping and banging. Someone was trying to enter the outside door of the tower. He looked out from the single slim window on to a scene lit by flashes of light. Below him stairs wound around the base of the tower and men were running down them.

'They're trying the cellar door,' Jorge said. 'We need to leave. Don Reza...'

The surgeon picked up his medicine satchel and sat on the edge of the broken floorboards. He passed a lighted lantern down and then followed it, Kasha taking his weight.

'Fabio,' Jorge ordered and the red-faced man stepped forward. Ben turned back to the window.

Outside the battle raged, as the corporal led his men against the battlement wall and the archers upon it found themselves attacked from behind. A black-bearded man, wearing a wide-brimmed hat and high boots was leading its defence, striding up and down the parapet lunging and slashing with a pair of glittering swords, one in each hand, the metal reflecting the lightning flashes. Ben's stomach clenched - this man was deadly.

With a shout the swordsman leapt from the battlement into the fray below. Untouched by weapon or hand, he forged a path through the soldiers, striking without mercy, towards the corporal, who was bending to help a fallen comrade.

'Look out!'

His shout was lost in the din. Without a second's hesitation the villain's sword swept through the corporal's neck and he stabbed the injured man with his other sword as the corporal fell.

Then the man glanced up to the window.

Instinctively Ben drew back. The man's gaze was full of malice. In the fracturing light he looked like the very devil.

Was this Raul Ramirez of whom Rebecca spoke?

He returned to the window, but the man had gone.

'Here, Isaacs, your turn.'

The room was almost empty, all but he and Jorge had gone down into the cellar. Ben dangled over the edge of the floorboards and hands from below gripped his legs and guided him down. Jorge leapt down after him.

There was a pounding on the cellar door. Lantern light showed planks stretching from one door jamb to the other. He could hear muffled voices and sounds from outside.

'Is there another way in?' Ben asked.

'Not into the tower,' Fabio answered. 'Into the caves...who knows. Come on, if we're to catch up with Anna and the others we ought to get going.'

He raised the lantern and Ben saw an opening in the floor next to the rocky wall. Dusty wooden steps disappeared downwards into blackness. Fabio started down them.

'Here' Kasha handed Ben a lighted lantern. 'Go.'

The pounding on the door began again and Ben didn't hesitate, however unwelcome the darkness seemed.

At the foot of the steps a rocky floor sloped away, down into the mountain. Beyond the pool of lantern light the blackness was total, save that, up ahead, he could see the flickering reflexion of another light on the rocky walls. Fabio's lantern, he was already further along the tunnel. Behind him he heard Jorge and Kasha descending.

The passageway was dry and sound was muffled, even his own footsteps and the drip, drip of water as it trickled off his clothes. Ben noticed flakes of red-painted wood on the uneven floor, forming a trail. Someone had gone ahead of them, Nathan perhaps?

There was light ahead and a new sound, growing louder.

254

The passage opened out into a cavern. Its roof was lost in darkness and through it roared a river in spate. On a shelf of rock above the roiling waters Fabio, Luis and Don Reza stood looking across the torrent.

'Look, there are markers on the far bank!' Don Reza pointed. He was leaning out over the surging water. 'They must have crossed before it flooded.'

But now there was flickering torchlight on the far side of the cavern. About a dozen men was descending to a ledge on the other side of the river. The hairs on Ben's skin rose. The black-clad swordsman was there, torch flames reflected on his black leather clothing. It was clear that the group had seen them but, for the moment, could not get across to them. For now they were safe.

'There are other entrances to the caves,' Fabio yelled. 'They must have known...'

On the opposite bank there seemed to be some discussion, then a man reached down and scooped up one of the wooden markers. He handed it to the black-clad man.

The swordsman took the piece of wood, then looked across the rushing water at them, smiling.

Don Reza shouted, moving forward and Kasha grabbed him, pulling him back from the brink.

They had found the trail. Ben caught his breath.

They would follow it and find Nathan, Atta and the others. Ramirez was going to catch them and there was nothing he, or any of them, could do to stop him.

255

30.

Retreat

'Fabio,' Jorge shouted over the noise of the torrent. 'Do you know a way across? Or another path through the caves?'

The smith, who was peering at the far bank, shook his head. There men were leaving, following the wooden markers, while more were entering the   cavern.

'Then we go back to the tower,' Jorge said.

'No, we can't...' Don Reza began. He looked close to collapse, at the end of his endurance.

'He's right, Sir,' Ben said, as gently as he could above the ceaseless noise. 'It's the best thing to do. At least there we might be able to help. There's nothing we can do here. Please...'

Don Reza acquiesced and Fabio too was persuaded to leave. All returned through the tunnel to the tower.

They found the cellar door barricade was still intact. Jorge climbed upon Kasha's shoulders to get up into the tower and secure a rope to bring everyone up. The barricade at the inner door was also unbreached.

Ben peered out of the single window. In sheeting rain El Zagal was rallying his men to the wall's defence. Archers fired arrows from the battlement embrasures, their bows angled downwards. So the assault was concentrated here now, the soldiers having crossed the outer ward. Of his companions who had climbed down the precipice he could see no sign, but many bodies lay in the churned mud of the inner compound.

Surely, there were fewer bandits on the ramparts than he'd seen before?

'Your comrades need our help,' said Jorge, standing by his side.

'There aren't as many defenders,' Ben said. 'I'm sure there were more before.'

'You might be right. I can't see any of Don Raul's men at all,' Jorge leaned out of the window slit. 'Maybe they followed him into the caves to escape. Perhaps El Zagal's new ally has abandoned him.' His smile was grim. 'It doesn't help us. Those battlements will hold all day.'

'We need to open the gates.' Another voice said.

Fabio had joined them at the window. He was hefting a large hammer. 'If you can cover us, Kasha and I can open the heavy bolts.'

Jorge nodded.

'Barricade's clear.' Luis called. He grasped the handle of the door. 'Everyone ready?'

Luis pulled the door open and leapt through. Ben followed.

The tower room beyond was empty. Broken furniture littered the muddied floor. The external metal door lay on its side.

'They got this far, but no further,' said Kasha.

258

'The barricades took too long to break down. They were probably called back to the fight.' Luis said.

'Here.' Jorge handed Kasha a heavy claw hammer, as he strapped on his own sword. 'The plan is... we all run to the gates. Then we'll defend the two of you while you work.'

'What about these?' Ben pulled down an old-fashioned wooden shield from the tower chamber walls. The first fell apart in his hands, but the second and third were more solid. 'They're better than nothing. Could we use them to shield Fabio and Kasha from the archers?'

'We can try,' Don Reza said, as he took the longest of the shields.

'Right,' Jorge said. 'Ben, Don Reza, hold the shields to protect Kasha and Fabio, Luis and I will do the sword work,'

'The gates open inwards,' Fabio said. 'There are ground bolts to pull up and the middle bolts slide to the right.'

'Straight to the gates, with as little noise as possible,' said Jorge. 'With luck none of the defenders will see us, they'll be focused on the soldiers outside. Everyone ready? On my mark.'

Ben braced himself to run, weighing the old shield in his hand. The arm loop had rotted, but there was enough left to hold on to.

'Three, two, one. Mark!'

He dashed forwards, through the door and down the steps around the tower. Jorge was first, with Fabio and Kasha behind him, then Luis, himself and, finally Don Reza. Their footsteps rang on the stone stairs, but the din at the wall must have been much greater, for none of the bandits turned around.

259

No one challenged them either. So far so good. But they would almost certainly be spotted when they started working on the bolts.

'Get started,' Jorge hissed when they reached the gates.

Ben drew his sword and stood, the old shield held at an angle above his head, rain splattering on it, as it protected himself and Fabio from the archers on the bastion to the left. Tall Don Reza did the same on the other side, shielding Kasha.

Jorge and Luis faced outwards, their backs to the others, swords and daggers drawn.

There was a grinding noise from behind him, it was one of the heavy ground bolts being lifted by Kasha.

'Hey!'

They'd been heard and seen.

Ben's arm shuddered as an iron arrowhead thudded into his shield. The old planks splintered. It wouldn't take many of those to reduce it to matchwood. To his right Luis parried a sword thrust and made a jab of his own. Weapons clashed.

Bandits were running towards them, waving swords. One headed straight for Ben, slashing his weapon. Parry!

It was all he could do to swipe the sword away and still hold the shield aloft. Another arrow thudded into it, arrowhead protruding through the wood. The bandit made a thrust forward and he stepped to the side, bringing his own sword down on the other's weapon. Luis, his wet hair in his eyes, finished him off with a short stab. That was well done, but, at this rate he'd be skewered soon, he couldn't hold up the shield and fight effectively at the same time. Already another bandit was running into the attack.

Hurry up and get those bolts drawn.

He steadied himself, but was almost knocked off balance by Fabio, who was hammering at the cross bolt, again and again. The grinding sound was repeated.

The next assailant didn't run in and slash, he danced to the left and aimed a blow to Ben's rib-cage. Ben had to turn to counter-strike, forcing his opponent's blade to the ground and an arrow whizzed past him, into the wood of the gate, as he twisted from its path. His breath was coming quickly now and shallow. He was tired. Too tired to continue for much longer.

'It's coming!' Fabio shouted. 'It's coming! It's open!'

'Run!' That was Kasha's voice and Ben was shoved forwards. 'Re-form at the tower!'

Behind him was a great shout – the soldiers outside had seen that the gate was opening.

They had done it.

Ben lowered his shield and ran, jumping over bodies, sliding in the mud until he reached the curving stone walls.

But the bandits were fighting to defend the gates, as soldiers tried to enter. At El Zagal's command they formed a line, several men deep, across the opening to fight off the incomers. The battle could still go either way.

He glanced around. Jorge was by his side, hair slicked back from his forehead, still gripping his weapon. The others stood just beyond. Luis was leaning forward on his sword, blood coming through his hand as he held his face. Kasha was impassive as always, but even he was panting. An arrow head stuck out from Fabio's thigh as he leant on Don Reza. The other shield was nowhere to be seen.

261

Would Jorge demand that they attack again?

Could he do it?

He would have to. The man who couldn't keep going in a battle would die. He cast the shield aside, it was too heavy. Gripping the wet leather of the hilt of his sword with both hands he prepared to run at the bandit lines.

'Look!' Jorge pointed to the battlements.

Soldiers had gained the parapet and were fighting hand to hand with those defenders remaining on the walls. The men before the gates had seen them too. They would be surrounded if they remained where they were, but they had no-where else to go. Except the route through the caves.

Jorge was already moving away from the tower, pulling Luis behind him.

'Get to the cliffs! Through the boulders!' Ben yelled. The ropes would still be there.

Kasha and Don Reza helped a limping Fabio and Ben followed, protecting their rear. But the bandits didn't give them so much as a glance.

Twenty or more men were running, pushing and shoving, intent on getting to the tower, to seek escape through the caves. King's archers fired at point blank range from the battlements into the melee and bandits toppled. Granadans swept down on them, scimitars flashing.

Even those who got into the tower would find out soon enough that the way was barred.

Ben leaned back against a boulder. He could barely stand upright he was so tired. Slowly he slid to the ground.

It was over. All bar the mopping up.

It was over.

Against all the odds, they had won.

But what of Nathan and the others?

31.

In the Caves

Nathan raised his lantern as high as the roof of the tunnel would allow. Jagged rock pressed in on both sides, snagging the leather and wool of his clothes. Oppressive and narrow, it was barely wide enough for them all to pass.

His clothes were damp against his skin where he held Miguel, wet with blood. But it was Atta who, being taller, bore more of the weight, his shoulder beneath Miguel's right arm and his arm about Miguel's waist.

Johanna was up ahead, but he'd lost sight of the lantern she carried.

They seemed to have been passing through the caves for hours, leaving markers to indicate their route. Yet there was no sign of the others.

Why hadn't they caught up yet? Had something gone awry?

'When this widens out again we need to stop,' Atta said, his voice strained.

Nathan grunted in response.

If it widens out again.

Sometimes he felt as if he was being buried alive, that there was no way out.

Then he saw light ahead again.

The sides of the tunnel opened out into a cave, lit by Johanna's lantern. On the far wall the black mouth of the passage lead onwards and to the right a low aperture reached into the dark.

Johanna set Nathan's lantern on a flat rock beside her own. With a sigh of relief, Nathan helped lower Miguel to the cave floor. The young man's breath rasped in his chest and he could barely stand unaided. He needed to rest.

Sitting back on his haunches, Nathan rolled his cloak into a pillow and placed it under Miguel's head. Miguel groaned, the sound echoing in the chamber. Yet there was something else, another noise – a continuous rumbling sound.

Nathan watched as Atta took a bottle from his satchel and gauged the level of the liquid within. He hesitated, then replaced it.

'I can't give him any more.' Atta's hands fell limply onto his knees.

'But... for the pain,' Johanna said. 'No?'

Atta shook his head.

'Atta, are you sure?'

'Yes. We need him to stay conscious. We have to get him out of here and we can't carry him through these caves, not even when the others arrive.'

'I'm all right,' Miguel said in a weak voice. 'Just give me a few minutes to rest.'

Nathan met Johanna's anxious glance across the body of the injured young man.

266

'We'll wait for a while anyway,' Nathan said.

Miguel needed to rest and it might be better to wait. Moving him was difficult and the others would help. Besides, he was concerned about that noise.

He picked up one of the lanterns and wandered over to the opening in the cave wall. He needed to bend almost double to walk a few steps inside. The rumbling grew louder, becoming a distinct, rushing sound, as he crept along. Soon it drowned out any other sound.

The floor of the low passage ended, falling away into darkness. Nathan halted and raised his lantern. Its glimmer reflected far below in   running, tumbling water.

Dropping to one knee, he held the lantern further out. Its light pierced the blackness of a huge cavern, its roof only feet above him. Beneath, beyond the racing water he could see a flat rocky shelf.

His eye was caught by a flash of red upon the floor. What was that?

It was one of their wooden markers. They must have passed this way. Yet they hadn't forded a raging torrent, there had only been a small stream.

So they hadn't got far at all, just doubled back upon themselves, only much higher up. They were no nearer finding the way out. Suddenly Nathan felt weary.

Carefully, he withdrew the lantern and retreated back to the cave.

Johanna was peering into the narrow passage through which they had just passed.

'Nathan,' she said. 'Look. I think I can see lights. It's the others.'

Maybe it was, but... something didn't feel right.

'Come away.' Nathan grabbed Johanna and her lantern, pulling her over to one side of the cave.

'What...'

Atta looked up too.

'The stream we crossed earlier is in that direction.' Nathan pointed back into the gap. 'And it's a foaming torrent now. It's the rain, the cavern has flooded.'

'But...' Atta shot a glance at Nathan. 'My father, the others - would they have been able to cross?'

'I don't know. These flash floods can happen very quickly.'

'But if they couldn't... who's behind us?' Johanna gestured to the passageway.

'I don't know,' Nathan said as he glanced around the cave.

He sensed danger. Better get out of the caves as soon as they could. 'We must move on.'

'Help me,' Atta said. Nathan picked up a lantern and slipped his right shoulder beneath Miguel's arm. Grunting with effort, he straightened up as they lifted Miguel.

Johanna carried the rope and a lantern. They followed her into the next tunnel.

'Do you think it's the bandits,' Atta half whispered.

Nathan nodded, his face tense.

'Father... the others?'

What could he say to reassure his friend?

'Oh!' Johanna exclaimed.

'What is it?' Nathan called.

'It's a dead end.'

He could see for himself now, the passageway opened, but in front of them was a wall of rock.

'Hush!' Atta said. 'I think I can hear someone coming.'

All were still but there was no sound besides Miguel's rasping breath.

Nathan looked around the little cave. If the bandits were behind them, this place would be a trap. It was only a matter of time before they would catch up and they'd be cornered.

It seemed the same thought had occurred to Johanna, for she held her lantern up to examine the rock face, seeking a way out.

'Look,' she pointed upwards. 'There's a ledge and...' The lantern flame guttered in a slight breeze. 'The air is moving. I think this links with the outside, we've just got to get up over this rock face. It's the way out.'

Nathan stared upwards, straining to see.

They seemed to be standing in a vertical shaft, its sides rising up and up. But there was a deeper darkness in the rock wall in front of them, several feet above the height of a tall man. It could be a ledge. Johanna was right. If they could climb up to it, there might be a way out. He fancied that he felt a slight breeze upon his face.

'Go,' Miguel said, struggling feebly to free himself from their grasp. 'I'll never get up there. Leave me.'

'No.' Atta said, flatly. 'Hold him.' He instructed Nathan as he slid from beneath Miguel's shoulder.

Nathan staggered as the whole weight of the injured man fell on him.

Atta was feeling the rock face for handholds.

269

'I'll climb up,' he said. 'Secure the rope and drop it down. Anna, you come up next, tie a lantern to your back. Then we'll haul Miguel up.'

This was ridiculous. Atta couldn't climb. He had always been afraid of heights.

'Atta....'

No, Atta was the one who had been climbing mountains. He'd manage.

'Be quick,' Nathan said.

Atta took the rope from Johanna and slung it across his chest. Joanna laced her fingers together.

'You'll have to be quick,' she said as Atta placed his foot into her hands. 'I won't be able to hold you for long.' She grunted as Atta shifted his weight and began to climb.

Like a long-limbed spider Atta drew his body upwards, his feet finding cracks and juts for support. His legs and arms stretched across the rock face, as he climbed up into the dark.

There was a noise in the passage behind them and shadows swayed as Johanna turned round to look, she had tied the lantern to her back.

'I'm going to have to let you go,' Nathan whispered to Miguel. 'Here, lean against the rock.'

'Right.'

Carefully, he lay Miguel against the wall of the shaft. The injured man slithered sideways and Nathan reached out to catch him, but he righted himself.

'I'm all right,' Miguel said, clutching at his chest. He didn't look it, his face was shiny with sweat and there were dark smudges beneath his eyes.

Nathan drew his sword and faced the opening into the passageway.

'Anna!' Atta's voice echoed down the funnel.

Nathan grimaced. He looked at Anna. 'Go. And when you get there, tell him to be quiet.'

Nathan watched over his shoulder as Johanna caught the rope's end and began hauling herself upwards, hand over hand. The light around him dimmed, he had only one lantern now.

Voices.

He could hear voices, but not what they were saying. All he could tell was that a discussion was taking place. Were their pursuers in the cave where they had rested only a few minutes before?

These people weren't their friends, he was sure of it. They would have seen the lights up ahead and would be calling for them. No, they were more likely to be bandits looking for a way of escape.

It wouldn't be long before they came along the passageway, though perhaps they would look to see where the other tunnel went first.

'Hsst!'

Nathan glanced round to see the rope snaking down the last few feet to the rock floor. It had a noose in it now. He placed his drawn sword on the floor.

He wound his cloak around Miguel's chest and looped the rope on top of it.

271

'In a moment they're going to pull you up the rock face,' he whispered as he worked. 'The noose will pull taut beneath your arms. It's important that you don't let yourself slip out of it.'

Miguel nodded. 'I'll try,' he said. The young man's face had a sheen, his eyes were bright - with fever, or excitement, or with fear.

'I'll take your weight, support you as Atta and Johanna pull you up. You can put your feet on my shoulders.' Nathan grinned. 'Though I've never been very tall.'

Miguel half-smiled in response.

There was a noise in the passageway.

'Use your feet against the rock if you can,' Nathan shuffled them both over to the rock face.

A voice echoed from the tunnel.

'You! You up ahead!'

Say nothing. Gain a few seconds more.

'We know you're there! We can see your light.'

'You cannot pass,' Nathan answered. 'There are soldiers of the King here, try another way.'

'It's not a way out we seek,' another voice called. It was refined and cold. 'We want the man you took from the dungeon.'

'What do you want with him?'

'That's my business,' the voice was drawing nearer. 'Give him to me and you and the others can go free.'

'I don't believe you.' Nathan could hear more noise in the narrow tunnel.

Keep him talking. Play for time.

272

His eyes were on the tunnel but he felt the rope round the young man's chest tauten. Nathan let him go, bending to cup his hands together and boost him upwards.

'I promise you,' the cold voice was closer still. 'You won't be hurt.'

'Don't come any further. We're armed.'

Miguel's feet were on Nathan's shoulders. His weight lifted.

Nathan grabbed for his sword, gripping the hilt with both hands. He braced his feet apart on the stone floor of the cave.

'The passageway's narrow, you can only come through one at a time and the first man through gets a sword point in his guts.'

Why did he have to sound so young? And weak.

'Without a chance to defend himself?' The voice was much nearer, the man must be almost upon him. 'Are you a coward then?'

'Stay back. Or you'll find out.'

There was a muttering. Voices were conferring.

'Nathan,' there was an urgent whisper from Johanna above. He turned and saw the rope drop down the rock face.

Miguel must be up.

Get out. Now!

He began to climb, his own blood smearing the rope. He had sliced the pads of his fingers as he'd jammed the sword back into its scabbard.

Pull yourself up. Hand over hand, feet against the rock face.

He was half way up when he heard someone enter the chamber below and glanced down.

It was Carlo, the youth from the tower, gripping a sword as he yelled. 'You!'

Then a figure shouldered him aside. It was Raul Ramirez. His long hair fell in waves to his shoulders and his black leather clothing reflected dully in the lantern light. With a shout, he swept his sword at Nathan as he spied him climbing away.

Nathan pulled up both his legs and the sword swing passed beneath them, slicing the rope in two.

Keep climbing.... keep climbing! Don't fall!

He pulled himself up, hand over hand, finding footholds in the rock.

Such an effort. His arms were burning with it.

But the rope being pulled upwards too.

He looked up to see Johanna's face above him.

'Come on,' she said, staring at him, watching every move. 'Not far now.' She flinched as his fingers, slippery with blood, slid on the rope. Her stare intensified. Then her expression changed to one of horror.

A searing pain shot through his left shoulder, slicing though his body. He cried out with pain.

His feet had lost their grip and he hung, one handed, from the rope.

Beneath him someone laughed.

'Hold on! Hold on!' Johanna called.

The rope began to move more quickly.

He had to hang on. He had to. The top of the rock face was only inches above him now.

Hands clutched his wrist. Sinewy, long fingered, strong hands, Atta's hands.

274

With a heave, his shoulders were dragged over the edge and he was pulled away from the drop. He sagged with relief, all strength leaving him.

'I'll pull the blade out,' he heard Atta say. 'Be ready with something to staunch the blood flow.'

Nathan saw a bright, white light. His body was on fire.

Someone screamed. There was a fierce throbbing pain in his shoulder.

The white light receded, replaced by the yellow glow of the lantern. He lifted his head.

Miguel, his face haggard, was lying against the rock wall only a yard from him. A slim throwing knife lay on the rock floor. He felt Johanna's hands beneath him, passing fabric around his chest and over his shoulder.

'It's a flesh wound,' he heard Atta say. 'You'll be alright.'

'I don't feel alright.'

'You will.' It was Johanna's voice. Nathan twisted round to look at her. She returned his gaze with a merciless glare that brooked no denial.

'On your feet.' Atta hauled him upright. 'Your legs are all right, you can walk. Come on.'

'But, I.....'

There were sounds from the cave below, someone was climbing up the rock wall.

'Time to go,' Atta said.

Johanna went ahead with their one remaining lantern, then Atta supporting Miguel.

275

Nathan swallowed and stepped forward. He was the last. His head swam. Blinking hard, he made himself focus on the passageway ahead as he forced one foot in front of the other. It was dark.

'Keep up!' Atta shouted. 'Come on! There's too much water, it's going to flood.'

He reached out to balance himself against the rock wall. Surely its surface was wet. His vision blurred. The floor of the passageway seemed to be moving. He stumbled, struggling forward as the passage twisted this way and that.

He had to keep up.

There was a thumping from people in the passage behind him. Or was that in his head? No, he was sure he could hear them in the blackness. They were coming.

It was so hard to move. His shoulder burned with pain. If he could just rest....

Now the rock walls gleamed and flickered. He could hear the sound of water. Were they back at the torrent?

The light came from a lantern and there was Atta's face, anxious and frowning. His friend reached out to take his arm.

'Quick,' he said. 'Hurry. The cave mouth's just up ahead. Lean on me.'

'They're catching up,' Nathan said. 'I heard them.'

'Come on! Here, up here.' The light grew stronger and the passageway widened into a vast gallery.

Strange crystalline shapes glittered in the half-light. Cascading rock sculptures dripped from the ceiling and crystal columns reached up from the cave floor. Where was the light coming from? The cave was beautiful, but it hurt to look up.

Easier to look down at his wet feet, where he was sloshing through a stream which was getting deeper by the second. The sound of running water grew louder.

Atta reached back and grabbed Nathan's hand.

'Come on!' Atta shouted. 'Up here. Away from the flood.'

He was pulled on to a sloping mound of earth and boulders.

'Climb!' Atta yelled at him.

Nathan began to grasp at the rocks, pulling himself upwards with what strength he had left. The cave seemed to revolve around him.

Up there. Daylight.

It must be the entrance. Keep going - it was the way out.

A shout came from below him.

From the mouth of the passageway men were trying to force their way against the flow of water, now waist-deep, as they tried to get to the slope as he had done.

Climb. Keep going.

Nathan staggered. There was even more water.

'Nathan!' Atta yelled.

Nathan reached up his right hand and was hauled to the summit of the slope.

Here the rock floor was dry and, about fifty paces on, there was daylight.

Johanna reached out for him and he fell into her embrace. But she wouldn't let him rest, pulling him on towards the cave entrance. He raised his head to look back.

Men were still trying to climb upwards, but the water seemed to be coming from everywhere at once, splashing, a foaming mass, onto the boulders, streaming to meet the flood below. Their shouts barely heard, first one man, then another, was swept away, taken by the torrent as it grew, bouncing from rock to rock.

One man had reached a rocky outcrop, an island above the waters which surged around it. Nathan recognised the bulky form of Carlo, his sword sheathed, his hair slicked to his skull.

He tightened his grip around Johanna's waist.

Another man was climbing up to join Carlo on the rock. It was Ramirez.

At first Carlo tried to pull him up, then realised that there wasn't room for two. The last thing Nathan saw before he staggered out into the daylight was Carlo's body tumbling away into the maelstrom.

32.

After the Battle

Rebecca drew her knees up beneath her cloak as she sat in the doorway of the shepherd's hut. She fingered its hem, teasing the stitches apart.

From her eerie high up on the mountain side she could see the saddle of the pass which led into El Endrinal. Beyond the ridge were the mountain peaks.

Behind her, inside, the wounded guard was as comfortable as she could make him. Getting the arrow head out had been a gruelling task, its tip was barbed and she only had Antonio's knife to work with. The shepherd had held the wounded man down while she cut around the wound, the hot blade slicing into the flesh, until her patient lost consciousness. Only then could she work without fear.

She had sat there for the rest of the day, staring out at the rain as it lessened into drizzle and then stopped. Birdsong sounded amidst the slow dripping of water as weak sunlight struggled through the high cloud. The storm clouds had passed.

What was happening beyond that grassy slope? So much of her world was at stake.

The light would start to go in a few hours.

If no one came to them by dusk, they had agreed that Antonio would return to his village and get help while she waited in the cave with the guardsman. If the *bandeleros* had won, or escaped, there would be little help to be had. No village would be safe from them.

Yet, right now, all she could was wait.

On the *Teresa* it had been different. On the *Teresa* she had been a boy. She blinked back tears of frustration. From now on, she vowed, if she got out of this alive, she would determine her own fate. Accommodate the tenets of the world, yes, but somehow find a way to do what she wanted to do, regardless.

She looked down at her hands. The edge of her cloak was now ragged, the fabric unwoven.

Then a figure crested the saddle of the pass, a lone horseman.

Her heart skipped, then began to beat faster.

'Tonio,' she called, getting to her feet.

The shepherd's eyesight was keener than her own. She should keep in the shadows, at least until it was clear who the rider served. Yet all her instincts were to call out, to attract his attention and ask him for news.

Antonio came to her side.

'I see him,' he said, shading his eyes with his hand. 'He's a King's soldier. Wait...!'

Antonio's voice was lost on the wind as Rebecca ran out onto and down the hillside.

'Hey! Hello!' She shouted and waved her arms, as she hurried down the slope.

The rider halted, then kicked his mount into a trot towards her.

He wore the badge of the King. He was one of the Lieutenant's men.

'What's happened?' she demanded. 'Is the fortress taken?'

'Are you all unharmed?' The soldier spoke at the same time. 'Yes, the bandits are destroyed.'

Rebecca felt the tension leave her. It was going to be alright.

'We're up in the hut,' she pointed back behind her to where Antonio was standing at the door. But her gaze was drawn beyond the soldier. Cresting the ridge was a column of riders.

Where was Nathan? Where was Miguel?

She saw the Lieutenant, the Granadan officer and the Major. There was Ben and Jorge, both of whom waved as they caught sight of her; and Don Reza and Atta. Next was Nathan, riding just behind his friend, someone else alongside. He kicked his horse's flanks and cantered down towards her.

Her eyes filled with tears as Nathan halted. He almost fell from the saddle.

'Nathan!' She embraced him. 'Nathan. I...I don't know what to say.'

'Don't say anything,' her cousin hugged her in return. 'No need.'

He seemed exhausted and he wore a bandage underneath his shirt. Had he been wounded?

'It's only a flesh wound, Atta assures me,' Nathan held her hands in his own. 'I'm going to be all right. I'm going to be all right.'

Then she remembered Simon.

'Oh, Nathan, your father... He's been injured and needs you. You have to come home now, you must come home!'

'I know, I know,' Nathan put his arm around her shoulders. They began to walk back to the column of riders, Nathan leading his horse. The column halted and riders were dismounting. Two covered wagons circled and stopped. 'Atta told me about Father. Don't worry, I'm coming home. I'll tell you about everything. Who are you looking for?'

'No-one,' she answered, dragging her eyes back to her cousin's face. 'Do you have more wounded? Were more people hurt?'

'Yes.'

Please, please don't let it be Miguel.

How could she ask about him? What could she say?

'Rebecca.' It was Atta.

'Atta!' Rebecca grasped his hands, but let go as he winced and pulled back. 'Your hands!'

'They'll heal,' Atta replied. 'Come, come with me.' He drew her into the swiftly forming camp, Nathan following.

'Hey, I want to...' Nathan began. He glanced back at the riders and glared at Atta.

'Yes,' said Atta. 'I know. But that can wait. Rebecca is helping me.'

What did Nathan want? And why was Atta being so mysterious?

'All right, all right,' Nathan backed off.

'Look, I'll help Atta then I'll come and find you. All right?'

'Yeah, look for me.' Nathan was frowning. 'But don't be long, we'll be moving out soon.'

She watched him stalk off into the camp.

Oh dear, they had only been re-united for half an hour and already they were at odds.

'Come,' Atta said, leading her through the groups of soldiers, as they gathered around the cook fires. 'There's someone who wants to see you... and who you might want to see.'

He must mean Miguel. Surely.

'How do you...?'

'Doesn't matter.'

They came up to one of the covered wagons and Atta bent and cupped his hands together to help Rebecca into it.

His poor hands.

Reluctantly she lifted her booted foot.

'Up you go,' he said.

On the tailboard of the wagon, she ducked beneath its covering.

Inside Miguel lay, pale-faced and wan, propped up on pillows.

His chest and arms were swathed in bandages. His battered face was bruised purple with one eye puffy and closed above blood crusted cuts. He was so hurt, so broken.

Poor love. Her chest tightened.

But he was alive, at least he was alive!

He turned towards her and his lips parted. He began to smile and struggle to sit up.

Within an instant she was at his side. He reached up and she held his hand in both of her own.

'Barely a fortnight without me and look what happens to you,' she said, blinking back tears. 'How on earth did you think you would manage on your own?'

Miguel reached his other hand to her face and placed his finger upon her lips.

283

'I thought I'd never see you again,' he said. 'It was Ramirez, back from the dead, intent on revenge.'

She wiped her nose with the back of her hand. 'I know. Jorge told me about it. He'd joined the bandit leader. That's why the Granadans decided to attack with us.'

Miguel frowned.

Of course, he knew nothing of what had happened. She would tell him later.

'It doesn't matter. Nothing matters now. I love you.'

'And I love you,' he said. Rebecca felt her heart leap. His hand brushed her wet cheek, wiping away the tears. 'But...'

'Yes, I know, it's impossible. You're a nobleman and I'm...I'm a runaway.. and a Jew they call a sailor's drab.'

'They'll not say that in my hearing.' He smiled. 'As for you running away – if you hadn't I would never have met you.'

She wanted so much to hear his reassurances that none of it mattered.

Miguel's hand dropped to the coverlet. His face grew even paler. 'But there's something I must tell you.'

Surely nothing, nothing could spoil her happiness. Miguel loved her.

'Then tell me.'

'There is a girl...'

What? Rebecca recoiled.

Someone else.

'Listen to me, it's not what you think.' He held her hands and wouldn't let her go. 'My brother, Juan, your cousin's friend...'

'I know, knew, Juan.'

284

Miguel inhaled deeply.

'My brother – well, it seems that he wed this girl, in secret. Now he's dead and she's pregnant. She, or rather her mother, is demanding that I take his place.'

'But... you can't....'

He couldn't. He just couldn't. She wouldn't let him.

Yet even as her heart railed against it, her mind recognised that this was common practice. Family was all.

'But what could mean more to you than our life together?' Rebecca dragged her hands free.

'Rebecca...hush...'

If he loved her, how could he marry someone else? Or did he think...?

She would not be any man's concubine. She wouldn't share him with anyone else.

She edged back towards the back of the wagon.

'Rebecca!' He pushed at the pillows, struggling to reach forward, forced himself upright. 'I'm trying to explain. I love you. It's nothing.'

'Nothing!'

There was another woman expecting to marry him and he called it nothing.

The canvas flap at the rear of the wagon lifted and Atta climbed in, holding a vial of medicine. He looked from Miguel to Rebecca.

'That's long enough,' he said. 'I can't have you tiring him out. I've more poppy juice for him, he needs to rest. And I believe your cousin is still expecting to talk with you.'

She should go. Yes, she should.

285

She looked back at Miguel. He had fallen back on to the pillow, his eyes half-closed. He needed Atta now, not her.

And she? She needed to think.

Rebecca scrambled to the backboard of the wagon and jumped down.

33.

Returning

It would go more smoothly if he managed to keep his temper.

His father was weakened, he had been wounded, it was for him, Nathan, to be magnanimous.

Yet there was no chance, he suspected, of his father allowing any illness or wound to soften his attitude. If anything it would make him worse.

The thought of home, of returning to the little compound, with its house, smithy and stables was very appealing. A place of safety, of warmth and comfort, in which to rest. Yet also a place of confinement, a place he had run away from. He shifted in the saddle, his shoulder ached.

He had run away, he knew that now. Just like his cousin.

He had to return and face up to things.

Nathan stole a glance to his right.

Johanna rode beside him. She caught his glance and smiled, her nose crinkling upwards in that way that it did. He returned her smile.

Nathan turned, wincing at the pain in his shoulder, to look back at the long column of riders and wagons.

287

It wound its way down the valley, occasionally crossing ridges and passes, but always getting closer to the plains. They had parted company with the detachment of Granadan soldiers, who were returning home, going back across the mountains.

Now the column marched steadily downwards. The harsh landscape of the mountains was behind them and they travelled through vine-covered foothills. Ahead lay the plain, with the city beyond. Out-riders trotted ahead and to each side, but the mood was relaxed, everyone else was going home too.

'You look deep in thought.'

A voice broke into Nathan's reverie.

It was Atta, his horse trotting up to Nathan's left.

Nathan smiled in greeting. It was good to be in his company once more.

'Oh, just thinking about how to handle things at home.'

'Your father?'

Nathan nodded. Atta looked down at his hands, resting on the saddle pommel.

'Perhaps it won't be as difficult as you imagine.'

Nathan raised his eyebrows.

'I mean, you might find that things have changed. We're none of us the same as before this war.'

Atta was right.

They had all changed. Including him.

For a while he'd lost himself, become detached from reality.

'Juan..' he began.

'Yes, I think about him too. I still haven't really got used to his death.'

Yet Atta, Rebecca, his father and Don Reza were alive. And he was alive, despite all attempts by death to claim him.

He glanced to his right again. She was still there.

The others had come through too, Kasha and Luis, Ben Isaacs and Miguel Delgado.

'How is Miguel?'

'I've treated his wounds, but...' Atta grimaced. 'He's not improving as quickly as I'd hoped.' He stared hard in front of him. 'I'll be glad to get him to a place where we can care for him properly. He saved my life, you know, on Eagle's Crag.'

'Yes.'

Nathan remembered the sight of his friend plummeting from the precipice, then Miguel tumbling after, buffeted against the mountain.

'I still don't know how you came to be up there in the first place. It's ridiculously high and you've never liked heights.'

Atta began to grin. 'I sometimes wonder myself. It just...happened.'

Nathan knew how that could be. He still wasn't sure why he had stowed away on the *San Fernando*, why he had crossed to the galley and why he had run from his friend.

He suspected that he hadn't quite been in his right mind. Sleep walking in daylight. But now he was awake. Ever since the ambush he had felt more like himself.

'How's Luis?' His friend had received a nasty sword cut across his face.

'He'll mend,' Atta answered. 'The scar will match his broken nose. He and Kasha are heroes again.'

289

'Maybe this time they'll stay in Jerez.' He hoped so.

'Along with our other heroes,' Atta said and gestured towards Ben Isaacs, who was riding immediately in front of them, by Rebecca's side.

'He won't be going anywhere.' Nathan grinned. 'He's much too sweet on my cousin.'

'Yes, but Nathan...' Atta's face assumed an interesting expression, part exasperated, part amused. He gathered his reins in his hands, as his horse skittered to one side. 'Perhaps he's not the only one.'

Eh? Since when had his cousin become so attractive?

'Who?'

'Miguel.' Atta was looking at him strangely. 'Don't you think?'

'Miguel Delgado! No.' Where had Atta have got that idea from? It was ridiculous. 'Look, she hasn't been anywhere near him, other than that one time to help you.'

'Yes,' Atta seemed distracted. 'It's true, she doesn't seem to be... interested.' He frowned. 'Maybe I've got it wrong?'

'Completely.'

'I've made quite a habit of getting things wrong, recently,' Atta said.

Nathan waited for him to go on, there was clearly more that he wanted to say. In the end he gave up the wait and asked.

'Like what?'

'Oh, nothing. Just me being stupid.'

Nathan studied his friend's face.

Atta had never been one for sharing his every thought and opinion, but they hadn't kept secrets from each other either. He sensed that there was a lot behind that brief dismissal. Yet there was no point in forcing things, Atta would tell him when he was ready.

'Only one more night bivouacking in the open,' Nathan said. 'Some of us haven't slept in a bed for a while, though at least it was warm last night.'

The group had accompanied Antonio when he returned, with some of those most badly wounded in the fighting, to his village. Grateful villagers had entertained them with the best they had. Nathan had slept in the smithy, with the other soldiers, but Atta and Don Reza had stayed with the shepherd.

'Yes, it was good to sleep indoors again,' Atta smiled. 'Carmen insisted that I stayed with them, you know. And Father wanted to thank them. I think Jorge wanted to see them again too, if only to prove that he wasn't a villain, though I don't think Carmen was entirely convinced.'

'He was a good friend to both of us,' Nathan said. 'Even if we didn't know it at first. Your uncle must value him highly.'

'I'm sure he does,' Atta said. He looked like he might say more, but did not.

Nathan didn't pursue the subject. Jorge had ridden off first thing that morning, going who knows where.

The haunting cry of birds split the silence and Nathan looked up, shielding his eyes. Vultures were hovering and swooping, high above them, fighting over prey. One had a small creature in its beak and the other sought to take it, stooping down, its talons reaching out. Beautiful and fine birds, but pitiless, without compassion or kindness.

'Will you stay?' Nathan asked, ' When we get back to Jerez, I mean?'

'We'll stay for a while,' Atta said. 'At least until my uncle has fully recovered.'

'Your father would be welcomed back at the hospital.'

'I know. But the city's changed, Nathan, and who knows what will happen. There may be more war.'

'I thought your uncle was supposed to be negotiating a peace.'

'He is, or was,' Atta suddenly looked careworn. 'But who knows...nothing's certain. Do you know what you will do?'

'No, not really. I'll stay in Jerez I think, though I'm not sure where...'

'Your father will welcome you,' Atta said. 'I'm sure of it. He missed you so much.'

'So that's something that you are certain about.'

'Yes, that I know.'

Nathan shrugged and looked down at his hands.

His friend might be right, but it wouldn't make it any easier.

Part Three

Home

34.

Father and Son

Nathan turned north along the narrow lane which skirted the Alcazar, in the direction of Plaza Plateros.

Up ahead the square in front of the hospital was full of bright sunlight, they had left the rain behind in the mountains. Townsfolk were going about their daily business, none of them giving him a second glance.

He was alone. Until he had prepared the ground with his father, Johanna and Fabio would stay in the Alcazar. Rebecca was there with them now.

Maybe he should look in at the hospital and greet Senor Thomas? It had been three weeks since he had last spoken with the surgeon, though it seemed longer, so much had happened since. It would be good to catch up.

No. Thomas might not even be there and anyway, it was only putting off going home.

It couldn't be avoided. It had to be done.

He stretched his legs, striding across the square and into the shaded maze of streets beyond. Here tradesmen sat outside their shops and women stopped to chat and gossip. They watched him as he passed, but there was no one he recognized. All were newcomers.

Up ahead was the sunlight of Plaza Plateros.

Nathan's steps slowed.

What would his father say? How would he react when he saw who had returned? Maybe he should have agreed to let Rebecca accompany him?

No, Rebecca's presence would only complicate matters, this was something between him and his father. She would come home to Plateros later.

The square looked the same as ever. Leaf buds were already forming on the jacaranda trees. Spring wasn't far away. Children sat on the lip of the dry fountain.

Nathan fished inside his pocket for his key. One turn in the lock and the blue painted gate opened to reveal the familiar courtyard before him.

The shutters on the ground floor were closed tight, as was the smithy door, but the porch door to the house was ajar and the upper window shutters were open. He wrinkled his nose in distaste at the pungent tang coming from the stable, it needed cleaning out.

Crossing to the house, he walked through the vestibule and into the living room.

It was dark inside and almost as cold as in the courtyard. The air had a musty smell.

He pulled open the courtyard window and thrust the shutters open. Sunlight flowed into the room.

The furniture stood where it always had, but the hearth was cold and empty. His father had not been looking after the place. But then, how could he? It was only six days since the ambush, since he had been wounded.

Above his head the wooden ceiling creaked. Was that Father? He summoned up his courage and turned to face the wooden stairs. Someone was descending, coming into the light.

It was Thomas.

Nathan exhaled.

'Hello, am I glad to see you,' the Englishman grinned and came forward, his hand extended. 'The messenger reached us last night.'

Nathan took his hand and smiled.

'Back in town, bringing trouble,' he said.

'No,' Thomas replied. 'Just at the right time. Your father will feel so much better for seeing you. Come.'

Nathan followed the young doctor back upstairs and along the landing to his father's bedroom.

'Simon, I was right,' Thomas called. 'You have a visitor.'

A figure lay propped against pillows in the large wooden bed, a heavy coverlet pulled high over his chest. He wore bandages around his head, above a gaunt face, the taut skin stretched over his cheekbones, shadow in the hollows beneath. Sunlight glinted on the silvery stubble on his chin. His grey eyes seemed huge.

He looked so much frailer than Nathan had imagined and older. When was the last time he had really looked at his father?

'Nathan.'

The throaty voice was the same.

'Father,' he said as he crossed to the bed.

Simon lifted his arms from beneath the cover and opened them wide.

Nathan bent into the embrace. He closed his eyes, ignoring the pain in his shoulder. Here was warmth, safety, love and completeness. How could he have forgotten this?

Some things might not be easy, but this would carry them through. Things were going to be alright, just as Atta had predicted.

The embrace was weakening and Nathan drew away. His father's right hand grasped his own, the grip still strong, but was not as it had been.

'I'm weak and feeble,' Simon said, as if he had divined Nathan's thought.

For a moment he couldn't speak, his tongue seemed too large for his mouth.

'You've been injured,' he said. 'And abed.'

'Thomas insisted,' his father said, loudly. 'He's worse, even, than your cousin, when it comes to giving orders. We came across her, with Ben Isaacs, on our way back to the city. Is she...?'

'She's well. They found us.'

'I was worried.'

'Yes.'

'And about you.'

'Yes, I know, I...'

All the speeches he had prepared melted away.

Outside a bird sang and chirruped, filling the silence.

'I've done some thinking, lying here,' his father said. 'I know what they'll say, in the town, about foolish Simon Calamiel and his wayward niece, who should be soundly beaten. And now his son's gone too - shows what sort of a house he keeps.'

'Do you think that? That Rebecca should be beaten?'

'No,' Simon sighed. 'Your cousin knows I don't. But you going too...?'

The assumptions his father had made, his insistence that Nathan would follow in his footsteps as a silversmith. His father's refusal to listen to any other view - the orders, the prohibitions... this was the opportunity to say all of this. But he couldn't. Not to this man in the bed.

His father was waiting for him to say something.

'It's difficult to explain.'

This would be hard, he had only recently begun to sort it out in his own mind. He wasn't sure he could explain, he didn't have the right words.

'A lot of it was to do with what was happening. Everything was being destroyed. Juan was dead, Atta gone, Rebecca too, and all those people dying and suffering. And it was how I felt...' His father remained quiet so Nathan continued. 'Powerless, there was nothing I could do – nothing any of us could do – to stop it. Even at home I had no say and I'm not a child anymore.'

'I'm your father, it's my job to keep you safe. You can't tackle the wrongs of the whole world Nathan. You don't understand it.'

'I understand more than you think,' Nathan said, slowly. Choose your words with care, he told himself. 'I've seen things, such things you wouldn't believe.....and I've come through. If this is my home, I want to be able to make my own decisions, or at least be able have a say in what's decided.'

Nathan gritted his teeth, awaiting the explosion.

'Yes, I thought that you might say something like that,' his father said. 'We need to discuss this properly.'

Did he understand? Could he?

'But if you want to be treated as an adult you have to behave like one. No more disappearing without a by your leave and turning up looking like a vagabond. There'll be customers to consider and...'

'But not now,' said Thomas, as he returned, carrying a cup of water for his patient. 'That's enough for now. I take it that you're staying, at least for a time?'

'Yes,' Nathan answered.

'Then let your father rest, you can talk later.'

Nathan allowed himself to be ushered out of the room, but he looked back from the doorway and smiled. It wasn't all going to be easy, that was clear. His father's pride wouldn't allow it. But they would work it out.

'Come on,' Thomas urged him along the landing. 'He'll sleep soundly now.'

'You gave him something?'

'Poppy juice.'

'I'll make a fire and get the house warm,' Nathan said, as they went down stairs. 'Rebecca will be on her way.'

'Good. I haven't been able to do much to keep the place up, I've been too busy at the hospital. Now it'll be more like home. He's been worrying.' The doctor's eyes travelled over Nathan's shoulder. 'And not without cause I think.'

'A flesh wound only, Atta says.'

'Well, no doubt he's taken care of it. Nathan...'

'Yes?'

'Simon needs looking after. Proper care and attention. Can you give him that?'

'Yes, of course we can.'

The doctor hesitated, then spoke.

'Nathan, how long will your cousin stay? Will you be able to look after your father on your own?'

Rebecca wasn't going anywhere and, besides, Johanna would be here and, maybe, Fabio.

'What do you mean?'

'It seemed, that is to say, we thought... the Captain and I... that Rebecca might have formed an attachment,' Thomas met his gaze. 'Miguel Delgado is clearly in love with her and... well, she seemed to feel the same about him. We thought that, perhaps, they might... marry.'

Atta had said something similar. Could it be true? Rebecca and Miguel were... what? Lovers?

'No, at least.... she hasn't said anything to me about it.'

'Would she?'The doctor asked.

Nathan considered. Maybe in the old days she might have done.

'Maybe not.' Nathan drew his brows together. 'You haven't said anything to Father about it have you?'

'I may have mentioned it, just as gossip, that's all. Delgado is noble and rich, it would be a good match.'

Oh no, gossip would be the last thing his father would want to hear about Rebecca. And Miguel Delgado, however rich and fine his family, was Christian.

The courtyard gate slammed. That would be his cousin now.

Rebecca came into the living room, her face flushed and anxious.

'How is he? Have you seen him?'

'Yes. He's sleeping now. We spoke briefly.'

'You didn't argue, didn't upset him further?'

'Give me some credit for how to behave in a sick-room.' He snapped. It had gone so well, but now things seemed to be spiralling out of control. 'Anyway, your news is hardly likely to soothe him.'

'My news? What do you mean?'

Nathan failed to catch the physician's eye, he'd get no help from Thomas.

'Thomas tells me that you have an admirer, a lover perhaps? Miguel Delgado...'

His cousin became very still. She stared at the wall, as if commanding her thoughts and then glared at the Englishman, who flushed guiltily.

'Thomas? What have you been saying?'

'I...er...well...'

'Perhaps you should mind your own business, not mine.'

Two spots of vivid red came to her cheeks and Nathan leapt back as she charged past him, stamping up the stairs. The door to her room slammed shut behind her.

What was going on?

Nathan looked at Thomas, who seemed just as surprised. The doctor shook his head.

And he'd thought that father was the worst of his problems.

35.

At the Ambassador's

Once Atta and his father had passed through the city gates it seemed entirely natural that the first place they visited was the hospital. The wounded had to be settled and tended and, after all, where else would they go?

Now, as darkness began to fall, the sound of bells echoed in the deep stone recesses of the building.

His father stood, gaping in amazement. Atta remembered his own astonishment the first time he had heard the Angelus bells.

'You'll hear it all over the city, church bells tolling to summon the faithful to prayer or to tell the hour,' Atta said.

'Noisier than the muezzin's call,' his father replied. 'Though, now I think on it, I haven't heard the call to prayer since we've been back. Is it no longer permitted?'

There was no way of cushioning the blow, it was better that he knew.

'There are no muezzins any more, nor mosques neither,' Atta said. 'Aside from us, Mustafa and his guard, there are no

Mohammedans left in the city. There is a place in the residence where we can pray privately.'

'None at all?' His father raised both eyebrows. 'Are they all gone? Everyone?'

'Yes. In the end they had no choice, I was told. The King exiled them all.'

Don Reza shook his head. His father would realise soon enough just how different the city was.

Yet here at the hospital, more than anywhere else in Jerez, Atta felt most like he had before - before the war, before the siege. It was like being at home, watching his father go along the line of beds, followed by a trailing orderly, tending the sick and wounded. This was the right order of things, it was how things should be. For the first time since they had left the city months before Atta felt whole. He felt complete.

Senor Thomas entered, ducking beneath the lintel of the low doorway to the square. He caught sight of them immediately.

'Welcome home,' he said, clapping Atta on the back and shaking his father's hand. 'I'm glad you're back, there's still plenty of work to be done here.'

'So I see,' Don Reza said. 'But what of those who returned before us? My brother? Simon?'

'Your brother is improving,' Thomas said. 'The arrow was extracted quickly and cleanly.' Thomas looked at Atta. 'Thanks to your son. But Mustafa's trying to do too much, too soon and does not take instruction well.'

'My brother would not be a good patient,' Don Reza answered. 'I don't envy his doctor.'

'I'll gladly let you take over now,' Thomas grinned. 'I've just come from Plateros, Simon's wound is healing well and he'll benefit from Nathan's return.' Then his eyes scanned the newly occupied beds. 'Are there many killed?'

'We buried seven,' Don Reza replied. 'Of those who set out from Jerez. The injured you see.'

But not Miguel Delgado, who had been taken to his own house; Thomas may not have heard about his friend.

'Thomas, you should know that Miguel, Miguel Delgado, was badly hurt,' Atta said. 'Two broken ribs and other wounds. He was... tortured by one of the leaders of the bandits. A man named Raul Ramirez, whom I believe you know.'

Thomas' expression darkened.

'I thought I'd rid us of that villain,' he said. 'I shot him with my longbow, during the sea battle.'

'Well, we're rid of him now,' Atta said. 'The floods in the cavern took him.'

'I hope you're right. He escaped the waters once before,' Thomas said. 'But you should go now, you've done enough. Get some rest. I can manage here.'

'Yes, it's about time I saw my brother,' Don Reza said quietly.

Atta looked at his father, whose thoughts seemed far away. On the journey home he had told him about how Mustafa had been courier for the money that the Emir had sent King Alfonso, gold which the King had used to wage war on Jerez and the other southern cities. Money to pay the soldiers, who had killed Juan and so many others.

To his amazement his father had not seemed surprised, though even more surprising was that he was not outraged.

'It's wrong,' Atta had prompted. 'He helped finance the war and all the killing.'

'It is,' his father said. 'But we should understand better before we condemn, Atta.'

Since their conversation, Atta had sensed his father watching him whenever Mustafa's name was mentioned. Was his own disenchantment with his uncle so obvious?

Now he wanted to lighten his father's mood.

'You'll be amazed when you see where we're living,' he said. 'Such luxury, private bath rooms and heated floor tiles.'

'Private baths, you say?' His father began to smile. 'I'd appreciate a good bath. There were none in the mountains.'

'All is of the very grandest, there is no expense spared. Your brother does very well for himself.'

'My brother is your uncle, Atta,' his father said, his face becoming grave. 'You used to be so proud of him.'

'I know, but.... I thought him so brave and honourable...'

'He is brave. You told me that he'd saved your life, at risk to his own.'

'He did, but...'

It was difficult to explain.

It was partly his own fault, because he had idolised his uncle, expected too much. Mustafa was a man like any other, imperfect as everyone was and probably better than most. Atta tried to be dispassionate.

And yet... the resentment didn't go away. Mustafa had not even trusted him enough to share his plans, to tell him about Jorge.

'Come, it's time we went to find him,' his father said. 'And I want those baths.'

It was but a short walk through the lamp-lit streets to the Ambassadorial residence. Torches burned on either side of the heavy wooden entrance doors to the old palace, lighting the coat of arms carved into the stone above it.

One of the door guards exclaimed in amazement.

'Atta! Welcome back.'

His colleague strode off, going to inform his master of their arrival.

He must have told others too, for people of the household spilled into the hall, smiling and welcoming them. Atta's hands were shaken, he was clapped on the back and surrounded by smiles. Beyond the circle of well-wishers his father stood, thin, his black robes dusty, unrecognized.

'Come,' Atta said, taking his father's arm. 'He's in the salon, working.'

Heavy curtains covered the windows against the dark and cold, but the room was brightly lit and warm air rose from the brass grilles in the tiled floor. Mustafa was seated at a table, conducting a meeting with two other men, his massive presence dominating the large room. When he saw them enter he rose and the others left.

'Reza!'

In three long paces his father reached and embraced his brother. Atta hung back.

'I am so glad to see you,' Mustafa said as he pounded his brother on the back. 'I doubted if I would ever see you again!'

So his uncle had been worried all the time and he, Atta, hadn't seen it.

Mustafa settled on to a couch and Atta crossed the tiles to join the brothers, sitting next to his father on the divan opposite Mustafa.

'Uncle,' he said, glancing over the bandages beneath his robes. 'How are you?'

His uncle's posture was stiff, his shoulders stooped so as not to put pressure on his wound. He looked well enough, but the shadows beneath his eyes told of pain.

'Well, Atta.' He struck himself on the chest but coughed, involuntarily. 'It'll take more than an arrow in the shoulder to kill this old bear.'

Now it was up to him, Atta, to make things right between them.

'That arrow was aimed at me,' Atta said. Kneeling, he reached for his uncle's large hand and raised it to his brow. 'Thank you, Uncle, you saved my life.'

Mustafa pulled his hand free and gripped Atta's head.

'Think nothing of it,' he said. 'I would do it all again.' He flopped back, giving a little sigh, as he let Atta go.

Atta resumed his seat. He had acknowledged his debt. It was a first step.

His father was asking about the treaty negotiations. Without a treaty there would be more conflict, more death.

'There's no treaty yet,' Mustafa replied. 'I suspect that the King is seeking allies, in Al Andalus and beyond, before he agrees to give up claim to more territory. Who knows how long the peace may hold.'

'King Jaume may give him more support.'

King Jaume of Aragon was father to Alfonso's Queen and had fought alongside his son-in-law in the past.

'Maybe, though Alfonso may try to draw England in.' King Edward of England was married to Alfonsos's half-sister. 'Though England has his own problems, de Montfort leads the rebellious Barons against him.'

That his Uncle knew such things was no longer a surprise to Atta. He had, it seemed, been kept well informed, even while on his sick bed in an 'enemy' town.

'Sirs?' A servant had entered the salon and was hovering.

'Yes.' Mustafa looked over to him.

'A visitor,' the man said. 'Nathan Calamiel. Shall I show him in?'

This was unexpected. Why was Nathan here so soon? Something must be wrong.

'Yes, show...'Mustafa began.

'No, I'll come.' Atta rose to his feet. 'I am glad to see you well, Uncle.' He looked at Mustafa. 'Truly.'

He turned to follow the servant out.

'Atta,' his uncle called. 'You must say nothing of what we have discussed here.'

'I know Uncle.'

Nathan was pacing back and forth across the tiled floor of the hall. When he saw his friend he hurried forward.

'Atta,' he said. 'I need to talk with you.'

'Yes, yes, come in....'

'No, we need to go.' Nathan gestured towards the doors. 'You were right maybe....'

What was it now? Was there a problem with Simon?

'Right about what?' He took his cloak from the servant who had brought it and pulled it around his shoulders, nodding his thanks. 'But where are we going?'

'To the Delgado house,' Nathan replied. 'I need to talk with Miguel Delgado.'

36.

Understanding

Nathan hastened out of the residence and strode out along the lamp lit street. The more he thought about his cousin's reaction to what he had said, the more he needed to talk with Miguel Delgado. If Thomas and the Captain had noticed their attachment, how many others had too? How might this affect his cousin's reputation?

'Nathan, what is it?' Atta's voice sounded from back down the street. 'Why are you in such a hurry? What's so important? Is it your father?'

He hadn't realised how quickly he'd been walking.

'I'm not... it's just... Atta, I want some answers. Senor Thomas believes, as you did, that Rebecca and Miguel Delado were... that there was something between them. I must find out what's going on.'

'And your father? How is he?'

'My father...' His anxiety about seeing his father again seemed ages ago now. 'My father's recovering well, thank you. Our reunion was... good, in the end. But he looks so much older, Atta.' Nathan resumed walking, more slowly now. 'I've only been away a few weeks, but he seems to have aged. Oh, I forgot to ask about your uncle. Is he...?'

'Yes, he's doing well.' Atta said, dismissing the topic. 'So, Thomas thinks as I did?'

'He does. Tell me, did my cousin... did she confide in you?'

'No.' Atta fell silent, pensive. 'When Miguel believed that he was going to die.... he said some things. But he made me promise...'

'To keep it to yourself?'

'Something like that.'

'But there is something between them.'

'He certainly believed so, he mentioned a ring...'

'A ring.'

So it had got as far as that. Yet there was no talk of an engagement. Why? Surely Miguel was a man of honour.

The Delgado house was well lit, its large windows blazing with light over the courtyard wall. Nathan and Atta entered the forecourt to find one of the main doors to the house was ajar, open to the night.

Nathan looked at Atta, but his friend just shrugged. They climbed the steps to the door and entered.

Inside, the tiled hall was empty. No one came to speak to them. Where were the servants? Somewhere deep within the house Nathan could hear a woman's voice protesting.

'Hallo?' He called.

A plump housemaid burst into the hall, skittering to a halt on the tiles. It was Mercedes, they had often seen her when they called on Juan. Behind her a thin, red-haired man, dressed in a lawyer's black robes, appeared from a corridor.

312

'Mercedes, go and help attend to your master,' he ordered.

The girl stepped back but didn't leave the hall, while the man stood, feet apart, in the centre of the room, a forbidding look upon his face. 'Can I help you?'

Nathan hadn't expected to have to explain himself, he and Atta were known here, they were Juan's friends, they had always been made welcome.

But Atta was speaking. 'I am Senor Delgado's medical advisor. I am here to ensure he is adequately settled. Al-Mansuri is my name.'

The lawyer looked askance at Atta, pointedly observing his dirty travelling cloak and dusty boots.

Nathan glanced down at his own clothes, he didn't exactly look presentable. His boots were filthy with dried mud and there was a sweaty tang about his jerkin.

'I have been attending him on the journey,' Atta continued unperturbed. 'I gave instructions that he should bathe. His bandages will need changing.'

'Er, he bathed almost as soon as he returned,' the man answered, his eyes narrowing. He was suspicious. Why?

'Good. I need to see where he is situated, please take us to him.'

The man hesitated. There was a silence, as they waited.

'Very well,' he eventually said. 'Mercedes...'

The servant girl stepped forwards and gestured for Nathan and Atta to follow her.

She led them along an arched corridor, looking back over her shoulder to whisper. 'You're Juan's old friends aren't you. I remember.' Her eyes were anxious. 'The master's unhappy and

313

careworn. They've been on at him ever since his return. They won't leave him alone.'

They reached a tall pair of doors, which she opened with a flourish.

'Visitors, Sir,' she said as she entered.

The wood-panelled room was bright with candle light and a log fire crackled in the wide hearth. An immense desk dominated the space, but in front of it a day bed had been placed near to the fire. Miguel lay upon it, his dark chestnut hair curling damp against the pallor of his face.

'Atta, Nathan, come in, come in,' he strained to lever himself upwards amid the cushions. 'I am glad to see you. Thank you, Mercedes.'

The serving maid scurried over to catch a falling cushion which she stuffed back behind Miguel before she left the room. Miguel had a protector, that was clear.

'If I may examine you...?' Atta said. He sounded Miguel's chest and flexed his arms forward and to the side. Opening Miguel's shirt he checked the bandages. Miguel bore it all patiently and was, eventually, allowed to sink back onto the couch.

'Sit, please,' Miguel indicated chairs and offered wine.

'No, thank you. We – I, need to speak with you privately,' Nathan said, perching on the edge of one chair. 'It's important.'

A faint frown creased Miguel's brow and he raised an eyebrow. He looked so like Juan when he did that.

How to begin? Nathan leaned forward with his forearms laid across his thighs, hands clasped together. He swallowed hard.

'I must ask you a personal question,' he said. 'As a matter of honour.' That sounded like something his father would say. 'The Calamiel family isn't a noble one, nor wealthy, but it is respectable and respected. I cannot allow my cousin's reputation to be damaged, or her feelings. I speak of Rebecca.'

At Rebecca's name Miguel's face grew even paler, if that was possible.

'Yes,' his voice was barely above a whisper. 'I understand.' His voice dwindled.

Nathan cleared his throat. There was no going back now.

'It seems to me that you and she... have strong feelings for each other, but that you aren't making the customary arrangements, that is, to, er... marry. What are your intentions? Have you let her down?'

'Let her down, no,' Miguel shook his head. 'Never.' His vehemence brought a look of concern from Atta. 'I love your cousin and I have told her so. I want to make her my wife. My intentions were, are, entirely honourable.'

Nathan sat back in his chair.

So Atta and Thomas were right. But then why hadn't matters been taken forward?

'Have you proposed to her?'

Miguel looked sick. He stared into space. 'Before I left Jerez I intended to ask Rebecca to marry me,' he said. 'Then to speak with your father on the journey to the hills.'

So there had been no proposal, but surely she knew, she must have guessed.

'But you didn't,' Nathan prompted.

'No. I left it too late, more's the pity. And then, just before I set out I received a visitation. It concerned my brother.' He paused. 'You were Juan's friends, you know what he was like, impetuous, good hearted. Perhaps easily imposed upon.'

Impetuous, yes, good-hearted too... generous to his friends. But easily imposed upon?

'Juan was no one's fool,' Nathan said.

'I agree,' Atta supported him. 'He always knew what he wanted.'

'Maybe you knew him better than I did,' Miguel went on. 'I saw little enough of him. Well, it appears that he wanted a girl. Her name is Dolores Verde and she, and her mother, came to make claim upon me. Dolores is pregnant. She states that the child is Juan's.'

What?

'I had her claim investigated and it appears that a ceremony took place,' Miguel was tight lipped now. 'She has evidence, Juan's silver ring.'

'Have you seen it?'

'Oh yes, it's Juan's ring all right.'

It wasn't possible. It just wasn't. Juan would never have done such a thing and kept it hidden from them. He glanced at his friend. He could tell Atta didn't believe it either. Nathan began to shake his head. There was no way that this was true.

And anyway.....

'How does that affect my cousin?'

Miguel took a deep breath. 'Dolores, or rather her mother, wishes me to marry my brother's widow,' he looked at the wall. 'As

316

you know, it is often done in aristocratic families. My lawyer urges me to it, to protect the family name and bring up the child.'

'And you have told my cousin this?'

'I did,' Miguel swallowed laboriously. 'But I also told her that I had not agreed to it... she and I can still be wed. Somehow I will manage things, to avoid further scandal.'

A bastard child, was that such a scandal, especially in war-time? Or was the scandal his marrying Rebecca? Was his cousin not good enough for the Delgados?

'You don't have to marry this girl,' Atta spoke. 'Especially if you love Rebecca.'

'I know,' Miguel gave a deep sigh 'And I do love your cousin.' He was staring intently at Nathan now.

The door flew open with a crash. A tall and buxom figure, wrapped in swathes of green damask stood in the doorway, the serving maid hovered behind her, hands fluttering.

'Where is he?' The woman demanded, gazing in imperious fashion around the room. 'Who is imposing on our invalid?' Long, dangling earrings swung as she looked from Nathan to Atta.

She swept into the room, followed by the pinch-faced red-haired man from the vestibule.

'Senora Verde,' Miguel spoke slowly and deliberately. 'I will decide who enters my own house....'

'Yes, of course,' the woman interrupted, as she bent, smiling, over Miguel's sick bed. 'I'm sorry.' She took up position behind the couch, her hand resting on its head and glared at them, looking down her nose. 'Would you introduce me to these people?'

317

'He claimed to be a doctor,' the red-haired man pointed towards Atta, regarding them warily.

'And so he is.' Miguel's response was sharp. 'May I present Atta Al-Mansuri. I owe Atta my life.'

The red-haired man nodded a surly acknowledgement.

'And we're all grateful, I'm sure,' the woman smiled with her lips but there was no warmth in her eyes. 'Come. Come in, daughter. Your place is here.' She raised her arm to summon another woman forward.

So this was the girl. Juan's supposed wife.

She wore a sleeveless surcoat of rich maroon velvet, over a loose, pale gown, which fell in thick folds from her distended belly. Her brown hair had been braided with seed pearls, framing an oval face, then caught up into a fine net of what looked to him like silver wire. Her face was expressionless and pallid.

The young woman's eyes swept the room.

Atta rose, relinquishing his chair to her.

'Atta al-Mansuri, Nathan Calamiel, may I present Dolores Verde and her mother Constanta,' Miguel said. 'Atta and Nathan were very close friends of my brother.'

Nathan sensed the girl's head turn sharply to look at them, but he was watching her mother. The woman had become very still and, he could have sworn, there was uncertainty in her eyes, which slid sideways to rest upon the lawyer, just for a moment.

'He must have spoken of my daughter to you,' she leaned forward across the back of the couch. 'If you had been real friends I'm sure he would have done.'

'He did not,' Nathan replied.

There was something suspicious about this, he was sure of it. He glanced across at Atta, who looked like he wanted to be somewhere else.

Nathan understood. They needed to talk about what they had learned. Yet he was reluctant to leave Miguel with these people. They were clustered around him like vultures at a corpse.

'Atta, you'll be back to tend me tomorrow?' Miguel asked as Atta rose.

'I will and I'll bring more medicine,' Atta said.

Good. That would gain them entry and they could find out more.

'Good,' Miguel said. He looked in Nathan's direction. 'And we need to speak further.'

Nathan nodded and they stepped towards the door.

The girl had half turned, watching them leave.

Nathan frowned. She looked familiar, somehow. Take away the fine clothes and jewels and......

In the courtyard Nathan halted. It didn't seem right to leave.

'Nathan, come on,' Atta said. 'We have to let Miguel handle his own affairs and we'll be back tomorrow morning. What can happen before then?'

'I don't know, but I don't trust that lawyer. He's in league with the woman. Juan would never.....'

'I don't believe that story for a minute,' Atta said. 'We would have known. Juan would never have kept it from us.'

'I know. But then how did she get Juan's ring?'

'I don't know.' Atta looked at him, a question in his eyes.

'How far gone is the girl? Her pregnancy?'

'I can't tell with any certainty. The siege, the lack of food, could have made a difference to the baby's development. I don't know.' He shook his head. 'We're not going to say anything to Rebecca right?'

'No, not until we know more,' Nathan said. 'Especially about what Miguel intends.'

Surely one night wouldn't make any difference? So why did he feel such foreboding?

Anyway, there were other things to think about. Tomorrow he was to bring Johanna to Plateros and introduce her to his father. He had to prepare himself, it was so important that their first meeting went well.

'Will you call for me in the morning?'

They had reached the place where their paths diverged. Atta nodded as he turned towards the residence and Nathan watched his friend walk away before resuming his journey.

There was something very wrong here, that he knew, but there was nothing to be done until tomorrow.

37.

Plateros

'So have you met this Johanna, Rebecca?' Simon asked.

Oh dear. She didn't want to pronounce on the suitability or otherwise of the young woman Nathan had chosen. Her cousin had left earlier to fetch Johanna and he was taking his time about it.

Rebecca brought her uncle a dish of hot oats and small beer on a tray. He was seated in a wooden armed chair by the hearth with a rug across his legs. The living room was warm and bright, the morning sunlight streaming in through the windows and a fire crackling in the fireplace.

'Yes. She's someone Nathan cares about very much,' she answered. 'Here, take this on your lap.'

'Where did he meet her?'

Rebecca sighed. With unerring instinct Simon had homed in upon the least palatable aspect of the tale of how Nathan had met Johanna. Well he would have to know sometime...

'In the bandit camp,' she said. 'Now don't jump to conclusions. She's not a bandit. Her father was, is, a smith. He was forced to work for them, just like Don Reza.'

'A smith, eh?' Simon blew on his spoonful of oats. 'A blacksmith?'

'Yes, I believe so. I spoke to him only briefly on the ride home,' she sat at the table and took up her spoon. 'He seems a decent man. He helped Nathan and the others escape. Johanna had been serving as Don Reza's assistant.'

She sneaked a look at her uncle. He was looking thoughtful, a faint frown creasing his forehead. Why hadn't he asked Nathan these questions?

She had seen little of her cousin since they arrived home the day before. Last evening he had gone out to find Atta and his behaviour seemed odd when he returned. Probably nerves about introducing Johanna to his father. More than once during supper she'd sensed his eyes upon her. In the end she had ignored him.

At least Simon was cheerful. He was pleased that she and, especially, Nathan, were home once more. She didn't know what had passed between father and son but it seemed to have done him good. For the first time in months her uncle looked optimistic.

Where was that cousin of hers?

She rose to take the breakfast things into the kitchen.

Simon lifted his mug as she reached for the tray, but looked up at her. He rubbed his hand around his chin.

'Maybe, should I shave?' He said, tentatively. 'I wouldn't want to let Nathan down.'

Let Nathan down......

She placed the tray on to the table and hugged her uncle tightly.

'You won't,' she murmured.

'Well, I need to get ready.' Her uncle grumbled, but his voice betrayed his pleasure at her show of affection. She stepped back.

The latch of the outside gate rattled.

That must be them. No time for uncle to shave.

Hurrying into the kitchen Rebecca dumped the dishes into the washing pail and stood in the doorway, smoothing her skirts. She watched as, with careful courtesy, her cousin presented Johanna to his father.

'Please don't get up,' the girl said, as she bent to take his hand.

And my cousin you already know,' Nathan said, gesturing towards her as she entered. He clasped his hands, then unclasped them. He seemed not to know what to do with them.

Johanna straightened up and gave her a nervous smile.

'Here, Nathan, get a chair for Johanna,' Simon said, gesticulating.

Time to make herself scarce. Better to leave them to it, without her looking on. Maybe she would go to the hospital, where she could be useful and with any luck, the Lady Beatriz would be there.

Rebecca caught her cousin's eye, gesturing to let him know that she would be going outside. She closed the inner door behind her as she carried the pail of crockery into the courtyard.

She wished Nathan happy, but she didn't want to see such happiness right now.

As she cleaned the dishes she went over what Miguel had said to her in the wagon, again. She felt a trembling in her chest when she remembered how he had looked, his pallor and his wounds. The damage she had done.

And yet.. what was she to think? He told her that he loved her, then, in almost the same breath, said that there was someone else, another girl he was being urged to marry. Was she held so lightly in his affection that he would set her aside?

Her instinct told her that his love was what mattered, but she had learned that the world's judgement mattered too. It had a way of intervening, shifting the ground beneath the feet. She had done nothing wrong or improper during her time on the *Teresa*, her deeds had been brave. If she had been a man she would be feted as a hero. Yet she had been ostracised.

Someone knocked at the gate. Wiping her hands upon her apron, she crossed to open it.

It was Ben, looking startled, as if he hadn't expected her to answer.

'Come in,' she said, stepping aside to allow him entry. 'Please. Nathan and Johanna are here, please come.'

'Yes.' Ben stepped into the courtyard. 'That is to say, no. It's you I want to speak to. Alone.'

Oh dear, what now?

She glanced at him. He was looking at her intently, anguish in his eyes.

'It broke my heart,' Ben began, barely audible. 'To learn that you loved someone else, that I couldn't ever be the first person in your thoughts.' He began to walk back and forth. 'It is hard. Very hard. Perhaps, maybe, now you know how that feels?'

She opened her mouth to retort, but closed it again. He wasn't gloating and besides, she had hurt him badly. But how did he know how she felt? Were her feelings so obvious to everyone? And how did he know about Miguel and the other girl?

'In a way I don't blame you,' he continued, with a wry smile. 'I was arrogant, I took your acceptance for granted, thought myself such a catch... Little did I know that your sights were set even higher.'

No, he still didn't understand. That wasn't how it was at all.

'It wasn't a matter of setting sights,' she said. 'Really...'

'It doesn't matter anyway,' Ben said. 'I accept that you don't love me. But plenty of marriages start out like that. It doesn't mean that your feelings can't change.'

'Or yours.'

'Or mine,' Ben conceded. 'But I don't think that's likely.'

'Ben, you don't understand'

Ben nodded, slowly. 'No, maybe I don't.'

He reached inside his jerkin and withdrew a ring.

'Miguel Delgado is to marry Dolores Verde, it's the talk of the town. My sisters told me, even our maid knows it. So, if you can't have the man you want, maybe you'll make do with me. I want you to know that this is yours if you want it.' He reached out for her hand.

Was he proposing? Again?

She wouldn't be left on her own. She could marry Ben, have a home, a house and children. He wasn't an ogre. She had thought of him as her future husband once. Plenty of Jerez girls would be more than willing.

325

The house door opened and Nathan, Johanna and Simon came out laughing. They stopped at the threshold, open-mouthed at the scene before them.

Rebecca snatched her hand back and metal rang as the ring struck the cobbles, rolling away towards the drain.

'No!' Ben tried to catch it, casting aside the crockery in his attempts to stop its progress.

'That's it!'

The shout came from the doorway. It was Nathan.

'I've remembered. I must go. It's important, I'll explain later,' he said to Johanna. He grabbed Rebecca's arm and strode across to the gate, pulling her after him. 'Come with me.'

'What....?'

She tried to free herself but his momentum carried them forward. The gate slammed behind them as Nathan dragged her out into the street.

38.

In the Delgado House

Miguel shivered.

The fire was dead. Why had no one come to replenish it? No one had opened the shutters either and the candles were burnt down. Where was Mercedes?

He tugged at the blanket, pulling it further up over his body. His head pounded with a deep, aching rhythm, a pummelling in his skull. It felt for all the world like a hangover, as if he'd drunk a vat of wine, but he hadn't touched a drop.

Maybe it was Atta's posset? He'd ask him what was in it later. He could remember drinking it, though, in truth, the events of the previous evening were somewhat hazy. Just like a hangover.

He licked his dry lips. He was parched. The carafe standing on the low table next to the day bed was empty.

Miguel levered himself upright and reached for the little hand bell. Its ring echoed as he flopped back against the cushions. Why did he feel so weak? He seemed so much worse than yesterday, when he came home. Was it some sort of delayed reaction?

He stared upwards at the wooden carvings in the ceiling and tried to recall the events of the previous day. It had been good to see Atta and Nathan. He owed his life to them both. They had been close friends to his brother, now to him. It had been good, too, to tell someone how much he loved Rebecca and sharing his predicament with someone made the burden lighter.

It was a pity he hadn't been able to offer Nathan more assurance in the matter, there and then, but he couldn't in all conscience talk about Rebecca in front of the Verdes, especially Dolores.

And Bonifaz - the lawyer was much too tight with Senora Verde, who certainly seemed to have made herself and her daughter at home in his house since he had been away. He would move them to one of the country houses, perhaps, somewhere private for Dolores to have the child.

The door opened and a manservant entered.

'Open the shutters please,' Miguel said. 'And lay a new fire. Where is Mercedes? She should be about these duties, is she sick?'

'Don't know, Sir.'

After a moment of fumbling, the man let in the daylight. Miguel raised his hand to shade his eyes.

The man wore a house servant's livery, but he looked unfamiliar. The clothes were clean, but the skin of his brawny neck looked unwashed and there was dirt beneath his fingernails.

'Are you new here?'

'Yessir.'

At the hearth the man swept the ashes, but succeeded only in raising a cloud of dirt. Miguel coughed.

'Not like that! Get Mercedes, she knows how to do it.'

'I think she's gone, sir,' the man looked at the floor, not meeting Miguel's eye.

'Gone. Gone where? Her family has served in this house for three generations, wherefore would she go?'

'Dunno, sir.'

The servant was useless.

'Go and replenish my water,' Miguel ordered. 'And send Don Ludovico to me if he's returned.'

As the servant left Miguel swung his legs around and placed his feet upon the floor. He flexed his toes and the muscles in his calves. His legs were still weak, but now he was back home he could start a regime of exercises. He would discuss this with Atta later.

Wobbling slightly, he stood. His legs were working alright, though the skin across his chest felt taut and fragile. The throbbing in his head had lessened and he felt more clear-headed.

One foot in front of the other.

His limbs protested, but he could walk.

Behind the desk he sat, with relief, in his father's high-backed chair. That was better. Now it was time to find out what had been going on in his absence.

The door opened, but it wasn't the servant returning, it was Senora Verde and Dolores, with Bonifaz bring up the rear.

'What! Up and about!' The woman exclaimed, coming towards him. 'You should be resting.'

Miguel raised his hand to forestall her approach.

'Where is Mercedes?' He asked. 'And I wish to see my steward. Find Don Ludovico for me, Bonifaz. This morning. There are estate matters to discuss.'

'Don Ludvico's not here,' the lawyer answered. 'He's gone into the countryside.'

'Then send a messenger after him and get him back,' Miguel said. 'And where is Mercedes, she was here yesterday?'

'She was dismissed,' Bonifaz replied. 'I...'

'For what reason?' Miguel glared at Bonifaz.

What did the lawyer think he was doing? He didn't have the authority to dispense with servants and retainers.

'I dismissed her,' Senora Verde said, a haughty look on her face. 'She deliberately flouted my instructions and she was impudent to my daughter.'

This was insupportable. Who did she think she was?

'You have no such power in this household, madam,' Miguel directed a cold glance at the woman. He addressed Bonifaz. 'Find Mercedes also. Clearly matters have gone awry in my absence. They will be put right.'

He emphasised the last four words through gritted teeth. His head felt constricted, as if an iron band was pressing round his skull.

'But I am to be your wife,' Dolores spoke up. 'As your fiance I have the power and my mother was only doing right.'

What was this now?

'Do not confuse what you wish with what is, Dolores,' Miguel tried to keep his voice under control, to speak calmly and patiently to the girl. It cost him an effort.

'Show him the contract,' Senora Verde commanded Bonifaz.

The lawyer produced a key from inside his jerkin. He unlocked a drawer in one of the cabinets and drew out a roll of parchment.

'We reviewed it last night,' he said in an unsteady voice, as he brought the document to the desk. 'You decided to sign it.' He unrolled the parchment and held down two of its corners.

What was this?

His signature was on the document in front of him.

It couldn't be.

But there it was. The marriage contract signed, witnessed by Bonifaz and Constanta Verde. All that remained was to sanctify the contract before God. Miguel's vision swam.

He hadn't signed it. He couldn't have. He had every reason not to. But his signature was there. Was it a forgery? No, it looked real.

The script seemed to move before his eyes, crawling across the page.

'He is ill again,' Dolores said, tearfully, as she rang the bell. The burly manservant came running. 'He needs to lie down. Take him to bed. I will bring his medicine.'

Miguel glared at the man, who hesitated.

'Now sir,' Bonifaz's voice was in his ear. 'You're not well. You bride has only your welfare at heart, sir.'

'My bride...nonsense. I don't know how you got me to sign that paper, but I wasn't in my right mind when I did so. Don't touch me!'

The lawyer and the servant moved to haul him from the chair.

'Stop!'

The shout came from the doorway.

He dropped back into the seat and gasped as a shard of pain shot through his ribs.

Nathan and Atta stood in the doorway. Atta made to approach him, but Senora Verde blocked his path.

'Who let them in here?' She said, her voice commanding.

'Let me pass.' Miguel heard Atta's cold voice, though could not see past the woman. 'Or things will go even more badly for you.'

'Who are you to say what will or will not go well for me,' she said, equally coldly. 'Your sort isn't wanted here anymore. It'll be you who will find things going badly.'

'I don't think so.' That was Senor Thomas' voice. The Senora stepped aside and he could see the English doctor.

Atta was by his side now, pulling something from his satchel.

'Tell Miguel what you told me,' Thomas prompted Nathan.

'The girl, Dolores, I've seen her before, but yesterday I couldn't remember where,' Nathan spoke urgently. 'This morning I realised where it was - in the courtyard of the Alcazar, just after the bastion was destroyed, just after your father and brother were killed.'

What?

Senora Verde, Dolores and Bonifaz were all staring at Nathan. The manservant backed away.

'You were there, you were both there, searching through the rubble of the fallen wall,' Nathan spoke to Dolores and her mother. 'So was I, and Atta. We were searching for our friend Juan, Miguel's brother. You were searching for.... who or what? Whatever you could get perhaps? That's when you found the ring.'

The ring. Nathan had seen Dolores come upon the ring.

'My father!' Dolores face was streaked with tears. 'We were looking for my father.'

332

'How dare you upset my daughter,' Senora Verde reproached Nathan. 'Given her delicate condition.' She looked around the room for support. 'Who is he to question my daughter's word? A nobody and a Jew. Him and his Islamic friend here. They forced their way in yesterday.' She directed her gaze towards Thomas and her voice became conciliatory. 'You've been deceived, sir.'

'Have a care, lady,' Thomas replied. 'The King has reason to be grateful to Nathan and his family and Atta is the nephew of the Emir's Ambassador. Whether you like it or not, they will be listened to. I will see to it.'

Senora Verde sniffed, her nose in the air. 'Where is the proof?' She said. 'He could be mistaken... or lying.'

Nathan wouldn't lie. Though they would say he, as Rebecca's cousin, had good reason to.

'I know what I saw,' Nathan said, raising the palms of his hands.

Perhaps it wouldn't be enough. How to get at the truth?

'Dolores,' Miguel looked at the girl. She returned his look, but he sensed that her confidence was failing. 'You told me that my brother gave you the ring, the one you now wear on your finger, is that right?'

She nodded, half raising her left hand. The simple silver ring was there, eclipsed by others of greater weight and decoration.

Her mother interjected. 'We've explained all this....'

'Please allow your daughter to answer,' Senor Thomas said. 'Miguel...'

'When he gave it to you,' Miguel continued. 'What did he tell you about it?'

333

Dolores shrugged. 'It was a betrothal ring, he didn't say more than that. He put it on my finger.'

There was a commotion at the doorway. Mercedes and some of the servants had pushed their way in and, just beyond, was Rebecca. Her face was pale but she was watching closely. His eyes met hers and he saw the question there. Well, he would sort this out for good and show her.

With an effort he turned his attention back to Dolores, who was looking increasingly uncomfortable. Her gaze flitted around the room, finally resting on her mother.

'He didn't tell you about the others then?'

'What others? There's only this one. My ring.'

Miguel nodded to Nathan, who reached inside his shirt and drew out the chain which held his ring. Dolores flinched at the sight of the ring on the chain.

'No,' she stuttered, her demeanour desperate. 'Yes. Now I remember. There was another, he told me.'

Atta began to draw out his ring too. The girl's gaze flitted round the room from face to face. She wasn't a very good liar.

He didn't believe her and neither did anyone else

'Is it true?' Bonifaz hissed. He moved away from Senora Verde and her daughter. 'Is what he says true?

'What do you care?' The woman spat back. 'You were happy enough to accept it when you thought you'd benefit.'

So, Bonifaz had colluded.

'I asked you to investigate,' he said to the lawyer. 'You said there was a marriage.'

334

'There was a priest,' Bonifaz answered, passing his tongue over his lips.

'Probably bought and paid for,' Miguel answered. 'What is his name and where does he reside?'

'Father Ignatius, but... he's not there anymore.'

'Documents? Registration?'

Bonifaz shook his head.

'So there is no proof of any marriage of this girl to my brother.'

'The ring...' Senora Verde began.

'Wasn't given to her at all,' Miguel replied. 'She, or you, found it. Probably on my brother's body.'

'But you've signed the marriage contract,' the woman pointed to the parchment lying on the desk. She wasn't going to give up.

His glanced toward the doorway. Rebecca's lips parted and her eyes glistened.

'I don't remember signing any document,' Miguel said firmly, looking Rebecca in the face. 'I don't know how my signature got there. It was after I drank the medicine....'

Senora Verde protested noisily but Mercedes was shouting too. Bonifaz was inching towards the door. Nathan's lips were moving, though Miguel couldn't hear what he was saying.

Miguel focussed on the face in the doorway, pale under the brown of the sun, grey eyes watching.

Don't turn away. Don't go. See this for the fraud it is. Believe me.

Rebecca smiled.

It was going to be all right.

'Silence!' Senor Thomas demanded and the noise subsided. 'What medicine did you take? Miguel.'

'What? Oh, the potion Atta delivered late yesterday,' Miguel said. He looked up at Atta, who shook his head.

'I brought no medicine,' he said. 'Nor sent any.'

'Drugged,' Senor Thomas said as he examined Miguel's eyes. 'Yes, you bear the signs.'

So that was why he felt so unwell this morning.

Senora Verde had grabbed her daughter by the wrist and was pushing her way to the door.

'Don't let them escape!' Senor Thomas ordered and the servants reached out to stop them.

'No, let them go.'

Everyone turned to look at Miguel.

'I just want them out of here,' he said. 'Let them take what they have, but no more. Except the ring, I want my brother's ring.'

Senora Verde drew herself up, pulling down her rumpled sleeves.

'Come, daughter,' she said and, with a vicious glance at Miguel, swept from the room.

Dolores tugged at her finger, removed the ring and placed it into Nathan's outstretched palm. She scurried after her mother, hurriedly replacing the other rings on her fingers.

'Sir, I didn't know, I swear,' Bonifaz was pleading, wringing his hands.

'Pack your bags,' said Miguel.

'But...'

'Think yourself lucky that you're being allowed to go.'

The lawyer backed away and hurried from the room.

'Right, now, please leave everyone.'

Suddenly he felt very tired and he wanted to be alone with Rebecca.

The servants were already withdrawing, their voices echoing in the vestibule. He was helped to the couch by Nathan. Atta felt his ribs and pulled up his eyelids.

'I'm fine,' Miguel said. 'Really. Thank you. Thank you all.'

Go, just go.

Mercedes hovered.

'Can I get anything? Does the master need anything?'

'If he does, I'll deal with it, thank you,' Rebecca said.

One final thing.... Miguel pushed himself upright and reached for the marriage contract which lay on the desk. Looking at Rebecca, with an effort he tore the parchment in two and threw the pieces into the fireplace.

'It'll be useful kindling,' he said and held out his hand to her, looking into her eyes. After all this, would she take it?

There was a pause.

Rebecca walked over to him and placed her hand in his.

Epilogue

Ten Years Later

Nathan strode along the quay side, through crates, casks and bundles of unloaded cargo. The ship he was bound for was at the end of the harbour and it didn't surprise him to see its crew was busy loading for another voyage.

'Bella, be careful!' He called to the small girl running ahead of him. She had reached the jetty and the gangway leading to the ship. 'Wait for me.'

'I can do it, Dada. It's only a gangway.' She protested as he caught her up into his arms.

'Serve you right if you fall in,' Nathan said.

'Doesn't matter, I can swim.'

Nathan walked up the gangway, noting the new gilding on the ship's name, *Teresa*. When they reached the deck he put his daughter down. She immediately ran off into the hurly-burly of a crew preparing to sail.

'Isabel,' he called.

'She'll be all right, don't worry.' The bo'sun approached and shook Nathan's hand, inclining his head towards the rear of the ship. 'Your cousin's in her cabin.'

'Thanks.'

Nathan picked his way across a deck crowded with ropes and barrels. He glanced up to see his daughter half way up the mainmast, accompanied by a sailor and a young boy, slightly older than she was, his chestnut curls ruffled by the sea breeze.

'Hello!' The boy called and waved. 'Uncle Nat.'

Nathan returned the wave. He ducked beneath the low lintel through to the large cabin which occupied the width of the rear of the ship.

Rebecca sat in a wide winged chair, the light on the sea sparkling behind her. Her long hair was pulled high on to the top of her head and she wore a shirt and jerkin over an ankle-length skirt. She put down the little garment she had been sewing and made as if to rise.

'No, don't get up.' Nathan bent to embrace her and planted a kiss on her forehead.

'I'm not ill,' she said. 'I've had a baby, that's all. It's not the first time.'

Nathan leaned towards the crib at her side, to see the new-born, face scrunched like an ancient, eyes closed and mouth open, asleep.

'A girl this time,' he said.

'Yes, a half sister for Miguel.'

'Have you chosen a name yet?'

'Beatriz Rebecca.'

Nathan nodded.

340

'I thought...' Rebecca avoided Nathan's eyes, busying herself putting away her sewing things. 'I thought Simon might have come with you.'

'He's been ill,' Nathan replied. 'He doesn't travel far these days.'

There was a small silence.

'It's difficult to think of Simon as old and weak,' his cousin said.

'Well, that's what he is. Why don't you come back and stay for a while? He would love to see you, Miguel and the baby?'

'We sail on the Spring tide,' she replied.

Nathan hadn't really expected a different answer.

Rebecca's home was on the *Teresa*, she had only returned to Cadiz so that Atta could deliver her child. The ship was, he supposed, where she had been happiest. The house in Plateros was his, Johanna's and Isabel's now.

'But tell me all the news. Have you heard from Ben? Is Simon still telling you how to run the forge?'

'Between him and Fabio, I've have more than enough advice.' Nathan gave an exaggerated sigh. 'Ben was in Jerez recently, to visit his mother and sisters, but he's another who didn't stay long. It looks like there'll be more fighting, King Sancho is determined to destroy Granada. '

Ben would be travelling with the army. He was a Major.

War was a constant fact of life, bringing higher taxes and, sometimes, shortages, but at least it was being fought on the other side of the mountains.

'You'll need new tenants for the Delgado house,' Nathan said. 'It's empty again.'

'Find some. I'd like the place to be lived in, not a mausoleum. It will come to Miguel in time. I've started teaching him how to manage the estate. He's learning quickly.'

'He's a clever boy,' said Nathan. 'Though adventurous.'

'Like his father,' Rebecca said.

In the silence Nathan could hear the sea slapping against the quay.

'Doesn't being here remind you....'

'Yes, but they're good memories.' Rebecca said.

They had so little time together, Nathan thought. Miguel never really recovered.

The cabin door opened and Captain Morientes entered.

'Nathan.'

Nathan grinned and reached out his hand.

'Cristobal, congratulations!'

'Thank you. I was told you'd come aboard. Come to see my new daughter.'

Rebecca lifted the new-born from the crib.

'She has your eyes,' she said, smiling, as she handed the baby to him. 'Blue as the morning sky.'

The Captain held his child as if she was made of diamonds but would shatter at a touch. It was clear that he adored her. Nathan remembered that feeling, the sheer astonishment at becoming a father, mixed with pure happiness and some terror.

Atta had delivered Isabel too.

'Tell me, is there any sign of Atta finding a wife?' Rebecca asked. She could always guess his thoughts. 'Isn't it about time he had some children of his own?'

342

'No. Too busy, he says. Don Reza is ageing, so he has the hospital to run and there's the new school, to train physicians. I wrote to you about it,' Nathan was never sure if his letters arrived.

'Yes, I remember you financed some of it with money from our farms.'

'So, where will my new goddaughter first travel to?'

'We carry wine to England,' the Captain replied, jiggling his child up and down. 'Thomas awaits us in Bristol. He is to be her other godfather.'

'He is well?'

'His letters say so. He thrives and has been summoned to the English court on more than one occasion,' Rebecca answered. 'Queen Eleanor likes to speak of home and her half brother. Though I think he's had enough of being a courtier.'

Nathan remembered the tall Englishman who had turned up at the house in Plateros over ten years ago, apologising for being with the King's army and embarrassed to be billeted upon them.

'Tell him hello from me,' Nathan said as he got to his feet. 'And send greetings from your uncle, Rebecca.'

'I will.' Rebecca rose and came over to embrace him. 'We will be back in Summer and I will come to Jerez then to see Simon and you and Johanna.'

'Isabel might have a little brother or sister by then,' Nathan said.

'Nathan, that is so typical. You leave the best news 'til last and then make your getaway!' She put her hands up on to either side of his head and shook his ears, just as she used to do when he was small.

Nathan smiled. It was good to see her happy again. Beyond her the Captain was smiling too.

Time to go.

'Where is that daughter of mine?' He kissed his cousin and raised a hand. 'Time I took her home.'

The Captain accompanied him out on to the deck.

'Have a good voyage and keep safe,' Nathan said.

'I'll send to let you know when we're on our way back. She loves her uncle dearly... it's just that the town is so full of unpleasant memories for her.'

'I know.'

'We will come next time. She should see Simon and he should see his new grand-daughter.'

'He'll look forward to it.'

They strolled towards the gangplank and Isabel and Miguel ran up.

'Look Dada!'

Shouts came from the quay as a cow was hauled up in a harness. His daughter was entranced.

'We'll be off then.' Nathan shook the Captain's hand and tousled Miguel's hair. 'Goodbye Miguel.'

''Bye Uncle Nat,' Miguel answered. 'Remember, you're my godfather too,'

'I seem to be acquiring godchildren as quickly as I get my own,' Nathan laughed. 'Come on Bella.'

He ushered Isabel in front of him on to the gangplank and they crossed to the quayside.

'Miguel is going to marry me when we get older,' she said, looking up at him.

What had they been talking about?

'You're Miguel's cousin, that means you can't get married,' he explained, as they turned to look back up at the *Teresa*. 'You'll just have to be friends.'

The Captain stood at the rail, his hand on Miguel's shoulder. Both waved.

Nathan lifted Bella up and they waved in response.

She squirmed in his grasp and he placed her on the ground. He watched her skip away along the quayside.

'Home,' she sang as she ran. 'We're going home.'

Afterword

The Silver Rings and its predecessor, *Reconquista*, are fiction, works of the imagination. Nonetheless, historic characters appear within their pages and I must apologise, in advance, for any historical inaccuracies or infelicities, they are entirely my own.

A peace treaty was eventually signed by King Alfonso X of Castile and Leon and Emir Muhammed I of Granada in 1266, but both rulers were eventually deposed by their own sons, who chose not honour the treaty for long. War waged throughout Al Andalus until the final capitulation of Boabdil, last Emir, to King Fernando and Queen Isabel in 1492. The expulsion, or forced conversion, of the Moors and Jews soon followed.

The Sierra de Grazalema, in which much of the action of this novel takes place, is now a wild and beautiful nature reserve, very popular with hikers, climbers and pot-holers. It has always been the haunt of bandits and outlaws, some of them famous, and bandits were known to hide-out there until as late as the 1930s. The deep caverns and sinkholes are well known, though the underground cave systems are not fully explored. They flood quickly and dangerously, Grazalema being one of the wettest places in Spain, especially during the early part of the year.

Acknowledgements

I did not imagine, when I began to write the story which became *Reconquista*, all those years ago, that I would write not just one but two books about those characters. Once begun, however, I had to complete their stories. *The Silver Rings* does so and I do not plan to return to Nathan, Rebecca *et al* in the future.

I would like to thank my editor, Roz Morris, for all her help and her knowledge. Many thanks too, to those friends, especially Annette Souter and Myfanwy Garth, who have been unfailingly encouraging, even when major re-writes were needed.

Special thanks to Angustias Salgado Galan, my friend and neighbour in Jerez de la Frontera, with whom I first discovered the Sierra de Grazalema, a dramatic and beautiful area little known in the UK, but deserving of greater fame. We had tremendous fun, as did the dogs, Pizqui, Wendy and Relampago, walking the streets of Grazalema and Benamahoma. Thanks too to Mario Naranjo Molina for the loan of his books on climbing in the Sierras.

Although set in medieval Spain, in many ways this is a very English tale, rooted in those adventure stories which I devoured when young (and not so young), especially Robert Louis Stevenson, and whose authors I must also acknowledge here.

Finally, thanks to my husband, who read the early versions and the proofs, and cooked and tidied around me when I was far away.

Write a Review

If you enjoyed reading this book, write a review on Amazon and/or Goodreads.

About the author

J.J. Anderson lives in London and Jerez de la Frontera. She is Chair of the Trustees of Clapham Writers the organization which delivers the annual Clapham Book Festival. She curates literary events across London.

Julie blogs as 'JulieJ' at www.thestorybazaar.com . She reports on current cultural events and art exhibitions in London, places and people of historical interest, life and events in southern Spain and writing and publishing. You can find her on Facebook and she posts on Pinterest. Her Twitter handle is @jjstorybazaar.

www.ingramcontent.com/pod-product-compliance
Lightning Source LLC
Chambersburg PA
CBHW030553180626
46816CB00005B/1519